VAGABOND WIND

ISBN 978-1-7348488-0-9 Vagabond Wind paperback
ISBN 978-1-7348488-1-6 Vagabond Wind e-book

Library of Congress Control Number: 2020906045

Published by K.M. del Mara.

kmdelmara@hotmail.com
www.kmdelmara.com

Excerpts from the poems *Windy Nights* and *Happy Thought* are taken from *A Child's Garden of Verses*, by Robert Louis Stevenson. ©1929 and 1932 by The Platt and Munk Co, Inc.. It appeared first in 1889 under the title *Penny Whistles*.

Cover designs by the author.
Cover photos: photos of Red Dog by Marc Garstein, used with permission. All other images from the collection of the author.

K.M. del Mara lives in the wilds of New Jersey.

Other books by K.M. del Mara:

.

Beautiful as the Sky

.

Books in 'The Silent Grove' series are:

.

Whitebeam

.

Passage Oak

.

Willow Oak

.

To the memory of Mama and Papa Beckwith,
and to all souls who, no matter how modest their resources,
find a way to be generous in a distraught world.

All journeys have secret destinations of which the traveler is unaware.
– Martin Buber

PREFACE

Mark Twain wrote a preface to Tom's book of adventures, so it seemed only fitting for this adventure story to have one too. In his preface, Twain said he wrote his book for boys and girls, but hoped that adults would enjoy it too, that it would pleasantly remind them of what they once were themselves. I bow at the feet of Mr. Twain and would never presume to his status, but my hopes are the same, that these adventures of a girl and her dog will touch young hearts of every age.

VAGABOND WIND

THE ADVENTURES OF ANYA AND CORAX

August 1933

*O*n a hot August afternoon, a little devil breeze comes vagabonding through an old village in upstate New York. Swirling from corner to corner, it hesitates, no particular destination in mind. But it means to make something happen, somehow somewhere. It means to stir things up. It crosses the railroad tracks, spies a boy hobo scuffling over the canal bridge and spins the cap right off his head, as if he didn't have troubles enough. Sliding across a row of creaking porches, it sets empty rocking chairs a-rocking, blows somebody's dog-eared novel to the floor, and knocks over a pot of pink geraniums before it finally goes on its way, leaving who-knows-what behind, taking who-knows-what away.

The breeze has fish-scaled the waters of a broad canal that glides through the grittier outskirts of this village. Flowing past workshops, past stables and forges and grain silos, the canal slip-slides under the green iron bridge that is not far from the railroad tracks. In the heat of the afternoon, the canal's drab-colored waters beckon to all sorts of kids; to those who live in the nearby alley, to the children of bargemen, to footloose boys, and to dogs of every background. Well-brought-up village children, however, are forbidden to go near the canal, warned with stories of drowned cow guts and other items too putrid to name.

One such child is a girl called Anya Netherby. She can often be seen on a warm afternoon, hanging over the bridge railing on her way home from the library. She's there today, at the precise moment that the wind, that sly wind, spins a grimy newsboy cap through the air and drops it right at her feet. A dirty-faced boy runs up, stoops to pick up his hat, and speaks.

"Spare a nickel?"

She draws back. "What?"

"Can you give me a nickel?"

She hesitates, shakes her head. As he turns away, she presses back into the bridge railing, troubled by what she sees in his face, troubled by her own response, though she really does not have a single cent in her pocket.

For a minute, she stands quite still, her eyes following the boy as long as he is in sight. Then, believing she has put him out of her mind, she finally turns back to watch the local boys leaping into the canal. She likes seeing them splashing and rough-housing, and she is charmed by the spaniels who paddle alongside, their silky ears floating out like wings. Anya longs for a dog like that, but is forbidden to have one. She is also strictly forbidden to swim in the canal, though it would be a welcome relief from the hot little attic room where she sleeps. It's not as if Anya rails against any of these restrictions. No, she goes along, and she makes the best of things.

But that foxy wind, now, it's done some mischief. When it moves into the north quarter like that, it's a sign. The time is nearly right, and there *is* a something in the air. It's unmistakable. Maybe, maybe someday soon, some things that should happen, will; for it's an ill wind, they say, that blows nobody any good.

CHAPTER ONE

Anya Netherby lived in a rambling old house at the corner of Elm and Main with her grandparents, Mr. and Mrs. Netherby. The Netherbys were now in their golden years and were, judging by appearances, wealthy and respected residents. Appearances deceive, however. They were respected still, or acted as if they should be, but they were no longer wealthy and their golden years were dulled by discord.

Grandfather Netherby was a man of fine intelligence, mild-tempered but not spineless. He had possessed the fortitude to invest boldly in the stock market, until the Depression wreaked havoc on both his income and his confidence. But at no time had he possessed the strength to weather the tempests generated by Grandmother Netherby. In his youth Grandfather had been a gentle and happy-go-lucky man. Alas, that young man had retreated and no one knew where he had gone, Grandfather Netherby least of all.

About Anya's grandmother, Rose Netherby, people often said (out of her hearing) that she was "quite the piece of work". She had not been born to wealth. Her father had worked as an electrician in a coal mine in Pennsylvania and her mother had raised their four daughters and kept house. Her family was poor but they had never gone hungry. Every Saturday the four girls helped their mother clean house until every cobweb was banished, along with the cobs who built them. However, the family did not have the advantages of other people in their town and because of this, Rose Netherby was convinced that life had cheated her of something. Everything and everybody had disappointed her, with the exception of her grandson. It was only in Robert that she invested her hopes and affections. Alas, a happy house, at the corner of Elm and Main, it was not.

The house on Elm Street had many rooms, which was fortunate, as Grandfather and Grandmother Netherby did not live alone. Their grown daughter Helen and her twelve-year old son, the aforementioned Robert, occupied a spacious apartment on the second floor. Robert had a father, of that we can be reasonably certain, but who he was or where he had gone was never discussed. The family hadn't seen him in a very long time.

Besides Anya's Aunt Helen, Grandfather and Grandmother Netherby had a grown son named Jackson. Jackson was Aunt Helen's brother, and Anya's father. He also had not been seen in a long time, almost five years now. As a very young man, he had bowed to his mother's wishes and taken a job that made him a great deal of money. He had met and married the love of his life. But when his wife, pregnant with their second child, was killed by a derailed streetcar, he had disappeared into the west to mend his broken heart, get away from his mother, and study Anasazi cliff dwellings. It seemed obvious that he never intended to come back. He had placed his daughter Anya with her maternal grandparents in Lake Placid, and banked a substantial amount of money to pay for her upkeep and her private school education, when the time came.

The child knew nothing of this money, but it didn't take long for her Grandmother Netherby to find out about it. Little Anya hadn't lived in Lake Placid for more than a few weeks when Mrs. Netherby barged into town and swept the child and her bank account back to her house on Elm Street, giving this reason and that, and brooking no argument. So Anya grew up knowing almost nothing of her father or her maternal grandparents. All she remembered of the time after her mother's death was that there had been a lovely lake, and welcome comfort for her grief and confusion from people who seemed to like having her around. She had very few memories of her father. He had bequeathed to her his *A Child's Garden of Verses,* his old leather pouch filled with marbles, and a string of small pearls that had belonged to her mother. Then he had pried her little arms from around his neck and walked out. Anya treasured the postcards he occasionally sent, but she never saw him again.

*N*ow Anya lived on the third floor of her grandparents' Elm Street house, in an attic room way up under the eaves. She tried not to mind that her room was small and furnished with rather shabby cast-off furniture. From her little window she could see all the way out to where Main Street passed the cemetery and became a narrow road twisting through an orchard on its way to the city. Mrs. Wright, their housekeeper, had the room next to Anya's. It was just the two of them tucked away up there. The stairway to the attic was so steep and narrow that no one else ever came up. Not even Anya's cousin Robert found it worth the climb, no, not even for the pleasure of torturing her.

Anya wasn't allowed to have a pet, though she was a very responsible girl, and now felt nearly grown at age eight and three quarters. But she had to admit that no animal would be content in her room anyway. It was beastly hot in summer and frigid in winter. Still, it was a place where she could be by herself, a little hole she could crawl into when tempers flared downstairs. Thankfully, their housekeeper Mrs. Wright slept in the next room. It was she who tucked Anya into bed every night. And whenever red-eyed ghouls crawled slobbering from the night shadows, it was Mrs. Wright who annihilated them and stood guard until Anya fell asleep again.

When Anya was born, the Great War in Europe was long over, but hard times had fallen on almost everyone. The Netherbys were no exception. Grandfather Netherby had made some disastrous mistakes in the stock market, if the truth be known, though it was emphatically not generally known. It was a great secret that they could barely afford three servants. Mrs. Wright had been with them the longest. She had the job of keeping the entire house clean and functioning, all by herself. She accomplished this under a constant stream of criticism from Grandmother Netherby. Mrs. Wright politely ignored these complaints, in much the same way anyone would ignore embarrassing noises from overfed dogs. She would have appreciated more pay, but domestic helpers had few options in those days, and Grandmother Netherby took every opportunity to remind her that, in these dire times, she should be happy just to have a job.

In the kitchen, the woman who did their cooking was called Betty, and her husband Neil took care of gardening and maintenance. Betty and Neil Brendon lived in a small house on the other side of the orchard. Often, Neil would ask Anya to help him in Grandmother's garden. These were happy times for her. She and Neil spent whole afternoons in summer, puttering about the vegetable and flower gardens. Neil had, or claimed to have, a bad back, though how he managed when she was at school, Anya did not know. He would ask her to fill the watering can at the pump for him, or stab at the soil with a little hoe that he had cut to size, just for her. In the fall she helped him pull out the tomato plants, sow the last lettuces, and burn leaves. He paid her in return for this, small change mostly, but it was the only money she ever received. Her piggy bank was heavy, though, with the three dollars and forty-five cents she had earned in the last two summers. But even without the money, she would have worked willingly beside Neil because she liked him. Her favorite time came at the end of the afternoon, when he took her hand in his big sunburned one. They would walk about the whole garden together, admiring their handiwork and making plans for another day.

It was nearing the middle of August now and the garden was bursting. Every morning there were salad greens and tomatoes to be picked, tasks that Neil often gave to Anya. She was happy to be out in the garden with him because inside dwelt her cousin Robert. About

Robert, well, suffice it to say that life was more peaceful in the winter months when Robert was away at school. You would think a person would be happy to have her cousin home for the summer, but Robert Netherby (his mother had insisted he take her last name) was not that sort of cousin.

In fact, on this very evening, he was up to his usual tricks before dinner.

Anya entered the dining room just in time to find him with the wine carafe in his hand. He turned quickly, and seeing it was only Anya, tossed his head with a sneer.

"If it isn't the ugly attic witch," he exclaimed, pouring red wine two fingers deep into his mother's glass. He downed it in one long gulp and wiped his mouth with the back of his hand. "Don't you dare tell on me," he threatened.

"I don't care what you do, Robert."

"Huh. That's good. I guess you're not as dumb as you look." He glanced at the door and poured another splash of wine. He came towards her. "Here, I'll share with you."

"No thank you."

"Oh, Miss Goodie-goodie!" He dipped his fingers into the glass and flicked wine at her face.

"Will you quit it, Robert?" Anya said, taking a seat at the table.

"Oh, sorry. Accident." Hoping to get more of a rise out of her, he sipped some wine and spit it onto her dress. Big purple stains bloomed all down her front.

"Robert! Look what you've done!" She mopped at the stains

with a napkin.

"Really, Anya, you shouldn't be drinking at your age!" He gave a low shriek of laughter, setting the glass down at her place and hurrying round the table to sit on the other side, just as their grandmother came into the dining room.

"Anya?" Mrs. Netherby gaped. "What are you doing?"

"I told her to stay away from the wine, Grandmother," said Robert. He raised his eyebrows and smiled primly at Anya. She gave him a look that could have scorched those eyebrows right off his face.

Mrs. Netherby grabbed the napkin from Anya's hand and used it to swat at the child's head. "What do you think you are doing, you little sneak?"

"Ow! This wasn't my fault," cried Anya.

"Don't you dare lie to me! There sits the wineglass, right in front of you!"

"I didn't put it there!" Her voice rattled as her grandmother shook her by the arm. "No, Grandmother! I didn't do that!"

"Stop it! Stop it right now! Don't raise your voice to me!"

"Mother please," interjected Aunt Helen, who had just come in. "Let's just sit down and eat. Dinner will be cold, and besides, it's late. I have to go out tonight."

But Grandmother had worked herself into a tantrum. "No! Now I know who has been getting into my wine cabinet." She gave Anya another shake. "You've gotten away with this for the last time, young lady."

"Oh Mother, please don't fret tonight. Just sit down. Pass the carrots, would you, Bobby darling?"

"No, I'm going to make this child behave, if it's the last thing I do. You'll go to your room and stay there, Anya! Go! This minute!" her grandmother ordered.

"I didn't do this," Anya insisted.

"Stop the back talk! Go on." Grandmother pushed Anya away. "I can't abide such a miserable face at my dinner table. And now look! Here we are, ready to eat and no Grandfather."

"I called him. He's coming."

"That man will be the death of me. Where is he?" She took her seat and groaned when Grandfather Netherby came in and slipped quietly into his chair.

"Hello, Daddy," said Helen. "Have some potatoes, darling?"

"Thank you, Helen. Where is Anya going?" Grandfather asked.

"Never mind about her. You're late, Harold," Mrs. Netherby nagged. "You're late! I swear to heaven, you are no better than a child."

Anya, ignored by all but her grinning cousin, tried to keep her face composed. She managed to walk out of the dining room with her head up. Then she ran for the stairs. Up to the second floor, then up the twisting third floor staircase she went, as fast as she could. At the sound of her footsteps pounding up the steps, two little mice scurried under her desk and elbowed each other for a spot behind the wastebasket.

Yes, mice. Every house has them. But, always considerate of their human landlords, city mice take a special interest in children.

When these two mice saw Anya throw herself sobbing onto her bed, one stood wringing her paws in concern.

Her mouse sister eyed ruefully the hole they had chewed open behind the dresser, clear across the room. Here they were, trapped in the attic. They would miss an entire banquet of crumbs when the floor of the kitchen, a distant three flights below, was swept clean by that shrew of a cook, that harridan, that Betty.

So the mouse sisters had to tarry for almost half an hour, stuck behind the wastebasket, listening to a lot of very distressing weeping. But wait – more footsteps on the stairs. Mrs. Wright, the housekeeper, entered with a tray. Ew, Mrs. Wright. She presided over a terrifying arsenal of mops, brooms, obnoxious-smelling cleaning potions, and nasty snapping devices. Mrs. Wright was absurdly intolerant of any little mouse who tried to share the bounty of her cupboards.

Anya sat up and wiped her face with her handkerchief while Mrs. Wright set the tray on the desk.

"My heart! It's hotter 'n' Dutch love up here," said the housekeeper. "Whew! Those stairs are like to do me in. I hope this doesn't happen too often, Missy. What did you do this time?"

"It wasn't my fault, Mrs. Wright. Robert spit wine all over me, but I got blamed."

"He spit wine at you? Honestly, the things that boy gets away with!"

"Grandmother thinks he's a saint."

I don't suppose you ratted him out?"

Anya hung her head.

"Did you? No? 'Course not."

"I tried to tell them it wasn't my fault. Look at my dress. It's ruined."

"My lord. Here, wipe those tears. You know, you could stand up for yourself once in a while."

"I tried!" But not hard enough, apparently. She felt wretched.

"Oh, I'd give anything to see you put that boy in his place. Don't tell your grandmama I said that."

"It's hard, Mrs. Wright."

"Of course it is. I know. But there are times when you've got to show some backbone. Now don't fret. You'll get there. Just don't always be that shrinking violet kind of girl. You don't have to jump just because someone tells you to." She looked at Anya, whose chin hung on her chest, and changed her tone a little. "Now. Leave that dress out for me tonight. Don't worry, honey, I've washed out plenty of stains bigger than that. You hungry?"

"Not very."

"Well, you better eat. Betty sent this up special." She removed a cover from a dish. Good smells wafted forth, if you had a nose for such things. There was more elbowing behind the wastebasket. "Chicken and mashed potatoes. And these carrots?" She gave Anya one of her looks.

"I know. I'll eat them."

"You better. They're good for you." Mrs. Wright lifted another small cover. "Look what we have here. Devil's food cake."

Cake. And cake crumbs. There was a fiffle of sound behind the wastebasket, if you had an ear for such things.

"Betty said to tell you that a little bit of the devil's food might do you some good."

Anya grinned a shadow of a grin. She was far more hungry than she had realized.

"Now no reading tonight until after you finish your dinner, else you get crumbs everywhere and soil your pages."

"Thank you, Mrs. Wright."

"Yes, well. You've got to grow strong so you can stand up to that cousin of yours. I want to see a clean plate tonight, every morsel gone."

Every morsel? Humph. Though the two city mice cowered as Mrs. Wright's feet passed, though their eyes were full of the deepest dislike, they remained as quiet as – yes, they were very quiet.

As much as Anya loved summertime, she could hardly wait for fall to come because Robert would go back to school. He went to a private school while she attended the public school on Lincoln Avenue. She had once, on her way downstairs, overheard Grandfather and Grandmother arguing about this. There was a good deal of shouting behind closed doors, and suddenly her name was mentioned.

"And so should Anya!"

"Oh, keep quiet, Harold. Anya is a very lucky girl to get what she has. I never lived in a house like this when I was growing up."

"But that was Anya's money. Her father never meant it for

Robert. It's only fair, Rose."

"He's a boy and he needs a proper education. She doesn't."

"What are you going to tell Jackson? He wanted her at the Harley School."

"It won't hurt Jackson to help out with expenses, for once. We spent enough on his education."

"But Anya –"

"Harold, if you had not lost everything we had in the stock market, we might –"

"Stop throwing that in my face, Rose! I'm sick of hearing your –"

"And I'm sick of pinching pennies!"

"Don't give me that! You're tighter than the paper on the wall and you always have been."

"What choice do I have? If you would, at the very least –"

Anya went on downstairs. Poor Grandfather. No wonder he was so grouchy these days. His failings would take at least half an hour for Grandmother to enumerate, and Anya had heard it all before.

*T*he next evening, Anya crept into her grandfather's study and began a quiet game of marbles. Some people find it lonely to play by themselves. Anya didn't complain. It was just the way things were for her. Sometimes Grandfather would be in there reading or listening to the radio, but tonight she had the room to herself. She crouched in the corner where she wouldn't be noticed. She laid a circle of string on the carpet and tossed out a handful of marbles. She took out her father's old shooter marble, and began to play. She looked up when she saw Robert's feet coming across the rug. He scattered her marbles with the toe of his shoe and laughed.

"Hey!" She scrambled around on her knees, gathering her marbles back into their leather pouch.

Robert put his foot on her shoulder and pushed, knocking her sideways. "I just wanted to play with you, Puke-face. Look at you! You're so funny when you're mad." Again he pushed her to the floor.

"You leave me alone!" Anya leapt up in fury. She was no shrinking violet! She had plenty of backbone and she could prove it! She hauled back and let Robert have it, landing her fist right in his eye.

"Ow!" he howled, cupping his face. "You stinking brat! You'll pay for this!" He tried to grab her around the neck but she dug her fingernails into his arm and backed out of his reach.

"What is going on here?" Their Grandfather, newspaper in hand, came in. "What in the world are you two fighting about?"

"Look what she did, Grandfather! She punched me! I'm bleeding!"

"Oh, for heaven's sake, Robert. You know what happens when you tease a person. Now both of you, out! Go find something else to do. Jiminy, I'd like a little peace and quiet somewhere in this house. The President is speaking in a minute and it would be nice if I could hear him for once."

Grandfather bent over his radio and Anya fled.

"Look at my eye, Grandfather. Look what she did," whimpered Robert.

Grandfather tipped the boy's head back and looked. "You'll live, but you're going to have quite the shiner. Still, I daresay you deserve what you got."

"Did not," Robert sniveled. "Did not."

*T*hat night, Anya had another nightmare. The housekeeper, Mrs. Wright, pulled on a robe and came to sit with her.

"It was just a dream, Anya. Just a dream." She rubbed Anya's back. "How 'bout some cocoa?"

Anya sniffed and nodded.

Mrs. Wright took a lamp and went downstairs. At the bottom of the steps, she noticed a light on in the study.

Who was in there?

It was late, far too late for anyone in this family to be up. Wary, she put the lamp down, pulled an umbrella from the stand by the door, and crept over to the study doors. There had been burglaries in this county for over two years now. The thief had never been caught, but if he had managed to get into this house somehow, Lord help him! She'd bash his brains out! The umbrella shook in her hand, but Mrs. Wright steeled herself, raised it over her head, and nudged the heavy sliding door open a crack.

She stopped. Her eyes narrowed. Anya's Aunt Helen was in

there. The umbrella sank to Mrs. Wright's side. Lord Henry! What was Helen wearing? She was just untying a black bag. Mrs. Wright's eyes peeled wide open when she saw what Helen poured from the bag. As quietly as she could Mrs. Wright backed away, trying not to rattle the umbrella stand as she replaced her weapon. She snatched up her lamp and did not start breathing again until she was behind the kitchen door.

When the cocoa was ready, she went cautiously into the hall. Everything was dark now. No light shone from under the study doors. No light on the second floor either. Relieved that Helen had not seen her, she quietly opened the door to the third floor stairway. Still shivering from shock and confusion, she was glad, for once, of the heat in the attic. She steadied the tray with its cup and saucer and was about to make her way upstairs when she heard it. A door behind her, snicking closed.

Anya's Aunt Helen had a very busy social life. She never entertained anyone at home, but she was forever running out for afternoon appointments, always fashionably dressed – elegant suits, voluptuous fur stoles, stylish coats with matching hats. She also went out at night several times a month, often quite late, usually dressed to the nines, but sometimes not. Helen didn't seem to enjoy going out. She was always flustered and preoccupied, always in a hurry. More than once, as Anya passed her aunt's door, she had heard Helen fretting. She couldn't understand why her aunt bothered with a social life at all, if it caused so much anxiety.

It was the afternoon after her bad dream when, as Anya crossed the second floor landing, Aunt Helen came out of their rooms in a cloud of perfume. She wore a small lavender hat cocked above one eye, with a flirty little fluff of veil that came down just to the top of her lips. She was pulling on long lavender gloves, and Robert trailed behind.

"I can't listen to you now, Bobby. I've got to be somewhere."

Aunt Helen and Robert stopped when they saw Anya.

"Bobby, let her pass." She put a protective arm around her son and Anya felt the smallest prick of longing.

"I can't imagine what possessed you to hurt your cousin, Anya. You should have come to me if you were upset about something. There is no need for such violence. Now go. Go on."

She shooed Anya ahead, but not before Anya got a look at the stunning dark bruise on Robert's eye. It was only a small bruise, but she was pleased that it was so gratifyingly purple.

A couple of hours later, Anya climbed back up to her room and was furious to see Robert there.

She flew at him. "Hey! What are you doing in my room?" He held a handful of her marbles and the leather pouch her father had given her. "Give those back!"

"Get away! I'm keeping them. Mother says they were hers."

Anya snatched the bag from his hand. "They are not! Give me

those!"

Robert giggled and held a fistful of marbles over his head, out of her reach.

"Give them to me, Robert!"

Laughing crazily, Robert ran for the stairs, trying to jam marbles into his pocket. They scattered all over, some bouncing down the stairs.

Aunt Helen heard the commotion and opened the stairway door. "What's going on up there? For heaven's sake, will you two stop it?"

"She's throwing marbles at me, Mommy!"

"Anya, stop pestering him. Come on, Bobby, come down. Just leave her alone if she's behaving like that. And watch where you're going."

Robert picked his way down the twisting steps, carefully avoiding the marbles strewn about.

"Will you please pick those up?" Aunt Helen scolded Anya. "Someone could slip and kill themselves on these stairs."

CHAPTER TWO

*I*t was the next morning that the terrible accident occurred. Before Anya was even out of bed she heard a cry and a tremendous crashing on the third floor stairway. She ran out in her nightie to find Mrs. Wright lying in a heap at the bottom of the stairs, her leg and an arm at the oddest angles. Anya screamed and scrambled down the steps. She was sure Mrs. Wright was dead. Aunt Helen flung open the stairway door. Robert was right behind her. Helen gaped at the body of their housekeeper and put out an arm to stop her son.

"Bobby, don't look. Go get dressed."

"I am dressed." Robert knelt. "She's not alive, I don't think."

"Oh my god! We've got to call someone. Is she breathing, Bobby?"

"I don't think so." He looked at Anya, on her knees, crying. What a dork she was. Robert's hand went to his pocket. He fingered something there and thought of a plan, a way to really get back at his cousin for punching him. She'd be really sorry now, the stupid little goody-two-shoes.

"How did this happen?" Aunt Helen glared down at Anya. "Did

you see, Anya?"

"No, I just heard her fall. Will you call the ambulance, Aunt Helen?"

Robert stood up, and held something out for his mother to see.

She gasped. "Oh my god! Anya! Didn't I tell you to pick up these marbles?"

"I did. I picked them up. I know I did!"

Aunt Helen thrust her hand out. "Well, what do you call this?" Between manicured fingers she held Anya's father's shooter marble. "This is terrible. You," Helen scowled, "are in serious trouble."

*I*t seemed to take forever for help to come that morning. Mrs. Wright's body was very carefully lifted onto a stretcher and taken away in an ambulance. She was still alive, they said, but shook their heads in a way that frightened Anya out of her wits. Practically in a state of shock, she curled up on her bed and stared out the window.

Later, her grandmother ordered Anya downstairs to await her punishment in the study. She slunk in and sat down, her hands between her knees, holding herself rigid to stop the shivering. She was sick to her core, imagining Mrs. Wright in a hospital bed. How had this happened? Anya knew, she was absolutely certain that she had picked up every marble. The question was, if she hadn't left a marble on the stairs, who had?

She heard her grandmother and Aunt Helen come in. Afraid to look at them, she kept her eyes down, twisting her fingers in her lap.

The two ladies, mother and daughter, towered over her with arms crossed. When she did glance up, their faces were corrugated with frowns. Behind them, she glimpsed Robert peering through the partly-open door.

"Sit up, Anya."

She was cowering in the chair. She couldn't help it.

"I want to know what made you do such a thing, when you were expressly told to pick up those marbles?" her grandmother demanded.

"I didn't leave any marbles there. I didn't!" Anya felt her face crumple. "I know I didn't." She was trying not to cry in front of them but her chin shook with her effort.

Aunt Helen bent over her. "I just can't figure out what has gotten into you, Anya. First you get into the wine, then you attack Robert, now this incident. This isn't like you. What's going on?"

"It wasn't my fault! I didn't leave any marbles there! I didn't!" Anya's fists raked the tears from her cheeks.

Her grandmother gripped her by the shoulder. "They say it's very possible that the woman broke her neck when she fell. You do realize that? You realize what this means, Anya? Look at me! You know what this means?"

Anya shrunk away, making herself as small as she could. She shook her head.

"If she dies, this would be murder. You could be charged with murder, Anya."

This was too much. "No!" screamed Anya. She bolted upright,

gripping the arms of the chair. "No! I would never!"

Anya's fury made her grandmother draw back in surprise.

"I warned you, didn't I, that an accident could happen?" asked Aunt Helen.

"What ever possessed you?" cried Grandmother. "You are such a little pill. So disobedient, and after all we have done for you. I am completely disgusted with you!"

"I didn't leave any marbles on the stair! I didn't!"

The more Anya protested, the more worked up her Grandmother became. She pointed a sharp-nailed finger at Anya. "You are in big trouble now. There are places for children like you. You know what I'm talking about. Don't you!" Her grandmother's face was purple with fury.

Anya could barely shake her head.

"Reform school! Reform school for you, young lady." None of them heard Robert, now white as a sheet, slip away up the stairs.

"Reform school? What is it?" Anya whispered.

"They'll lock you up until you learn to behave. And believe me, they can make you behave."

"Jail?"

"Now Mother," reasoned Aunt Helen. "Wait a minute. Calm down a little. You don't mean that."

"She deserves it!"

"No. Please, Grandmother. Please."

"You've made your bed," her grandmother vowed, "and now you have to lie in it."

"Well, Mother, really, you're over –" Aunt Helen put her hand on Grandmother's arm.

"No!" Grandmother flung Helen's hand away. "She's got to learn! Surely she can't expect us to keep someone like her in this house. Who knows who she'll hurt next? What if it's me that gets hurt? Now you march right up those stairs, Anya. Sit in your room and think about what you've done."

"Mother, we'll talk this over – " protested Aunt Helen.

"I'm locking that stairway door and calling the police. Go on, Anya! Get out of my sight, this instant."

Anya flew up the broad carpeted stairs, then up the steep wooden stairs to her room.

Reform school. A place where they lock children up? What would they do to her there? No, please, this couldn't be happening. Her world had split wide open. One minute, she was safe, staying out of peoples' way, no problem to anyone. The next minute, she was a criminal. She stood in her room, her teeth chattering with a sudden chill, looking around frantically. What could she do?

Something, anything! Then, an image flashed before her eyes. That boy! The dirty boy she had seen on the bridge! She had wondered, that day, why a boy would choose such a life.

Now, she knew.

She yanked the pillow from her bed, tore off the case, and began stuffing clothing inside. A sweater, socks and underwear, a clean dress, the overalls she wore to work in the garden. She had to hurry. They were going to lock her in. What would she need? Her precious things. The book her father had given her, and his marbles. The little string of pearls that had been her mother's. She emptied the money from her piggy bank into a stocking. She stuffed her arms into a coat, laced up her gardening boots, and looked around her room.

I must go, she thought. But I wish ... no! Hurry! Why should I be sad, anyway, to leave this place? Especially if Mrs. Wright is not here. I just wish ... she didn't know what she wished. She only knew her heart was in her mouth.

She crept downstairs. She mustn't be seen! She raced across the second floor landing to the back stairs that led to the kitchen. Her grandmother and grandfather were in their room, arguing at the tops of their voices, but she didn't stop to listen. She couldn't waste a minute. At the bottom of the stairs, she cracked open the door to the kitchen. Betty the cook was gone. She had gone to the hospital to be with Mrs. Wright, and was apparently still there. Did this mean Mrs. Wright was still alive? Or not alive? Anya would have given the world to know.

She crept through the silent kitchen. In the pantry, she lifted a glass dome and took a heavy chunk of cheese wrapped in its cloth. She dropped it into her pillowcase. Frantically, she looked around. Corn muffins! She took two and wedged them into a tin of cookies. A bunch of carrots, three apples. Her pillow case bulged. She heard someone coming so she slipped out the back door and into the garage.

She squatted behind one of the cars so she wouldn't be seen, trying to think what to do next. Where could she go? Where, where? If only Neil were here! But there was no one she could ask for help.

Where would she find safety?

The back doorknob rattled. Someone was coming. They must be looking for her. Anya quietly opened a car door and slipped onto the floor behind the front seat. She hid face down, glad she was wearing a dark-colored coat, and held her breath.

One of the garage doors was flung open.

Then the car's front door opened, the very car Anya was hiding in. She'd been discovered?

The car door slammed, the engine roared. The car backed out of the garage and swung around fast, sliding on the gravel and speeding down the driveway.

Had she been seen? She wasn't sure. Were they taking her away now, driving her to the reform school, to be absolutely sure she was out of the house?

She lay quiet, not moving a muscle, uncertain whether she had been discovered, not daring to breathe. Maybe she hadn't been noticed. The car drove for several minutes before skidding into a sharp turn and braking to an abrupt halt.

Anya put her fist to her mouth, strangling the cry she felt rising in her throat. She braced herself, waiting to be pulled from her hiding place and thrown into a horribly dark dungeon. Locked in forever, cold, alone!

Someone got out of the car, slammed the door. She heard footsteps retreating. Police! They were going to get the police. Guards would drag her into the building. How could this be happening? Please, someone! Help me!

But there was no one to help her. She would be locked away, never to be seen again.

Slowly she peeked over the edge of the front seat of the car. Aunt Helen! It was her Aunt Helen that had been driving. It was Aunt Helen that she saw just entering a very large house. It looked like a mansion. It did not look like a dismal place. There was a sleek black car in the drive. Could this be the reform school?

Still, she mustn't wait to find out. Hurry, hurry, get away! Hide somewhere! She had never seen this house. She had no idea where she was, but she slid out of the back seat of the car without even closing the door, and ran for her life. She ducked into some shrubbery and crouched there, panting. It had begun to rain. What to do next? It was foolish to stay hidden in this garden. She must run.

So that is what she did. She ran, lugging her pillow case of food and clothing. She ran for her life into the woods, woods that she had never seen before. Fear bounded after her, a terrible beast on long legs, hungry to catch her, devour her! Run! Anya was blind to everything except escape.

She ran in what she hoped was the opposite direction from home. It would be useless to go home. There was no help for her there. She must get far, far away, as far as she could before it got dark. She saw nothing she recognized, no canal or train station, no library or school or church, no buildings of any kind. Where was she?

She forced herself to keep running, even when her side began to ache and she could barely pick up her feet. Perspiring, she stopped to tear off her coat, then ran on, holding her aching side. Her pillowcase bundle banged against her legs. Splashing through the rain, she went on and on. Whenever she had a choice between open space and woodland, she chose the woods. Get away from people. They would be searching for her, a runaway. A girl who should be locked up. A girl who had murdered. The woods were her only hope. Run, she told herself! Run!

Little did she know there was no one chasing her. Not yet. Back at home, Grandfather had finally calmed her grandmother down, had convinced her that reform school was a ridiculous idea. Still, Grandmother insisted on locking Anya in the attic, just as she had threatened. She marched over to the attic door, twisted the key in the lock and wrenched it out.

But of course by then, Anya had already gone.

CHAPTER THREE

*T*he sun was a pink fire slipping down from smoke-colored clouds. It had stopped raining. Anya slowed to a walk, trying to catch her breath. She had been running blindly. Now she began to look around. Dolorous trees everywhere, black giants, swaying, moaning in the wind. Wind pulling at the treetops, wind elbowing the clouds. She was deep in the woods, how far from a town? What if she had run straight back to their village? That was her deepest fear. Or it was her deepest fear until it began to get really dark.

Suddenly the enormity of her situation made her fall to her knees. Her fat pillowcase thudded onto wet leaves. No, she told herself! This was not the time to cry. Get up! She must find somewhere to hide. She got up and staggered on, and no sooner had she thought of shelter than she spotted a shed at the edge of a clearing.

She wanted to run to it, crouch down small and hide in there, get out of danger and catch her breath. She was bone tired. She must be careful, though, because she had no idea where she was or who was out here. Were the police searching for her now? She could hear nothing. No one had found her yet, no one but the roving wind. She moved closer to the shed, as quietly as she could. Raindrops blew out of the trees and ran down her hot face. Across the clearing from the shed was a house, more like a shack, really. She shuddered to think who lived there. No one very nice. A finger of smoke slanted from the chimney. She moved closer again. All she could hear was the sinister rumble of thunder. No dog barked an alarm. No one yelled a warning. She crept up behind the shed. Its door was on the other side, facing the house. Would she be able to get inside, or would it be locked?

It was fully dark now. The wind swirled and it was starting to rain again. Now that she had stopped running, she realized she was soaking wet. She couldn't very well stand outside all night. She inched along the side of the shed. She came around the corner and moved toward the door. She was in full view of the house across the clearing. Quick, quick get inside! she told herself. She pushed on the latch. It didn't move. Again she pushed it, hard. It held tight.

At this, she did begin to cry. She kicked the door. She'd never been allowed such a display of temper. What do I care, she thought – she kicked it again! Stupid latch! She leaned against the door and pushed with all her might. Open up! What did it matter how much noise she made now? She'd come so far! Open! She threw her shoulder against it. After she had run and run ... *scrape*. The grind of a rusty latch. She pushed it up. The hinges squealed and she stepped quickly into the shed. Breathing hard, she barely found room to stand, but at least she was out of the rain.

Inside, a furtive turning of heads. Footsteps halted in midstride, frozen in terror. Dark eyes, shocked and staring. Twelve little country mice barely breathed. They had homes here amongst the pots and bags, the tools and cans. This was their domain. Who was this now, this invader?

It was at this point that Anya realized there were a couple of things she hadn't considered. She had no light. It was black as pitch in here. She had no blanket to sleep under and she was wet and cold, though it was August. There was no space in this shed for her to lie down, or even sit. What had she done? This was a mistake, a bad mistake. She should turn around and go back.

Stop acting like a baby! she told herself. You had no choice! This dirty old shed is better than reform school. And it certainly can't be as bad as being in Grandmother's house tonight. Can it? But still, her own room and her books and – no! Don't think about that. Mrs. Wright wouldn't be there, would she? At the thought of the housekeeper, Anya's resolve collapsed. She put her palms against her eyes and sobbed. Mrs. Wright, hurting, lying injured in the hospital. Or even possibly, oh dear ... oh dear, please don't die! Please, Mrs. Wright! You can't be dead! Please please!

She tried to stop crying but a great well of misery had yawned open inside her. Every time she thought she had mastered herself, another low wail would rise unbidden. She clenched her teeth to keep from sobbing out loud, glad for the noise of the rain. Luckily, there was not a soul who could hear her.

Twelve puzzled mice crept to the edges of shelves and tried to figure out what all the racket was about.

Life was not always fair, Anya knew that, but when had the world become such a threatening place? Worn out with trying to make sense of everything, she wiped her eyes with her sleeve. I'm almost nine years old, she thought. Not a baby! I don't know what I'm doing. Or where I'm going. But I'll figure it out somehow. I will! She heard Mrs. Wright's voice in her ear. Get some backbone!

The shed was dark and smelled depressingly musty. She opened the door just a little and stuck a trowel under it to wedge it open. The wind slashed the rain in sheets. She could no longer even see the house across the clearing. Good, she thought. That means no one will be out and about tonight. She leaned her head on the door jamb. Safe. Safe here, for the time. That was all that mattered. Wasn't it?

With the door cracked open, she could make out some shapes in the dark shed. Yes, this was a wheelbarrow handle that was butting her in the small of her back. She felt carefully along its edge, then inside. It felt rough inside, but empty. She hoped it was empty. Leaving the door slightly open to get rid of the dank smell, she crawled into the wheelbarrow. Wait, no! If she left the door open, would a mouse, or something worse, come in? She got up and closed the door.

Twelve mice looked at each other and rolled their eyes.

Anya climbed back into the wheelbarrow and pulled her bundle in after her. This would have to do for a bed. She took off her boots and hung her wet socks on the handle of the wheelbarrow. Her coat was damp but it would serve as a blanket.

She folded her legs under her and propped her elbows on her knees with a sigh. She was out of the storm. The wind and rain pummeled the little shed, but at least it was dry. She would have to sleep in her wet dress. No nightgown tonight. Suddenly she realized she was hungry. She found an apple and the corn muffins.

Muffins? *Corn* muffins! The smell was almost too much for one of the mouse children. She would have fallen off the shelf in her eagerness if she hadn't possessed a tail and a mother quick enough to catch hold of it.

Anya knew it would be a long time, who knew how long, before her food supplies could be replenished. She ate only the muffins and an apple, and tried to formulate a plan for the next day.

She stared into the darkness. A plan? There was no one who could help her and she didn't even know where she was going. How could she plan? What was she going to do? She thought she had known loneliness before. She was used to being treated with a measure of indifference. She was, she believed, hardened to it. But no, she had known nothing of loneliness, nothing at all. In this shed, tonight, she was entirely and completely alone.

Twelve mice shifted quietly in the darkness and waited.

Mrs. Wright had told her many times that a new beginning often starts with a small tear. She felt that small tear now. She curled up in the wheelbarrow and pulled her coat across her shoulders. Her eyes dropped closed. Rain tattooed the roof like a crazy-mad drummer. *Paradiddle paradiddle.* Thunder cracked the cymbals. *Whap! Bam!* Anya fell asleep with her head on her bundle.

She woke up once in the night, crying from a nightmare. No one to comfort her tonight. All alone. Again, exhausted, she slept.

Twelve mice scooted across the shelves and down the walls, finally able to go about their nighttime business. The truth about country mice is that they rarely feel compassion. They have neither the time for it, nor the inclination. Tonight was no different. There was someone in their shed who made a frightening amount of noise with her whining and sobbing. They would just have to ignore her and carry on.

One little mouse did perch on the edge of the wheelbarrow, studying the sleeping girl. Not a single crumb of corn muffin? Really? Pity.

*I*n the morning, light fingered the edge of the shed door. Anya slowly came awake and only gradually remembered where she was. And when she remembered why she was there – that she had been branded as a criminal for something she did not do – she was crying again. What was she going to do?

She was afraid. She didn't want to run anymore. But if she stopped now, what would become of her? Was she the evil girl her grandmother had declared her to be? No! She must go on, go farther! She must keep running. But where to go? There had to be somewhere for her in the whole wide world.

She put on clean socks. Three mice slipped unseen from her boots just before she leaned down to reach for them. She climbed out of the wheelbarrow and peered outside. The rain had stopped. Across the clearing, nothing moved but a thin streamer of smoke sliding from the crooked old chimney. The sun was well up but she saw no movement anywhere. Maybe she could stay here, in this shed, safe and dry? No, she could not risk staying in one place for too long. Feeling dejected, still tired in every bone, she pulled her pillowcase bundle out of the wheelbarrow and gave a long sigh.

A dozen little mice peered from clay pots and watering cans. They sighed too, twelve very small sighs. Was this maudlin creature ever going to leave?

Anya closed the shed door and headed back into the woods, her bundle slung over her shoulder.

A dozen little mice tore across shelves and down walls, making a dash for her apple core.

The morning was clear and cool, and it lifted Anya's spirits a bit. She tried to remember where she had been when she had first seen the shed. I was over there, she thought. So I'll go on in the direction I was going last night. She had heard that people who are lost often end up walking in circles. I'll see my footprints again, if I do that. Her footprints in the mud! Anyone else could see them as well, and know where she was headed. Get moving!

The direction she took, the sun told her, was east. So in the morning she should follow the sun. In the afternoon, she should keep the sun at her back. That was the best plan she could think of right now. Just keep heading east, a random choice but the best she could come up with. Try to put as much distance as possible between herself and reform school.

The very words 'reform school' made her shudder. But this is what will keep you going, she told herself, this dreadful image of a dreadful place. Think how lucky that you are not there! This was the thought that gave her hope.

But that was enough thinking. She shouldn't let herself worry about Mrs. Wright possibly being dead. She must not let herself be consumed with upsetting thoughts about her grandmother and her aunt and her cousin Robert. She must handle these thoughts the way she always did – just put them out of her mind.

Walking in the morning woods helped clear her head. After a time, the trees stopped at the edge of a broad brown expanse of a farmer's field. Above, the sun was a hot disc burned tight to the cerulean sky. Raindrops from last night starred the sparse meadow grasses. Across a valley from where she stood was another woods that climbed a high hill. She looked around. That distant hill looked to be in her path to the east. There were no houses that she could see. At her feet, a breeze set the white blooms of Queen Anne's Lace dancing, and above the flowers, pale butterflies flittered, whispering, tattling secrets. Cold winds a-coming, they warned, sharp winds and long gray skies. How much longer would summer last, Anya wondered, and where would she be when autumn came?

Before her was the open meadow. She had to decide if it would be safe to cross it. Would she be spotted by someone? As she stood trying to figure out which way to go, a farmer and his plow horse came over the hill toward her. Anya shrank back into the woods. The man would certainly see her if she crossed his meadow. A girl, carrying a sack? Running? Running from what, he would wonder? He would know something wasn't right. A boy, now, that would be a different matter. A boy would be overlooked – out exploring, doing what boys do. But not a girl.

Well, here was a problem she could do something about. Anya reached into her pillow case and pulled out the overalls and cap she wore for gardening. Behind a tree she took off her dress, dirty as it was, and pulled on a shirt and the overalls. She tucked her hair up under her cap, and laced her boots again. She edged over to the far side of the field and, hearing the farmer call to the horse to turn, she began to run. The horse noticed her. He objected, yes, objected strongly to a stranger in his field. He tossed his head and rattled his harness. But the farmer barely glanced at her, though he did remind himself to lock his door against prowling hobos when he got home.

Such freedom! Life was different for boys! So for the moment no one knew where she was. A great weight lifted from her heart and she ran like the wind. Down she went, across the open field and through the line of trees. She stumbled across a low stone wall and started plodding up the hill ahead.

The sky had turned gray and the sun was low behind her by the time she struggled into the woods that crowned the hill. Her resilience evaporating, worn out with the climb, she sat down against a tree and looked at the way she had come. These were big hills. It had taken half the afternoon to cross from one hilltop to the next. She wasn't getting very far. If only I knew someplace I could go, she told herself, I wouldn't feel so bad. But where in the world *can* I go?

She took off her cap with yet another sigh and opened the pillow case. It had been a long time since she had eaten this morning. She unwrapped the cheese and realized she didn't have a knife. So she bit off chunks, devouring it hungrily and glad her grandmother wasn't there to see her deplorable manners. As she folded the cloth back around the cheese and put it away, a bird in the tree overhead set up a terrible racket. Had he been hoping for a bite? With the thought of a friendly woodland animal came the sudden fear of an unfriendly one. Night was coming and she had no garden shed to sleep in this evening. Suddenly worried, she looked around for shelter. The woods at her back had turned very dark. Nowhere safe to hide. Only rank upon rank of trees, a silent host, waiting, expectant. Waiting for what? What happened in a forest in the deep of night?

There was a maple tree near the edge of the woods, the only one she could find with branches low enough to reach. She climbed up and dragged her pillow case after her. She tried to find a comfortable position. If she did sleep, she might fall out of the tree and break her neck. She wriggled, trying to wedge herself tight between two branches.

The forest was restless. Faded August leaves shuffled and muttered, until, with sudden crescendo, they wailed against a rising wind. Anya thought of a poem about wind in her book. Its eeriness used to delight her. Tonight it gave her the creeps.

Whenever the moon and stars are set,

Whenever the wind is high,

All night long in the dark and wet,

A man goes riding by ....

Above her, the maple tree rocked creaking in the wind. A pair of tree frogs echoed each other in a tiresome chant. Then there was another sound, barely audible. Something down there. Anya dared not move. Her eyes flicked right and left. She heard a soft snorting and four deer, almost invisible in the dwindling light, paused beneath her tree. Their heads were up, their noses scenting the breeze. Finally one moved on and the rest followed warily. Just about to doze off, Anya sat up with a start. A long, long howl chilled her to her very bones. There it was again, from deep in the woods. It sounded like a woman, a ghost woman. A ghost crying long and loud, wordlessly, the pitch rising in terror. And again it came, a desperate keening.

Then, quiet. Not another sound.

Only the wind.

Anya's heart beat frantically. She could see nothing, hear nothing more. It was a long time before she could breathe at all, and much longer than that before she could breathe normally. She must stay awake. Watch carefully.

Deep darkness. The forest swaying and breathing. Sleep nudged her but did not come.

... Late in the night, when the fires are out,

Why does he gallop and gallop about? ...

Strange night sounds. Fears plucked at her and she had no defense. Where could she go to find safety? Mrs. Wright – what had become of her? Anya pulled her legs up close to her body and leaned against the maple tree trunk. The cramped little shed of last night seemed luxurious now. Even more so, her little attic room at home. Her books, her bed. In the garden, her hand in Neil's. Her head on Mrs. Wright's shoulder. Betty cooking three meals a day ....

... By at the gallop he goes, and then
By he comes back at the gallop again.

At dawn's first light, Anya climbed stiffly out of the tree. She was sore, chilled to the bone, and groggy from lack of sleep. She had dozed fitfully all night, roused by snuffling sounds below her, by the sudden crack of dry branches, something stirring among the leaves on the forest floor. And under it all rolled the sighs of the woodland, lamenting the long-ago nights when the whole world was a sea of trees. She had hardly dared to move all night. What would she encounter as she trekked over the hill this morning?

She sat down beside the tree and decided to eat a carrot for her breakfast, for a change from apples, and she allowed herself only one cookie. A bird of the same variety as last night began making a terrible noise again. Maybe he didn't like interlopers in his woods. Thinking him very inhospitable, she decided it was time to get up and get out of there. She dusted leaves off her overalls and was about to shoulder her sack when she noticed a number of black feathers on the ground. Some creature had obviously been in a fight, poor thing. Maybe it was he who was making such a fuss this morning. She looked around, and there, just above her head, perched a crow. He fluttered one wing and held the other at an awkward angle. He reached an open beak to her.

"Hello, little fellow," she crooned to him. "Are these your feathers down here?"

Ccccrrr-aaaxxx! said the crow.

"You're hurt then, aren't you?"

Ccccrrr-aaaxxx!

"Are you too hurt to find food for your breakfast? Here, I can give you something." She opened the tin of cookies and the bird screeched like a banshee, flapping one wing and dancing up and down the branch. Reluctant to give away something so valuable as a cookie, she still had to sympathize with a fellow creature in distress. She held out a tiny piece. The crow bent low and stretched his beak wide.

"Take it, take it. It's for you."

Ccccrrr-aaaxxx! The bird dipped and danced and fluttered his wings, but he didn't take the cookie.

"Are you afraid of me?" He seemed to want her to feed him, but she was afraid he would bite her. Finally she broke off a small crumb and dropped it quickly down his yawning gullet.

Ccccrrr-aaaxxx! Ccccrrr-aaaxxx! He wanted more. She fed him crumb after crumb, and he ended up eating half the cookie.

"That's all I want to share with you, baby bird. Your mother will be back soon." She put the tin away and picked up her bag. Seeing her walk away, the bird called frantically. She turned around and came back.

"Don't you see I have to be on my way? You must have someone to take care of you, don't you?" Anya stretched out a hand and was surprised when the crow immediately jumped to sit on her wrist.

"Well! You must be really lonesome. Did your parents leave you? Poor bird. Here we are, both of us alone. You could come with me for a while. Would you like that, black bird?"

Ccccrrr-aaaxxx!

Well, this was nice. A pet, or a kind of a pet. Not furry, but still, a friend. Anya held her hand close to her shoulder and, fluttering awkwardly, the crow moved to perch himself next to her ear. He swayed and squawked until he got used to her gait, and then was content to snooze when it suited him, or watch the woods go by.

They went along together all that day. Having a companion gave Anya something to think about besides her own troubles. She even found herself talking to the bird from time to time. When they came to the top of another wooded hill, she stopped at around noon so they both could have a bite to eat. When she opened her bundle the crow hopped awkwardly down her arm and squawked beseechingly.

"We're going to have to find you something to eat besides my food." What did young crows eat?

They had seen some farmers' fields that morning, but only a couple of lonely farmhouses. She was fairly certain they were still going in an easterly direction, and they soon set off again. A wind began to rise, never-ending wind, moaning through the valley like a lost soul. The temperature had dropped, very cool for August, but as long as they kept moving, Anya stayed warm enough. However, by dusk, towers of soot-black clouds were roiling across the sky and the wind's lament was a long, low sob. Anya heard the patter of rain in the treetops. She knew she couldn't last all night in the open. They had to find shelter.

But there was none. Anya and the crow trudged on through the woods. Her head was beginning to feel thick and heavy. She was hungry, exhausted, and irritated. The leafy roof of the forest was no longer protection from the rain, and even the crow looked wet and vexed. They came to an open space. Anya leaned against a tree and looked out across a hillside, wishing she could find some cover. Even a haystack would do. Then she noticed something in the tree above her.

"Look, little crow! A tree house." It was actually a hunter's blind, but Anya knew nothing of such things. If only she could get up there, they would be able to get out of the rain. The rickety cabin was slapped together with scrap lumber, but it had walls and a roof. Shelter.

There was a series of boards, like a ladder, climbing up the tree trunk. She leapt up to catch hold of the lowest board. The crow, clinging in panic to her shoulder, screamed in dismay. She could just manage to get hold of the board, but how to get her bundle up there? And the crow as well? She dropped to the ground again.

"Look, you'll have to sit somewhere while I find a way to get up there." She set the crow on a limb and put her bundle down. "You can't fly. I certainly can't fly. But we have to find a way to climb that ladder."

The rain was blowing through the woods by this time, and the sky grew darker. Anya tramped around, trying to find a log or something she could climb on. A fallen tree trunk lay nearby but no matter how hard she tried, she did not have the strength to move it.

"Dadgummit!" she swore, nearly in tears. It was an oath she had heard her grandfather use more than once. She was losing patience. "I'm so tired of being wet and cold! We've got to get up there!" The crow had moved out along the limb and was pecking at something. Anya dropped to the ground and leaned against the trunk of the tree he sat in. "What are you picking at up there?" She wiped her eyes on her sleeve. "Oh brother! Why am I talking to a dumb bird? You're no help at all!" she yelled.

The crow looked down at her and squawked.

"Just keep quiet!" She flung her arm at him and he fluttered his uninjured wing.

Listen to yourself, she thought. You're starting to sound like Grandmother.

It was then that she noticed the rope. The crow had been pecking at insects that crawled on an old piece of rope tied around a branch. She jumped up.

"Look what you found!" she exclaimed. She coaxed the crow off the rope. It had been there for a long time, old, dirty, and knotted tight.

"We need this," she said through clenched teeth. "I just have to get it untied! I ... am ... going ... to have this rope!"

"Ah, finally!" The knot released. The rope was only a little over a yard long, but she could tie the pillowcase closed with it. She made a loop, and hung it over the lowest of the slats that were nailed to the tree. She set the crow on the bundle. Insecure, he scrabbled for a grip. Now she had two hands free and with great effort, managed to pull herself up so she could stand on the lowest board. She moved the bundle up one step. The crow squawked and fluttered, trying not to lose hold of the pillowcase.

"Hang on!" she hollered. He panicked and tried to jump onto her hand. "Wait! Just wait!" Maneuvering clumsily, step by step, she and the crow got to the top of the ladder. Anya wasn't tall enough to get into the tree house but she reached for the crow and set him inside on the floor. Seeming worried, he watched her grunting with the effort of lifting the bundle in.

"Now how am I going to get in here?" The crow, unable to give an intelligent answer, walked in circles. Anya braced her elbows on the floor, wriggled one knee up, and finally pulled herself in.

They had made it.

She was completely exhausted. She just lay there on her stomach for a minute, trying to get her breath. She rolled over.

"What are you looking at, you dumb bird?"

He ruffled his feathers, protesting. Or trying to hide his wounded feelings. He fluffed and shook, rearranging every feather with his beak. He's trying to ignore me, thought Anya. He should ignore me. I'm being a monster.

Suddenly she was crying. "I'm sorry! I'm sorry!" She offered the crow her hand. "I don't know what's the matter with me. I didn't mean to be nasty to you. You're the only one I have to talk to."

And talk she did. The crow seemed to listen, cocking his head as though he understood. And maybe he did. Or he may have been thinking his own thoughts, as in 'Hey! Listen here, Sister, cuz I'ma say this one time only. Make with the food already!' Your typical crow talk, a little pushy.

Anya may have gotten the hint. "Are you hungry? Let's have cookies!"

There was one piece of furniture in the tree house, a low stool.

"Let's use this as a table. We'll put it in the corner here, where it's dry." The windows of the tree house were nothing more than holes in the walls, and rain was blowing in. Anya sat on the floor, sagging against the wall. She and the crow took turns eating all but two cookies and the very last carrot.

"Now we have a problem," Anya said to the crow. "I don't know what we'll eat tomorrow." She sighed.

A nasty storm was uncoiling from the black clouds. The tree house rocked and swayed, groaning like some ancient sailing vessel tossed by howling seas. Rain gusted through the window openings and drenched the floor. Anya cowered in the corner, the only dry spot. "Stay close, little crow," she cried. "I'm not sure this place is going to hold together."

They huddled there for a few minutes, listening to the raging of the storm and glad for what shelter they had. Anya finally took off her wet boots and curled up with her head on her bundle of clothes, using her coat for a blanket. The crow hid in the bend of her elbow, and it was only minutes before they both fell fast asleep.

*W*hen they awoke the next day, it was still raining as hard as ever. Anya's head felt achy and swollen and her throat was sore. Her body was a lump of hurt, her stomach empty.

"I can't go any farther today," she croaked. "I don't feel so very well." Besides, this was a good hiding place. No one would ever find them here, not in this weather. She peered out through each of the window slits.

"There is a lake way down there," she noticed. "But it's too far to go in this rain. I just can't make it, little crow." She dropped to the floor, put her bundle under her head, and thought of home.

Home. How very far away it seemed, and how very gloomy that thought made her. She had made a terrible mistake. She never should have left. She could not imagine turning around and going back. But there was no way to go forward either. She simply had nowhere to go.

That was a terrible feeling.

"I wish I had soup," she sighed. She was sure the crow wished the same, but there would be no food for either of them that day.

CHAPTER FOUR

And meanwhile, what was happening back in the Elm Street house belonging to Anya's grandparents? Oh, there was a great deal of upset. First there was the uncertainty about Mrs. Wright. Would she live? And, of utmost importance to the Netherbys, who would feed them? Betty was supplying them with simple dinners, but she spent hours at the hospital with the housekeeper. Were they to be expected to shift for themselves all day?

Also, there were gossiping neighbors to worry about. What would everyone say when they heard that the Netherbys were having troubles? They would gloat, surely. Should the family try to keep the housekeeper's accident secret? They argued and pressed their hands to their heads. It was all so sordid, quite embarrassing.

Then of course, on top of everything, was the problem of finding that miserable grand-daughter. They hadn't even realized she was missing until late the first evening. They had forgotten about her entirely until Betty came in and said she wanted to take Anya her dinner. When they unlocked the stairway door and Betty huffed up the stairs with a tray, they heard her shout the news. Anya wasn't there.

So this caused more consternation. How could that ridiculous child put them in such a position? She was probably hiding somewhere, just manipulating them for her own amusement, causing no end of grief. Grandmother Netherby's inclination was to let her stay out there, wherever she was. Don't even bother to look for her. After a night in the cold, she'd be back on Tuesday in time for breakfast, certain sure.

But of course she wasn't back for breakfast, or lunch, or dinner. To call the police would be yet another embarrassment, but by Tuesday evening, they had little choice. Mrs. Netherby phoned the major because he owed her a favor. She called him Major because she didn't know, or care, what title he went by, but she knew he had some authority on the police force.

Curiously, when she felt like it, Grandmother could be very charming. Tonight, she knew a pleasant manner would get her what she needed. She spoke in her sweetest voice.

"Major, my good friend," she implored him, "I know you're extremely busy, but I wondered if I could ask for your help? We need a favor, some sort of detective or other, I should think."

"Are you missing something, Mrs. Netherby?" The police chief braced himself, his fingers pinching the bridge of his nose.

"Yes, I'm afraid we are. My grand-daughter has disappeared." Grandmother Netherby had formulated a convincing lie. "We thought she had gone off with my daughter Helen, you see, and Helen thought she was with us. It turns out that no one knows where she has gone."

Ah me, he thought. "Did something happen that ... uh, ..."

"Well, we had a little accident here. It rather upset the child. Our housekeeper is in the hospital after a bad fall on the stairs and – and – and ...."

"Did you call the hospital? Maybe the housekeeper could help you."

"Helen phoned but got no help there."

"Maybe if you went down there?"

"To the hospital?"

"I imagine one of you will be going there anyway?"

"She's not family, this woman. She was a servant, a ...."

"*Was* a servant? Oh dear. Her fall wasn't fatal, I hope?"

"No. No, she seems to be hanging on."

"You mean she ...?"

"It was a very bad fall. To my knowledge, the woman hasn't regained consciousness. But listen! We need your help rather badly. You have to send someone to look for my grand-daughter. She is not a well child. We're worried – and Major, I must stress that this is a private matter – we're worried that she may cause harm to herself or someone else. I don't want to go into details."

"But the more we know, Mrs. Netherby, the better equipped we will be to help." Besides, thought the chief to himself, it has been a slow day here. He needed a good laugh.

"Well, the girl is dangerous, to put it bluntly."

"Dangerous."

"If you must know, we fear it was she who caused the housekeeper's accident."

"Really?"

"I'm afraid so."

"How old is the girl?"

"She's got to be, let's see ... well, I'm not sure."

"Ah." A pause of some length. "Can you make a guess, Mrs. Netherby, as to your grand- daughter's age?"

"Maybe seven. Or so."

"Seven years old?"

"Or eight. I'm not sure."

"An eight year old. I see. Well, at that age, she couldn't have gone far, could she?"

"No, I'm sure she's around somewhere. Maybe you could set some hound dogs on her, or whatever is usually done."

"Well, ..." The chief of police paused. Oh boy. "Why don't we start with some details."

"Details?"

"Time of disappearance, the girl's description, and so forth."

"Oh, Major, you know, I'm actually not feeling all that well tonight. I'm so very upset and I just don't have the energy to explain all that. Nor do I have the time to come down there to you. Could you send someone over here? Tomorrow morning would be convenient."

"You want to wait until tomorrow?"

"That would be the most convenient."

"I mean, a missing child – "

"Well, we're pretty tired tonight. The morning is best for us."

"Tomorrow. All right, ma'am. I'll get someone to come to your house tomorrow."

The chief hung up the phone, rested his elbows on his desk, and covered his eyes with his hands. An eight-year-old. He shook his head. Who to send? He didn't want to waste a good man when he was sure it was a case of a rich, spoiled grand-daughter hiding in a trunk in the attic. He picked up the phone again and asked for Officer Wallhanger.

*W*allhanger had been a patrol officer in the same little town for seven years. As a boy, he had moved with his family from Canada when his father, a chemical engineer, got a job at Kodak. After all these years, Wallhanger still did not feel like an American. He had never been able to fit in, especially at work. He was tall and slender, while the other officers could best be described as, well, meaty. He was a nice-looking man but rarely smiled when he was at the station. He did have a sense of humor, but somehow his jokes fell flat when he was there. He was just not comfortable kidding around with the guys, or not with these guys anyway.

The other men were harsh in their opinions of him. His attention to detail made everyone else look bad, and you couldn't get him to fudge a report no matter how sensible it would be to fabricate a lie. In spite of this, or maybe because of it, he had never advanced even to the rank of corporal. But hey, somebody had to sit at the bottom of the totem pole, his co-workers laughed, ain't that right? So why not give that distinction to Wallhanger, the dumb Canuck? That idea appealed to the other police officers. Call some other schmuck inept, and it makes you feel smart, right? Ain't that right? Of course, they never said he was inept because none of them knew the word. He was, in their parlance, just a wacko.

So this was the man assigned to the Netherby case. Wallhanger stood at the door of their Elm Street residence the next morning, waiting for someone to answer his knock. Finally Anya's Aunt Helen opened the door. The officer's eyes warmed, quickly taking her measure from head to toe. At first glance, anyone had to admit that Helen was a pretty lady, even beautiful, and that was assuredly Wallhanger's first impression.

She led him into the foyer. They introduced themselves. Officer Wallhanger held out his hand for a handshake. Helen touched it briefly with her fingertips. She gestured to a pair of chairs in the hall and didn't offer to take the policeman's hat.

"You'll have to excuse us this morning, Detective Wallhanger."

"It's Officer."

"Pardon?"

"Officer Wallhanger. Not that it makes a lot of difference, but I haven't made detective yet. I just wanted to be clear."

"So sorry. As I was saying, we're a bit slow today, with our housekeeper gone."

"Your housekeeper is missing, too?"

"No," said Helen carefully. "The housekeeper is in the hospital after a bad fall. It's my niece who is missing. I believe my mother gave your superior all this information last night."

"If so, the details were not passed on to me. So it's helpful to hear your side of the story, Miss Netherby."

"There is only one side to this story, Officer. My niece is missing and I don't know where to tell you to start looking."

"She is how old?"

"She'll be nine in a couple of weeks."

"You searched the house?"

"She is not in the house. Of that we are quite certain."

"Not in the house. I see." Officer Wallhanger made a note in his notebook. "And the garden?"

"She's not in the garden. Our gardener went over the entire property."

"You've spoken with her friends?"

"No. She's not – we're not aware of any friends."

The officer made another note. "Hmm. And have you established a motive?"

"The reason why she left?"

"Exactly."

Helen sighed. "I don't know. Something's been wrong with her lately. She has been troublesome for days. She physically attacked my son the other day."

"Your son is younger than she?"

"He's not – no, he's older."

Officer Wallhanger nodded gravely.

"Still, these altercations upset him."

"You're saying they fight?"

Helen leaned forward and Wallhanger stiffened. "Fight? My niece gave him a black eye. She taunts him, bullies him all the time."

"Your niece bullies her older cousin?"

"It upsets him terribly, how jealous she is of him."

"Ah," said Wallhanger, narrowing his eyes at Helen. "The green-eyed monster."

"Terribly jealous. We also suspect that she caused the housekeeper's fall."

"Really? How so?"

"The woman slipped on the stairs. And lo and behold, we found some of the child's marbles there."

"Marbles? Would you describe your niece as a careless girl?"

"No. She's normally quite tidy. We are sure the marbles were left intentionally. I'm sorry to say it, but it's true."

"So. You surmise that this accident was planned by the child? She did not like the housekeeper, Mrs. – ?"

"Mrs. Wright. Well, apparently not. Good point, Officer. No, I would say that, no, Anya does not like Mrs. Wright. At all." This was good. No shadow of blame could fall on Robert. Helen must make sure of that.

"The girl's name is Anya?"

"Correct. Anya Netherby."

"And Anya's parents?"

"Her mother passed away. Her father, my brother, is off gallivanting out west somewhere. Who knows where. He hasn't come home in years."

"Years. I see." The officer nodded and looked around the hall where they sat. "She's a fortunate girl to live in a house like this."

"One would think she would appreciate it, but she apparently does not."

"I see." Officer Wallhanger snapped his notebook shut and stood. "I'd like to see the girl's bedroom, if I could."

"It's ... it's not ... there is really nothing up there." Helen shook her head.

"It would help me get a sense of the girl, Miss Netherby. Perhaps there is some clue ...."

She sighed. "All right. If you feel you must."

They climbed with difficulty to the third floor. Helen stood in the doorway to Anya's room and watched the policeman. He wasn't over-hasty, she had to grant that. He looked at the one banged-up chair that was pulled up to the little desk. On the desk, a box held a collection of postcards. He turned one over. A short note, signed only "J". Three library books, due the next day, sat in a neat pile. He looked at the bed. The pillow had been thrown to the foot of the bed. No pillow case. The closet door was hanging open. Clothes spilled from yawning dresser drawers. On a shelf, a piggy bank had fallen over on its side. It was empty.

"You say this child is a tidy girl?"

Helen shrugged. "Normally, yes."

"How many of her marbles did you find on the stair?"

"Well, one."

"Only the one?"

"As far as I know."

"The chances would be slim, though, wouldn't they, that the housekeeper would step on that one marble? If it were left there on purpose, I mean."

"Well, it happened."

"Hmm. And the room next to this one?"

"That is the housekeeper's room."

"The injured lady? I'll just take a peek, if you don't mind." Nothing much to see there. The room was perfectly neat, nothing but a bed and a dresser with a couple of framed photographs propped on top, one of a little girl, and a much older portrait of a little boy. Wallhanger paused to study them.

"Shall we go?" asked Helen.

Finally, the policeman turned and inclined his head. Helen led him back downstairs. He stopped to look at a life-sized oil portrait in the hall.

"It's my son Robert," Helen said.

"Ah. And could I see a portrait of your niece?"

"I – I'll have to give you a description."

"That would be a great help."

"She has light brown hair, straight. Grey eyes, I would say. I'm sorry. I – I don't think I have a photograph of her."

"All right, then." An oil portrait of the boy. Not even a photograph of the girl?

"Is that all you need? Where will you start?"

"I'll visit the housekeeper. She's at the hospital, you say?"

"You can't speak with her."

"Indeed?"

"She's in a coma, close to death."

"Ah. Nevertheless." He pocketed his notebook.

"You can't speak – no!" insisted Helen. "It's useless to go to the hospital. The trouble, Officer, is my niece, not the housekeeper. This child is dangerous. It's possible she could harm someone else. She should be found immediately. My mother has even insisted that she be locked away."

"Locked away? Well, that would indeed be unfortunate."

"I agree, but still, ..."

"I hope it won't come to that. Don't worry, Miss Netherby. We'll find her, I assure you." Wallhanger bowed slightly, set a handsome white straw fedora on his head, and went down the steps.

Helen, frowning with worry, watched him go. What if Mrs. Wright had regained consciousness? What if she started talking?

*O*fficer Wallhanger went straight to the hospital and found Mrs. Wright's room. Betty the cook was sitting beside the housekeeper's bed, holding her inert hand.

"Oh Officer! I'm so glad they sent someone! Have they found the child yet?"

"I am just beginning my search, Madame. I have come to query this woman here." He leaned over and examined Mrs. Wright's still face, then turned to Betty. "Do you know if she has spoken to anyone yet?"

"She did rouse herself this morning, though I couldn't make a bit of sense out of her. Her head all bandaged like that, she can hardly get her mouth open."

"Ah? Perhaps you wouldn't mind if I asked you a few questions, then?"

"Certainly not."

"You're a friend of Mrs. Wright's?

"Well, yes. I'd say she is my friend, yes. We both work for Mr. and Mrs. Netherby."

"In what capacity?" Mr. Wallhanger looked up. "What job do you do, Ma'am?"

"I'm the cook. My husband is the gardener. We're – he's Neil and I'm Betty. Betty Brendon."

"Have you worked there long, Mrs. Brendon?"

"Four years, sir."

"And Mrs. Wright? Is she new to the household?"

"She was already there when we come along. She's been there a long time, oh, ten years, 'sfar as I know. No, prob'ly more than ten. Yeah, more than ten."

"So, the missing girl? I hear she's something of a problem child."

"Anya? No. No, never, sir. As sweet a child as you could wish for."

Wallhanger stopped writing and looked at Betty. "You are fond of her?"

"She's the apple of my eye! My husband, too. Anya's always

following him about."

Officer Wallhanger nodded, and pressed the end his pencil against his temple. "But Mrs. Wright and the girl do not get along?"

"Whatever gave you such a notion? Mrs. Wright is like a mother to that child!"

"There was no altercation recently?"

Betty frowned. "Pardon?"

"I mean, were there any recent arguments between them?"

"No!" Betty scoffed. "Everybody else in the house fights like cats. But Anya? No. She pulls back from all that. She has to."

"Has to?"

"It's just the way she is. She can't take it, the fighting. She's, well, she's a little mousy. A good heart, but mousy. Never complains. We try to get her to stand up for herself. But she's too much like her grandfather."

"Ah."

"But you know, there is something strange that happened the other day, Officer. I was thinking I should tell somebody."

"Do you want to tell me?"

Betty lowered her voice. "Well. It's passing strange. Very strange, I'd say, that the young Miss Netherby, you know, Anya's aunt, went tearing out of the garage in that automobile of hers that day, the very afternoon after this happened." She gestured with her head at the still body of Mrs. Wright. "The day Petunia was hurt. Miss Netherby come backing out of the garage, full speed. My Neil, she practically run him down, she was in such a rush. Now where was she going, I ask you? And isn't it odd that the child was not seen again after that? Not a sign of her."

"That is odd."

"Yes, I've been all in a knot, worrying about that. Because what if she took the girl somewhere and is just pretending her niece is lost? Yessir, I think she's just pretending because ...."

The door opened. Betty's face flamed red and her mouth dropped open. Helen Netherby stood in the door. Officer Wallhanger rose politely. Helen stalked into the hospital room. She opened her calf-length coat, a summer wrap of pale pastel linen, and put her hands on her hips. Wallhanger eyed those slim hips. Betty's eyes dropped to the floor.

Helen glared at her. "Go on, Betty. You were saying something. What was it?" she demanded. "Come on, finish what you were saying." In a quick motion, she took her hands off her hips and thrust them under crossed arms.

Betty's mouth snapped shut. "Wasn't saying nothing."

"You were voicing some idea about the girl's disappearance, weren't you?"

"I got opinions, Miss Netherby."

Helen's voice rose. "What makes you even think you're entitled to an opinion? You and your husband are hired help in our home, nothing more. And we can change that in an instant." She snapped her fingers under Betty's nose. Seeing Miss Netherby's diamond ring catch the light, Betty hid her red hands in her lap.

"Yes, I know you can, Miss Netherby," said Betty stolidly. "But we may save you the trouble, Neil and I."

"Don't you threaten me!" Helen looked suddenly at the policeman, as if she had not even noticed he was there. People often overlooked Officer Wallhanger. In fact, he counted on them doing so. Helen rubbed her forehead."You'll have to excuse me, Officer. This has all been dreadfully trying for us. We're all exhausted and short-tempered."

"Understandably."

"As you can see, what I said about the housekeeper is in fact true. She can be of no use to your investigation. The nurse has informed me that she may not last the night."

At this, Betty squinted up at Miss Netherby. She said nothing, but decided wild horses would not drag her from Mrs. Wright's bedside. Not this night.

"Come," Helen insisted. "We should let Mrs. Wright spend her final hours in peace. You too, Betty. Come along."

"I believe I'll stay for the duration, Miss Netherby."

"No. You have work to do at home. We must eat. I insist you come away."

"I'm staying right here."

"Betty!" Helen's voice rose and she stamped her foot.

Betty closed her eyes and shook her head.

Helen pressed her fists together. "Betty, I warn you. I can fire you. And your husband. Without pay. Is that what you want?"

Now all the world knows there are perhaps only two things a person should never do. Don't spit in the wind. And never ever push an Irishwoman.

And Betty, don't you know, was Irish.

"Miss Netherby," she said, "If that's the way it has to be, so be it."

Helen glanced again at Officer Wallhanger and tried to bring her anger under control. "I won't give you a second chance, Betty," she threatened in a softer voice. "You'd better reconsider."

Betty pointed at the floor. "I'm staying right here."

"I'm going to speak to the doctor," Helen huffed. "He'll throw you out of here so fast, it'll make your head spin!" She whirled, her coat flaring like a Vogue model's.

But Betty, knowing a thing or two about holding one's ground, made no reply. She hunched her shoulders and stared at Helen's retreating back as she slammed out of the room.

Officer Wallhanger stood up. He opened his notebook and scribbled something. "Let me give you my number at the station, Mrs. Brendon," he explained. "In case you have anything more to tell me."

Betty tucked the paper away. "Thank you, Officer."

He bowed. "I look forward to hearing how Mrs. Wright progresses. Please keep me posted." He left the room.

So, he thought, so. Somewhere out there, running from all this confusion, is an nine-year-old girl.

He stopped at the train station to ask if anyone had seen a girl carrying a bundle and walking along the tracks in the last couple of days. No one had. In the afternoon he got out his bike and cycled along the canal. He couldn't find a trace of Anya Netherby.

CHAPTER FIVE

*A*t the edge of a wood several miles to the southeast of their town, Anya awoke for the second morning in the tree house. The crow was still there. He apparently saw Anya as his best hope for survival, maybe because he had hurt his wing, maybe because he liked cookies. He blinked and ruffled his feathers when she moved, and let out a squawk of protest.

There were no cookies left. There was nothing left to eat. Nothing at all, and Anya had never thought about food so constantly in her entire life.

Her head was still stuffy and her throat a little sore, but she wanted to get down to the lake she had seen the day before. Maybe it was Lake Placid. And then, from the back of her muddled mind came an idea. Maybe she could find her other grandparents. They lived in Lake Placid, or used to, anyway. If only she could find them – what a relief that would be! She raised the crow up so he could look out the slit of window that faced south. She could clearly see the lake this morning, like a finger of silver lying between high, far away hills. Grey clouds still covered the sky but the air was mild, almost warm again.

"Do you think it is Lake Placid down there?" she asked the crow. He cocked his head from side to side. "If it is," Anya told him, "all our troubles are over. Look, it has stopped raining."

Getting down from the tree house was nowhere near as difficult as climbing up to it. Anya and the crow were soon striding over the ground, heading downhill toward the lake. In a couple of hours, they came to the bank of a stream. It looked clean so they both enjoyed a long, cold drink. Anya drank from cupped hands. The crow waddled cautiously into the stream, stretching his long black toes carefully ahead with every step. He bent for a sip of water, tilted his head back to swallow, and bent again.

There was still no sign of the lake. Anya looked long and hard but there were no houses that she could see, either. She had so hoped to see something that resembled her memory of Lake Placid, though admittedly, she had probably forgotten the exact details. And maybe the scenery had changed. Or maybe they weren't near Lake Placid at all. Anya put the crow back on her shoulder and they followed the stream downhill until, a little way along, she saw what looked like a small house among the trees.

"Shh!" she warned the crow. She crept through the woods for a better look. It was not a house at all, but some kind of wagon with a small house built onto it. Nearby, a horse was tied to a tree, pawing at a pile of hay that someone had left. A broad-shouldered man knelt beside a fire, humming a tune. And cooking.

Food.

The man had food. Wonderful wonderful smells! The crow

cawed, but Anya closed his beak with her fingers.

She crept away. "Let's sit for a minute behind that rock. I have to think what to do. And for the love of mike, keep quiet!"

She went a good distance along the stream and crouched behind a large rock so they would not be visible, in case the man looked their way. She opened the pillow case. There wasn't so much as a crumb of food left. The crow chased a fat moth along the ground. He gulped it down, but for Anya, there was nothing.

We'll have to figure out something pretty soon, she thought, watching the crow picking at things on the edge of the stream. We have to figure out how to get some food, and where we're going, and how we're going to get there.

She put her head in her hands. That man – I'm afraid to ask him for directions. She sat up and rubbed her hands over the legs of her overalls. But we have no choice, do we, little crow? She stood to gather her pillow case, but the crow was ignoring her. He began flapping his good wing and hopping up and down. Rrraxxx! he cried.

"What's the matter?"

He hopped awkwardly along the bank of the stream, turned to look back at her, then hopped away again, all the while cawing frantically.

"What is the matter with you?" Anya asked. He dropped down to the side of the stream and stood there, calling repeatedly. Mystified, she followed him. She peered over the bank and saw something lying at the edge of the water, something wet and furry. She clambered down. A puppy? A reddish-brown and white puppy lay there, panting in quick breaths. It didn't even pick up its head as she came close, but its eyes, full of fear, watched her warily. She bent to touch it. There was a thick rope around its neck, knotted tight, and when she looked she saw that the other end was looped and knotted around a rock.

Anya tried to pull the knot out of the heavy cord. She could not budge the rough rope. Still the dog did not move. It panted weakly, in small, shallow breaths, and never took its eyes off her.

"I have no knife!" she cried. "How can I help you?" She searched for a sharp stone, but could find nothing that would cut the rope. "Wait! I'll get help!" Slowly she reached to pet the dog, afraid it would snap at her, but it was so weak, it couldn't move. "Don't you worry. I'll be right back," she assured it. "You!" she said to the crow. "You'll have to stay here!" Unable to fly, the crow had to obey, but he protested vigorously as she ran along the stream bank.

Anya ignored the crow and crept through the woods. Hiding behind a tree, she looked for the man she had seen kneeling beside the cooking fire. He wasn't there. She crept closer, close enough to touch the wagon. She inched her way along its side, moving closer to his campsite. Suddenly he appeared, coming round the corner of the wagon. Here he was, right in front of her.

She jumped back in alarm. He was so astonished, he dropped the pan he was carrying.

"What the ...?" he cried.

"Oh please, Mister! Can you help us? We need a knife!"

"What?" he barked.

"I just need to borrow a knife for a minute. I promise I'll give it back."

"You must be kidding."

"No, please, it's urgent!"

"Get away. I'm not giving you a knife."

She had been taught to obey. Never talk back. Still, she had to have a knife! She clasped her hands together, begging. "Please, Mister. There is a little puppy over there. He's hurt. Someone tied a big rope around his neck."

"A dog? Why didn't you say so?"

"He's over here! But a knife! We need a knife!"

The man pulled a jackknife from his pocket.

"This way," said Anya. She pointed towards the stream.

"Shoo!" he yelled to the crow pacing up and down beside the dog. "Scram!"

"No, no! He can't fly. He's my friend. Look, see this?"

"What is this?"

"This rope has to be cut. Hurry, please hurry," she begged. "He can't breathe." Why wouldn't the man hurry?

"Is this your dog?"

"No," she said, impatient. "We just found him. See? See the rock he's tied to?"

"Looks like someone wanted to get rid of him. Probably couldn't afford to feed him anymore." The man finally knelt and began sawing at the thick cord. It frayed and fell away.

"Ah!" cried Anya. She slipped her hands carefully under the

puppy's shoulder and hind quarters. He was limp in her hands. "Oh, you poor poor thing," she cooed to him.

"He's a mess. Look at this. His muzzle, his paws – they're bleeding," said the man. "You won't abandon him, will you? I hope you're going to take him with you."

"I will. Thank you again," Anya mumbled. She held her hand out for the crow so she could set him on her shoulder, and bent to pick up her bundle.

"Hey, be careful! Don't drop the dog."

She was struggling to find a way to carry a limp dog, a crow, and a large bundle.

"I assume you don't have far to go."

"We're going to Lake Placid. I thought I saw it. Is it near?"

"Lake Placid? What? You serious?" The man frowned, incredulous. "No. It's not near. It's quite far, actually. How are you getting there?"

Shrugging her shoulders, she said reluctantly, "Walking."

"What? Who's with you?"

"It's – just us."

"Us who?"

"The crow and I." Her bundle was heavy. She set it down for a minute. "You don't happen to know the way, do you?"

"The way to Lake Placid?"

She nodded.

He squinted at her. "Where are you coming from?"

She gestured with her chin. "Up that hill."

The man looked, then turned back to her. He was almost afraid to ask. "What's the story here?"

Anya shrugged again. "No story."

"Aren't you a little young to be out on your own?" He'd been asked that very thing himself, back – how long ago? He never thought he'd hear that question coming out of his own mouth.

Without answering, Anya picked up her bundle again. She heard the jingle of coins that she had tied in her stocking, and that gave her an idea. "You don't have any food I could buy, do you?"

"Ah, I thought so." He swatted the air with his hand. "Yeah, don't give me that look." The man sighed mightily. Just what he needed, a kid hanging around. "All right. A cup of oatmeal, and that's it." He started back to his van. "Come on. Do you want oatmeal or don't you?"

"Yes please." She hurried after him. Not a nice man. But a man with food.

"Give me that." He took her bundle. The horse looked up in alarm as they came to the campsite. "Stay away from the horse. He bites. Sit yourself over there. I'll reheat this." He put a pan of oatmeal back on the fire. Anya's stomach growled.

She sat on the log he indicated, cradling the little puppy and speaking softly to him. The man went into his van and came out with a towel and a small kit of first aid items.

"Let me look at his feet." He arranged the towel across Anya's lap and picked up the dog's foot. "Whew. These are in bad shape. He must have been clawing his way to the bank of the stream and sliced them on the stones. He's quite the little fighter, this guy." The dog yelped and tried to pull his foot away. The man was very gentle with him. "Hey, don't worry, little one. I'll try not to hurt you." The man shook his head. "Not much point in bandaging his paws. I think I'll just clean the grit out and you'll have to let the wounds heal as best they can. He won't be doing any walking today, though." He stood up, handed her a bucket and pointed to the creek. "Here. Fetch some water so we can clean him up."

He helped her settle the puppy on the towel near the fire, and watched until she was a distance away. Then he picked up her pillow case bundle and looked inside. A few items of dirty wadded clothing, one clean dress. An empty cookie tin. Ah, a stocking full of money. He scooped some out. Less that five dollars there. He slid the money back into the stocking. It was just as he feared. The kid was on the road. Surely not tough enough for the road, though, or at least not hardened to it. He thrust the whole bundle back behind the log just as Anya returned.

"Here. Toast the bread while I rinse the dirt off his paws." The man handed her a long fork with a thick slab of bread on the end.

She moved to sit by the fire. The man swished the dog's feet in the water until they were clean. Then he gave the oatmeal a stir, and spooned some into cups. He poured the last of the milk into them. The crow watched closely, his mouth gaping open, shifting from foot to foot on Anya's shoulder.

"A cup for you." He handed one to Anya. "Let's see if I can get him to eat some of this." The man put the dog on his lap, dipped the tip of the spoon into the cup, then held it near the puppy's mouth. The little black nose quivered and a little pink tongue licked cautiously. The mouth made nibbling motions and the pink tongue came out again.

"Take it easy now, Buster. Just a bit at a time."

Anya had almost devoured her cup of oatmeal when the crow sidestepped down her arm and opened his mouth wide. Ccccrrr-aaaxxx, he beseeched her. She gave him the last of her oatmeal.

"Go ahead. Eat the toast. The dog won't eat it all."

Anya and the crow gobbled every last bit of toast. She looked up to see the man watching her. He was probably hoping she'd leave soon.

"Look," he said, "I've got work to do today."

She stood up, reached for her bundle, and took out the stocking that held her coins.

"Forget it. No money," said the man.

"No, I –"

He waved her hand away.

"Thank you, Mister." She put the crow back on her shoulder and bent to pick up the dog.

"Wait," the man said. He ran his hand back and forth across the top of his head, thinking. Yet another homeless kid. Lately he had been seeing children on the roads wherever he went. Heck, he had been like them once, himself. A vagabond, hungry, alone, wandering. Anyway, he wasn't going anyplace today. There was a sea of mud between his van and the track that led back up to the road.

His horse, Clodhopper, would never be able to drag the wagon out. "Maybe I could use your help, kid, just for today."

"Me?"

"I'm testing some new film. I could use a subject."

"What would I –?"

"All you'd have to do is sit still while I take a few photos."

"I should really … I have to get going."

The man scratched his bristly cheek. "I'll give you lunch and dinner." He saw her doubtful look. "And you can stay in the van. But only for tonight." He knew he had her interest. He pointed a warning finger. "Tonight only."

"All right. What do I have to do?"

The man handed Anya a dishpan. "First, get these dishes washed."

She went back to the stream and brought more water. The man swished some soap into the pan and handed her a towel.

"You dry. What's your name, anyway?"

Should she tell? "Anya."

"How long have you been on the road?"

On the road. How had he known?

He handed her the last bowl and waited.

She dried it industriously, not knowing how to answer.

"That's probably about as dry as that bowl is going to get."

She gathered up the clean dishes, ignoring his question. "Where shall I put these?"

"Come on. I'll show you." They carried the dishes to the van that had been built atop the wagon.

The van's dun-colored side was painted in faded red letters:

HUGH DURANT, PHOTOGRAPHER

1 PORTRAIT 10 CENTS

3 FOR 2 BITS

"Are you Mr. Durant?" Anya asked.

"Hugh."

He led her inside. There was a window set in the ceiling of the van so it was light enough inside, but it had a black shade that could be unrolled to cover it when he developed his film. In the front part of the van, Hugh kept, in exquisite order, his cameras and film and papers and chemicals, flash powders and trays, measuring cups and funnels, pens and paint brushes and scissors and cutting knives, cardboard mats of all sizes, a small work table, a fancy padded folding chair, a faded artificial plant, and a screen with a landscape painted in muted colors.

Hugh slid the folding screen aside, and behind it was quite a different scenario. A food cupboard hung open, half its contents crowding the small tabletop below. Another cupboard was jammed with books, mostly history books, as far as Anya could tell. A washtub hung on the wall, draped in towels, and a tired-looking easy chair was nearly buried under a jumble of clothes and a box of books. Indeed, albums and notebooks were scattered everywhere. Photographs fanned across a bed that stretched along the back wall. A couple of shirts and a clean pair of trousers hung above the foot of the bed, and, if you must know, a chamber pot was under the bed.

Hugh shifted a pile from the only chair to the floor. "Have a seat."

Anya sat down. "Your van is very nice," she said.

"Thanks. So." He clapped his big hands on his knees. "If I'm going to photograph you, we've got to get that face of yours washed. In fact, you know what? You could probably use a bath. Heat some water and give yourself a good scrub. You know, the hair, the works. You have something clean you can wear, don't you?"

She nodded. She'd put on her dress, the only clean thing she had.

"Fetch some water while I get my film loaded."

She followed Hugh out of the van.

"Look at this crazy bird. He's happy to see you." The crow was flapping his good wing and standing guard over the puppy, who was fast asleep on Hugh's towel.

"I can use him, too. Come here," Hugh said, holding out a finger for the bird. "His feathers, that dense black color. It'll make great contrast. Light and dark, just what I need." Maybe the morning wouldn't be a waste after all.

It took several trips to the creek to get enough water for the bathtub, and a long time to get it warm, or lukewarm, at least. While it heated, Hugh threw a blanket over his clothesline to make a screen for her bath, and found another towel and some soap.

"There's not much water. Just kind of toss it over yourself. Be quick. Wash those clothes, too, afterwards, in the bath water."

Soap and water. Anya had never realized how a bath can lift the spirits. She put on her clean dress and her mother's pearls. By the time she had inexpertly wrung out her clothes and hung them on the line, Hugh had prepared lunch. Ham sandwiches and hot tea.

"And pickles," said Hugh. "Gotta have that sour note on a ham sandwich."

Anya kept her thoughts about sourness to herself.

Hugh looked her over. Clean dress. And pearls? "Huh," was all he said. He handed her a sandwich.

The puppy had stirred and even tried to raise his head at the smell of food.

Anya started to feed him a piece of ham, but looked up sharply at Hugh. It was his food, after all, and she had done nothing to deserve it. "Is it okay?"

"Just this once."

"I can pay you for this."

"Don't worry. I'm going to make you work for it. So what do you call your crow?"

Anya shrugged and smiled a little. "Crow." She dropped a small piece of bread down his throat.

Ccccrrr-aaaxxx, the crow replied.

"Well he needs a decent name. And the dog too."

Ccccrrr-aaaxxx, cried the crow.

"Ha! Corax. Smart bird."

"What?"

"Corax. The crow wants the dog to be called Corax."

"Corax?"

Hugh spread his hands. "Never heard of him? Five centuries before Christ? In Italy. A philosopher, a scholar."

The crow bobbed up and down.

"And this one. How about Tisias, after Corax's student. Tisias the crow. Ha. Corax and Tisias? I just named your pets for you. How about that?"

"Okay," agreed Anya, her mouth full of ham sandwich.

"Finish up. You can leave the dishes until after dinner. I need you to pose for me while the light lasts."

Dinner. Anya closed her eyes and took a minute to savor the word.

Hugh rummaged in a box. "I've got some props. Somewhere in this mess. Here. A bow for your hair." He took a hank of her hair in clumsy fingers. "No. You'll have to tie it."

He brought out a stool for her to sit on and fastened his camera to a tripod. "Where should we do this? Over here, kid, in this little clearing. Yes, the light here is good. Sit nice and straight."

He ducked under the cover on his camera. "Don't move."

Over and over, Hugh moved them to different spots. He made notes on a pad and asked Anya to sit here like thus and there like so. She held Corax the puppy or Tisias the crow. She sat against Hugh's painted screen, she perched on a rock. Then, exhausted, she slept in Hugh's chair while he worked in his darkroom. When she awoke, she smelled dinner cooking.

"Did your film work out, Mr. Durant?"

"We'll see. The prints will be dry after dinner. Here's your plate."

"Thank you." Hot food, her first in days. She didn't think she would ever turn down a morsel of food again. She imitated Mr. Durant, mopping up gravy with a piece of bread. And again she was glad her grandmother wasn't here to see her.

When they had eaten, they sat by the fire in silence. Anya held little Corax on her lap and wondered what Hugh was thinking as he stared at the fire. He seemed a different man this evening, not as grumpy as this morning. Even his face had improved. It was actually, she realized, a handsome face. She hadn't thought that before. He had surprised her, too, in letting her and her pets stay for the night, a great kindness. How could a person change so much between morning and night? Or maybe it was her mood and the starry night, a fire of red embers, and the best food she'd ever eaten. Well, Betty's food was – no. She would not let herself think of home.

"You're a very good cook," Anya said.

Hugh seemed to snap out of some reverie. He nodded. "Thanks."

"Just about as good as Betty," she said, chattily.

Hugh leaned back against a log. "Tell me about Betty, kid."

"Betty?" Anya's mouth hung open. She had not meant to talk about any of this. Those people at home, Betty and Neil, Mrs. Wright. They weren't her real family. But how she missed them. She missed them so.

"Does Betty know where you are?"

"I don't know." She didn't want to talk about home. But what were they doing right now, she wondered? Especially Mrs. Wright. Was she –? Anya's eyes filled and she looked quickly away.

Hugh saw, and stood abruptly. "Now about tomorrow. If it doesn't rain, I need you to help me wash the van. Then we'll have to see if Clodhopper can pull us out of that mud before it hardens. If he gets us back up to the road, you can figure out how to get wherever it is you're going."

CHAPTER SIX

*O*fficer Wallhanger was again banging the doorknocker on the Elm Street residence belonging to the Netherbys. He had to knock three times before anyone answered. Grandfather Netherby flung the door open.

"What?"

"Good morning. I'm Officer Wallhanger. I'm investigating the disappearance of Miss Anya Netherby."

"Oh! Oh, our Anya! Has she been found?"

"Unfortunately, no sir. She has not."

"Oh dear. No bad news, I hope?"

"No, no bad news."

"We thought she'd turn up by now. I'm sorry. I'm a bit muddled today. Would you like to come in?"

"Thank you. I assume you are Mr. Netherby? I wonder if I could ask you a few questions?"

"Of course. Please, let's talk in here."

"That's very kind of you."

Grandfather Netherby ushered Wallhanger into his study. "Have a seat. Can I offer you some tea?"

"No thank you, sir."

"Good, because I'd have to make it myself, and then, even after my best effort, it would still be undrinkable."

"I understand your housekeeper has been hospitalized."

"She's been hurt very badly. Meanwhile, without her, everything is grinding to a halt."

"You haven't found a replacement for her as yet?"

"Apparently, well ...." Grandfather squeezed his chin and spoke softly. "Hmm. Well, I might as well tell it like it is. It seems there is no one who will work for what my wife considers a reasonable fee. In other words, for peanuts."

Officer Wallhanger looked appreciatively at the walls lined with bookcases. "The job probably entails a great amount of work. What about the other servants? One of them can't be persuaded to help out?"

"That's the darndest thing! We lost all of them at once!"

"Isn't that odd. Such a great number, leaving all at once?"

"Well, not that great a number of staff anymore, to tell the truth. I – we – like so many, I guess – it's been quite difficult. Quite difficult. Touch and go for us since the stock market took such a downturn. And now, all this."

"Ah, I'm very sorry to hear that, sir."

"Yes, well, don't tell my wife that I told you. Oh, here's my daughter. Helen dear, do come in. This is Officer ... I'm sorry. What did you say your ...?"

"I have met Miss Netherby." He bowed slightly. "Harvey

Wallhanger, at your service." He shook Helen's limp, diamond-studded hand.

"Mr. Wallhanger, of course I remember you. How could I forget? It was only yesterday that we spoke at great length."

"We did. And I thank you for that. But there is still something I need to ask you, Miss Netherby, if you don't mind."

Helen settled on the arm of her father's chair, leaning back and stretching her arm across his shoulders. "Go ahead."

"Can you tell me your destination on the afternoon of Monday, August 15?"

"My destination? Nowhere. I – no, I don't think I went anywhere."

"And yet, the back seat of your car was soaking wet."

Helen frowned at the officer. "Mr. Wallhanger, I didn't even speak to you for the first time until Wednesday. What makes you think my car got wet on Monday?"

"I happened to notice when I left the hospital on Wednesday afternoon, that the fabric of your backseat was soaking wet."

"You went through my car?"

"No, no." Wallhanger actually smiled. "Well, I did look in the window. I thought maybe you were waiting in the car. But I did see a very large wet spot on the backseat."

"What can that possibly indicate, I ask you?"

"That you may have driven somewhere on Monday afternoon, Miss Netherby, and left the back window open on the right side. Or the door."

"Left the window open? You're making absolutely no sense, Mr. Wallhanger."

"Do you usually keep your car in the garage?"

"Of course I do."

"So if it got wet, it must have been out of the garage on Monday afternoon. It rained that day, and didn't rain again until after I met you on Wednesday."

"Mr. Wallhanger, are you trying to accuse me of something? It's my niece Anya that you were asked to investigate, not me. Whatever you are suggesting, I assure you that you are way out of line."

"So you did not go out on Monday afternoon?"

"No, I did not."

"It must be my mistake then. I'm very sorry to have bothered you."

As Helen stood up, silently fuming, Grandfather Netherby rose quickly to cover her bad manners. "I'll see you to the door, Officer."

"I thank you, sir. Oh, by the way, Miss Netherby. One more question, if I may. On the day of your housekeeper's accident, who was it that found Miss Anya's marble, that one single marble, on the stair?"

"I – it may have been my son, Bobby. Or no, it must have been me. Actually, I really don't remember trifling things like that. At that hour of the morning – it was so early. We were – all of us were – we were all very upset that morning."

"I can imagine, yes. Well, I'll be in touch. Good afternoon." Harvey Wallhanger settled his hat on his head and left.

Had he uncovered a lie? Miss Netherby claimed she hadn't gone out, but Betty the cook said she had. He wasn't sure who was lying, but he finally felt he had his teeth into a rather intriguing case. He would wait to file his report. If it became known that he was investigating something interesting, the case would surely be taken away from him.

He didn't realize how right he was.

At the hospital that evening, Neil the gardener was sitting with Mrs. Wright while his wife went to get something to eat. Suddenly he felt the need to visit the bathroom. He probably shouldn't have drunk that iced tea that the nurse brought him. The need to go seized him with such urgency that he crept hurriedly out of the room and down the hall.

The night nurse knew that the tea would get to him. From her desk, she watched him pass and slid something from a drawer. Concealing it in her hand, she went to the door of Mrs' Wright's room. She looked up and down the hall. Quietly, she opened the door. The woman lay on her back, her eyes closed. The patient was asleep. Good. The nurse went in and closed the door.

She had been paid to do this, by a man she didn't know, and didn't want to know. She didn't like him. He frightened her. He said the woman knew things she shouldn't, and she had to be "dispatched". Whether it was right or legal to do what he asked, the nurse couldn't stop to consider. He promised she would be well paid and she needed money desperately. So just get this done, she told herself, and don't get caught. Uneasy, she crept to Mrs. Wright's bedside and carefully straightened the woman's arm. A sudden movement jarred her trembling hand. The patient was definitely not asleep.

"Nnn! Nnn!" squealed the housekeeper through her bandages. She twisted her arm back and forth, though she did not have the strength to raise it. She couldn't speak clearly with her jaw bandaged shut, but the sense of what she was saying was plain. She did not want an injection.

"Shh! Shh! Hush now. It's just a little shot. This will help you sleep, Mrs. Wright," cooed the nurse, trying to sound soothing.

"Nnn! Nnn!"

"Hold still, dammit!"

"Nurse! What is going on?"

The nurse looked up, startled to see Neil back so soon. "I'm trying to give her an injection."

"What is it for?"

"It's just to help her sleep."

"Nnn! Nnn!" said Mrs. Wright.

"She doesn't want it."

"She's upset. She needs it. Look at her! She's worked herself into a fit."

"The doctor said nothing about more injections."

"He told me to give it to her."

"Let's wait til he comes in to ask him, shall we?"

"I don't have time to sit around waiting for doctors. And I don't hardly need to take orders from you!" She poised the needle over Mrs. Wright's arm.

Neil gently lifted the nurse's wrist. "Just put it away, Nurse. It's upsetting Mrs. Wright. We'll wait for the doctor."

"I have a job to do. She has to have this medication."

"For the last time, take it away. You don't want me to start shouting."

The nurse darted the needle at Neil's arm, nearly jabbing him before she thought better of it. "If you don't let me do my job, the doctor is going to hear about it."

Neil swelled to his full height, took firm hold of her wrist and didn't let go. "The doctor most certainly will hear about it. Now get out."

The nurse jerked her hand away. With a last glare at Neil, she turned and slithered out the door.

Neil, a tall and hefty man, leaned against the bed, shaking. He wished he had been able to get hold of that syringe. He wanted to know what was in it. Mrs. Wright was making noises, desperately trying to tell him something, but he couldn't understand a word. He took her hand and held it tight.

"Don't worry, Petunia. Don't fret. I won't leave you." What in tarnation is going on around this place, he wondered? What kind of a hospital is this?

*T*he next day, Officer Wallhanger came into work late. There had been another burglary. He wasn't included in the investigation, of course. In two years, he had never once been asked to help with any of the burglary cases. But last night he had accidentally interrupted an office conversation about stolen jewelry, and he had stayed at the station for most of the night trying to find out what was going on.

Back in his office again this morning, he found a note from the Netherby's gardener, Neil Brendon. The note mentioned strange things that had gone on at the hospital, things that Neil thought Wallhanger might want to look into. He phoned the chief to ask for a security guard at the hospital, but couldn't get through. He left a message and then walked the eight blocks to the Netherby house. A maid, a very young girl, opened the door.

"May I see Miss Netherby?" he asked her.

"Certainly. This way." She led him to the second floor.

"You're new here, I take it?" he asked the girl as they climbed the stairs.

"Yessir. My first day." She grinned at him.

"Well, good luck. I hope the job works out for you."

"Thank you, sir." She knocked on Helen's door and opened it a crack. "Someone to see you, Miss Netherby."

"I'll be down in a few minutes."

"He's right here, Miss. I brung him up."

"What? You know better than that. I explained that you don't ..." Helen came to the door.

"It's entirely my fault, Miss Netherby," explained Officer Wallhanger, coming forward. "It was I who made so bold as to come straight up. Please don't blame this young lady."

"Nevertheless, Mary ...."

"It's Myra, Ma'am."

"Myra. Go on, go downstairs." Helen sighed. "I'll be down in a few minutes to go over your instructions yet again." She frowned. "Mr. Wallhanger, I'm not even dressed. I can only spare a minute this morning. I slept later than I wanted and I'm already late for an appointment." She turned with a practiced swirl of her satin robe, and sank into a chair.

Officer Wallhanger's eyes settled on the little shimmer of silky slipper that dangled off her shapely foot. Helen flipped her robe up to cover her lap and the flash of a diamond on her finger was large enough to distract Harvey.

His wits had scattered like butterflies. He collected them. "By coincidence, I was late this morning, too, Miss Netherby. We had quite a bit of activity at the station uptown last night."

"Oh?"

This had caught her interest, Wallhanger noted. "Yes, another burglary."

"Oh really?"

"Anyway, I won't bother you for too long this morning. I only have a couple of questions." He stopped and stared. "But you know, I've just noticed this array of family photos you have over here." He picked up a framed photo and admired it.

"Could we just get on with your question, Officer, so I can get dressed?"

"We shall, certainly. I must ask, though, about that other photo over there. This one. Some kind of family celebration, is it? This is you in the foreground. And who is that standing off to the side here?"

"Robert. That's my son, Robert."

"No I mean, well, Robert is a very handsome child. But this little girl here?"

"Oh yes, I can hardly see who you mean. That is Anya."

"Ah." He lifted that photo from the mantle. "You wouldn't mind my taking this, just for a day? How fortunate that you do have a photo of her, after all. I'd like to copy it, if you'll allow me."

"Take it."

"I promise to bring it right back."

"Fine."

"She resembles you, doesn't she, little Anya?"

"She does have the Netherby features."

"It's a fine shot of you too, Miss Netherby, in the foreground here." Beautiful jewelry, he thought.

"Thank you. And you said you have a question, Officer?"

"Well now, this does raise one question." He laid a finger on the photo. "I think this child might be the same girl as in the photo on your housekeeper's dresser. In her room upstairs. Isn't she the same girl?"

"I have absolutely no idea what is on that dresser."

"It just seems a bit strange, seeing as how you said the

housekeeper and the girl did not get along."

"Their disagreement is quite recent, actually. I told you. Anya has been very troublesome lately."

"I see. Did they actually have an altercation?"

"Mr. Wallhanger, I don't mean to rush you, but I do have appointments this afternoon."

"I'm very sorry. I'll be brief. My question was, well, firstly, can I assume you have had no word from Anya?"

"None whatsoever."

"Has her father been contacted? Does he know his daughter is missing?"

"Jack? My god, my brother is nothing but a playboy, Mr. Wallhanger. He has no interest whatsoever in the girl."

"You wouldn't mind if I tried to get in touch with him?"

"Whatever for? He's off in the southwest somewhere playing cowboys and Indians. God knows where. How can he possibly be of help?"

"You don't think the girl could be traveling to meet her father?"

"Not a chance. First of all, she has no money. Second of all, no one has any idea where he is. Besides, she hardly knows him."

"It was just a thought I had. I would be remiss if I didn't at least notify her father. Just in case she does turn up out there. If you could just give me a contact number, ..."

"Please, Mr. Wallhanger! Don't ask me to go searching for his address this morning. I'm in such a rush. Can it wait?"

"Certainly. Or perhaps you could tell me what firm he works

for?"

"I have no idea. The University maybe? The archaeology department?"

"He's in archaeology? So would that be Cornell University?"

Helen sighed. "I don't know. No, it was the University of Rochester, I'm fairly sure."

"Rochester?"

"Yes. I think so."

"And the name? Jack Netherby?"

"Jackson, yes."

"I'll follow that lead and see where it takes me." He gave a small bow. "I'm truly sorry to bother you when you are on such a tight schedule, Miss Netherby."

"I trust I have been of help." Helen rose and went to the door of her apartment. "You can find your own way out?"

"I think so. Thank you." Harvey Wallhanger stopped in the doorway. "Oh, there is one favor I might ask, if you don't mind."

Helen sighed. "What is it?"

"Would you allow me to just pop upstairs and borrow one of those photos from Mrs. Wright's dresser? My search would be a lot easier if I had a recent photo."

"You have the one –"

"I know I'm being a bit of a bore."

"Go ahead. Take whatever you need."

"Thank you so much, Miss Netherby."

Helen was about to shut her door when Harvey Wallhanger

turned back once more.

"By the way, I hear your housekeeper is getting some good news. They say they can take the bandages off her head soon. As I'm sure you've been told."

"Oh. No. I didn't know. I didn't. Thank you for telling me."

"Won't it be nice for her to be able to eat normally? And communicate? She's been through a lot. Poor lady!"

Helen's face froze. "Yes. Poor lady."

"Well, I won't keep you. Good day, Miss Netherby." Harvey vaulted up the stairs to Mrs. Wright's bedroom. He wanted a portrait of Anya Netherby, but he needed the family photo from Helen's room too, for another reason.

When he got back to the police station, he filed an urgent request for a security guard. Then he found the bureau photographer and asked him to copy the Netherby photos. Next, he put in a call to Cornell because, as far as he knew, the University of Rochester had no archaeology department. Then he spent the rest of the day looking through old files, those few that he was able to get his hands on. He had seen something in that Netherby family photo. A ring, a very singular ring, on Helen Netherby's finger.

*L*ate that afternoon, Helen Netherby, in spite of her various appointments, did manage to find time to visit Mrs. Wright at the hospital. Too much had gone wrong for Helen lately and she couldn't shake this feeling of vulnerability. She was nervous as she stepped into the elevator. She knew their housekeeper had seen her in rather suspicious circumstances – the middle of the night, that bag in her hands. Helen had cooked up an explanation to give to Mrs. Wright. Could she make it sound convincing?

As she rode the elevator up to Mrs. Wright's room, an impeccably dressed man, someone Helen knew quite well indeed, was going down, but he was using the stairs to avoid being noticed. Like Helen, he had also taken the trouble to visit Mrs. Wright. He did not know her. All he wanted to do was to confirm that the nurse he had paid had done her job. He was shocked to find instead a large policeman stationed outside Mrs. Wright's door. The man didn't dare go further. He put his head down and, avoiding the elevator, made haste for the stairway.

Helen Netherby came out of the elevator a few seconds later and saw the same policeman. She stopped. Why was Mrs. Wright's door guarded? Helen also panicked, turned on her heel, and caught the elevator back down to the lobby. The flurry of fear that raced through her was nothing, though, compared to the dread she felt when she exited the hospital. She saw a gleaming black car, a sleek and unusual car, speed away. She stared. A black Cord Phaeton. She knew of one Cord Phaeton in their part of the county. It was a very expensive car. There was little chance that there were two.

CHAPTER SEVEN

*T*hat night, back in the van beside Mud Creek, Hugh Durant lit a lamp and blew out the match.

"You sure you don't want to sleep on the floor?" Hugh asked Anya. "You'd have more room."

"I like this chair. Thank you for letting me stay here tonight, Mr. Durant."

"Kid, this 'Mr. Durant' business makes me twitchy."

"Sorry."

"Makes me feel old. Unless you want me to call you Miss ... did you tell me your family name?"

"Brendon," Anya lied, after a moment's thought.

"All right, Miss Brendon."

Anya curled up in the chair beside Hugh's bed, with Corax the puppy in her lap and Tisias the crow on the back of the chair with an old towel underneath him.

"Make that bird stay on the towel. You can't tell me he's not going to do what birds do," said Hugh.

"What do birds do?"

"They doo-doo."

Anya snickered. "I didn't know you were funny."

"I didn't know you could laugh."

"May I look at one of your albums for a while, Hugh?"

"You aren't going to keep me up all night, are you?"

In fact, Anya fell asleep so quickly, she never turned the first page. A little later, Hugh also called it a day and doused the flame on the lamp.

*I*n the morning, Corax the puppy surprised them by sitting up when he smelled eggs cooking.

"He's getting better!"

"He's a dog. His instinct is to get moving," Hugh said. "If you don't want him running away this morning, you'll have to tie him up while we wash the van. He's not going to like that."

Hugh was right. Corax did not like the rope in Anya's hands, not at all. He whined so pitifully at the sight of it that Anya could not bear to tie him.

"What should I do, Hugh?"

"I don't know. Work something out. I'm going down to the creek."

Anya stared at the dog in consternation. "Listen, puppy, little Corax. If you run away, I'll never be able to find you. Then we'll both be sad. Can't you stay here? Stay. Stay right here." She backed away, pointing a warning finger. "Stay!" Corax licked his nose, curled up and went to sleep with Tisias the crow nestled against his side.

While they napped, Anya and Hugh soaped the sides of the van and threw buckets of water at it to rinse it down.

"It looks nice, Hugh."

"Yeah, well. It's better. It's still a sad old crate. Hang these rags up to dry. I'll throw some sandwiches together. Then we'll see if Clodhopper can pull us out of here. And toss a log on the fire, would you, kid, so I can make tea?"

While Hugh sliced bread and ham, Anya tried to neaten the van a little, stacking his books and putting dishes away.

"Gotta get a move on," he called to her. "I want to buy some groceries before I hit the road." Hugh was a big man. He liked to eat well when he had the money. He stopped and looked at Anya. "So your plan is to head east this afternoon?"

"Is that the way?"

Aww, man, the kid doesn't even know where she's going. "East, then north."

"You said it was far away."

"Geez, kid. I worry about you. Okay, listen. You know what? I'm heading east too, working a few towns on the way to the Geneva fair. But then I've got to drive south. The opposite direction that you want to go."

"Oh."

"You can come with me as far as Seneca Lake. That's as far as I can take you." He saw the hopeful gleam in her eye. "That's the best I can offer. I've got this assignment coming up. In Maryland, see? So I have to turn south at Geneva."

"Would we be close to Lake Placid then?"

"Not really. You'd still have a long way to go. Pickles on your sandwich?"

"Yes please."

"Here you go. Eat up. None for you guys." He pointed to Corax and Tisias.

The dog and the bird sat at Anya's knee, looking longingly at her sandwich. After a minute, Tisias the crow waddled off, pecking and scraping in the leaves under a log. He came back with a fat black cricket in his beak. He dropped it in front of Corax. The puppy snapped up the bug, chewed twice and spit it back out. Tisias cocked his head at him, nosed the cricket, then gulped it down himself.

"So kid." Hugh sipped his tea and watched Anya. The last thing he wanted was to get her hopes up. He wanted her to understand clearly what his intentions were. "Too bad we're going in opposite directions, you and I," he said.

"I'll pay you for all this food, Mr. Durant. Hugh."

"No," he found himself saying, for no reason that he could fathom. "You'll need your money when you are on your own again. But if we're going to be together for a few days, I can use your help running errands for me while I work. Odd jobs. Stuff like that."

"I can do that."

"You're sure?"

Anya nodded.

"So what's in Lake Placid, anyway?"

She shrugged.

"Your parents?"

"No."

"No?"

"My mother died. A long time ago. My father's away."

"Who is taking care of you?"

Anya hesitated. "Me," she said, finally.

"Huh." Hugh chewed thoughtfully for a minute. "Yeah. I was out on my own at a young age too."

"You were?" she asked, moving closer to him.

"Not as young as you, though. And I was lucky. Somebody took me under his wing, eventually. Gave me a place to stay. Taught me about cameras."

"Why were you on your own?"

"We were poor, my family. There were a lot of us. Nine kids. I got mad about something. Left home. It didn't matter to them. Nobody really cared whether I was at home or gone."

"Same for me! We're poor now, too. Grandfather even had to let Sanborn go. He didn't want to, though."

"Who's Sanborn?"

"The butler."

Hugh raised an eyebrow. He put his sandwich down. "Ah, kid, kid."

"Yes?"

"What's going on? You'd better tell me."

She shrugged.

"Should I make you go back home? Cuz that's what I should

do. You know that, don't you? You're too young to – "

"No! No, no!"

"Look. I don't want any problems. People might think I'm kidnapping you. Any number of bad things. I don't need trouble."

"Then I –" Anya folded her arms. "I'll go on by myself. I'm not going back." She hung her head, her elbows on her knees.

Hugh sipped his tea for a minute. "Your family. They're probably worried sick."

She frowned, shaking her head and staring blackly at Hugh.

He put his tea down. "I should make you go back where you came from. I don't know what to do." Hugh finally threw his hands up, then folded them into his lap. "Okay." He sighed and shook his head. "Call me crazy. We'll leave it be. For now. Let's get this horse harnessed up and see if he can drag us out of here. He's had it way too easy these last couple of days."

*C*lodhopper the horse was an immense beast. In his younger days, before Hugh bought him, he had pulled more wagon loads of logs than he could possibly count, which is only an expression because, of course, he never could count. Or not as far as anyone knew. He was also extremely timid. It is difficult to imagine a creature of his size being afraid of anything, but in his old age, poor old Clodhopper had become as timid as a churchmouse caught under a pew on Sunday morning. He shied if a candy wrapper blew by, if someone fluttered a handkerchief, or if a patch of daisies tilted in the breeze. He hated this camping in the woods they'd been doing. He was sure he hadn't slept a wink all week. To say he was out of sorts today was putting it mildly.

So getting Clodhopper back in harness took some time. The trouble was, thirteen long years ago someone had buckled his bellyband too tightly, and by the end of the day it had chafed him raw. Clodhopper might not be able to remember that waving hankies don't bite, but the tight harness? That horse remembered it as if it were yesterday. Hugh had to work slowly and patiently when he harnessed him, examining the straps very carefully to make sure nothing would pinch or irritate him.

"I have to sweet talk him," Hugh told Anya. "So you're better off in the van, kid, and out of the way. You never know what he's going to do."

Near the camp site there was an old track that went up through the woods and onto the open road. Hugh walked beside Clodhopper, leading him up that track. But as they walked along, the horse was suddenly seized with a nervous fit. These strange sounds – where were they coming from? All this buzzing in his ears, those forest rustlings – had they become mysteriously louder, deafeningly loud? So much wind! All these fluttering leaves! They were making him dizzy. And here – right here at his feet – ferns clawed his ankles! Trembling, Clodhopper dug his toes in. He rolled his eyes and tossed his head.

"Come on, Old Hopper, come on," Hugh coaxed.

Clodhopper balked and his skin shook as if it was going to shed itself right off his body.

Just at that moment, a wild crow flew close overhead, eyeing the strange goings-on. Clodhopper threw back his head and shrieked. Tisias screeched too, in a frenzy at the passing crow. Seeing Tisias upset, Corax started barking, and the horse became convinced that the ogres of the underworld were rising from beneath the forest floor. He took off up the road with Hugh in pursuit and the van bouncing behind like a beach ball. Anya and her pets fell backwards off the seat. Clodhopper labored and bucked and steamed up the hill so fast that Hugh couldn't catch up.

At the top of the hill the dirt road ran alongside a pasture. With a thunder of pounding hoofs, with the van banging and rattling and making more noise than a cannon factory, the toiling horse, the van, the people, and the pets came lurching out of the woods. And it was here in the open meadow that Clodhopper, puffing like a runaway locomotive, nearly collided with the most fearsome danger of all.

Up ahead, in the dust of the road, a soft little rabbit hunched quietly, chewing clover and contemplating the universe. She was a smallish grey rabbit with smallish grey ears, round dark eyes, and a very small pink nose. The little creature had no idea that she was capable of stopping a ton of horsemeat in his tracks.

Then she beheld Clodhopper. His feet flying like a malfunctioning windmill, he was heading straight toward her. She dropped her mouthful of clover in surprise, as indeed, anyone would. She sat upright and stared. Clodhopper, suddenly spotting her soft white tummy, screamed in terror. His hoofs plowed furrows in the dirt and he nearly popped a puckering string trying to skid to a halt.

Just in time, the rabbit burst the spell that bound her and she high-tailed it into the meadow grass. As anyone would.

And thus did Hugh and his van and his friends and his horse come out of the woods.

While Hugh tried to calm poor Clodhopper, Anya let Corax sniff around in the meadow. He was much stronger today, though his wounded paws were still very tender. But wherever Anya went, he insisted on limping after her. When Clodhopper was finally reassured that he was safe from horse-eating bunnies, Hugh gathered them all back into the van and took the reins. They were on their way.

"I could use your help when we get to Pumpkin Hook, kid."

"Okay. Pumpkin Hook? Is that a town?"

"A village. All you have to do is hold a sign for me."

"A sign for what?"

"Telling people that I'm in town and selling portraits. Not hard."

"Will I be far from you?"

"Just down the road. You'll be able to see the van from where you stand. It's a very small village."

"What about Corax?"

"Keep him right there beside you."

*W*hen they got to the village of Pumpkin Hook, Hugh left the van in front of a dilapidated store and they went in to buy eggs, milk, and food for next day. There were four or five whiskery men lounging on the sagging front porch, apparently with nothing to do, even though it was the middle of the day and it wasn't Sunday. Everywhere you look, Anya noticed, you see men with that empty, worried look. The same look her grandfather wore, though at least her grandfather shaved.

When they entered the store, Anya stopped abruptly. Many of the shelves were almost empty. The store owner looked up sharply as they entered.

"Good morning," Hugh said to the proprietor. "Your peaches. They look good."

"Pretty fine. Expensive, though. Them's the last of 'em."

"I'll take two. And a loaf of bread. A wedge of that cheese. How's business around here?"

"Strugglin'. I seen your van. You thinkin' of sellin' your pitchers here? Not gonna get a lotta business in Pumpkin Hook, I can tell ya."

"No?"

"Not many here can afford no pitcher-takin'. Go down to Mertensia, why doncha? Good crowds comin' in on the trolley there. City folks. They still got a little money to spend, some of them."

"There's a trolley stop in Mertensia?"

"Rochester to Canandaigua Lake, stops in Mertensia. You get yer picnickers, yer sight-seers, yer bathers. But only for one more week."

"How so?"

"Closin' it down."

"The trolley? I should think it would be very popular, especially in the summer."

"Oh, it was. But nowadays them city folks gots automobiles. It's the danged automobile makers what forced the trolley right out of business. They wanna sell cars and don't want no trolleys. That's why the rest of us is gonna lose our shirts. Railroad too, closin' down soon. Hard times gonna get worse. People drive right past our village now. And all this, everything what we worked so hard for over the years, all of it's goin' down the drain."

"Sorry to hear that. As if times aren't rough as it is."

"Got that right."

"Sir, I wonder. Could I ask a favor? Would you mind posing in your store for a portrait? Hey kid, run to the van to get my Speed Graphic, would you? The smaller camera."

"I tell ya, ain't got no money for such things."

"I won't charge you. The government will pay for it."

"Naw. Go on!"

"Yes. They're starting to document the struggles of small farmers and businessmen like you."

"Document?"

"Make a record. They need evidence. Photographs that will prove their point."

"What fer?"

"President Roosevelt wants to convince Congress that people do need help. That's what he calls his New Deal."

"Naw, really? So that's what that danged New Deal is about?"

"He wants the government to create jobs for people."

"Naw. Since when do they care?"

"Apparently the president cares. His wife, too."

"It'll never work."

"Well now, give Roosevelt some credit. He has sent a dozen of us photographers traveling all across the country, to take pictures of people suffering hardship. I'm on my way to Maryland to photograph farmers who've lost their land, and fishermen, and shop owners, too, like yourself."

"What fer?"

"They'll show these photographs to Congress. Make them admit that there is indeed a real problem. They'll *have* to set aside money for aid."

"Yeah? So you wanna see hardship? See these shelves, half empty? Next week, there'll be nothin' there. Take pitchers of that. My store is good as gone. I'm done fer. A failure."

Anya came back with Hugh's camera.

"So you wouldn't mind posing, sir?"

"No! No. I don't want to. Too ashamed of my store anymore. Too ashamed."

Hugh looked at the man for a minute. "It's not you that has failed, sir. Stores like yours are struggling all over the country. You're not the only one. You're one of hundreds, and it is not your fault. Look, look at you. You've hung on all this time. I admire you for that. I want other people to see that. To see your spirit. I'd really like to try to capture this spirit of yours."

"Baw! Naw."

"I can picture you standing over here, sir. Just here. Your hand on this magnificent brass cash register. Standing straight and proud. I want people to see your courage in the face of huge difficulty."

Suddenly, Anya saw what Hugh was doing. The grocer was transformed. She looked up at Hugh, amazed.

"That's it! That's what I'm after. You've captured it," said Hugh. "Now stand tall for me. Good. If you lift your chin, sir, the light will catch your – yes, just so. Now. Tell yourself you're proud as hell, sir, proud as hell." Hugh's shutter snapped. "Let me get a couple more. And another. That's good! Just one more."

"Do I get to see your pitcher?"

As soon as he and Anya finished lunch, Hugh made a print and took it into the store. The man shuffled out from behind the counter and studied it for a long moment. Without a word he reached for Hugh's hand. There were tears in the grocer's eyes.

"*I*t's good we're passing through here today and not in a couple of months," Hugh told Anya as they drove away.

"The shelves in that store were practically empty."

"Hard times, kid."

"Why is it hard times?"

"Different reasons in different places. Around here, the railroad closes down. So all the railroad people will be out of work.

No trains, so the farmers won't be able to get their crops to market, and they'll be strapped for cash. No cash, they won't be able to buy things anymore. So stores have to close."

"Will things ever get better, Hugh?"

"They keep saying they will, but it looks to me like times are getting worse. Let's hope business will be better down the road."

When they pulled into Mertensia that afternoon, Hugh made a big sign for Anya to carry, out of lightweight matte board.

"You should glue some of your portraits onto the sign here, Hugh, so people can see how nice your photographs are."

"Good idea." Hugh riffled through his album. "This one turned out pretty well."

"No, no!" Hugh had captured Anya posing with Corax in her arms. "Not that one!"

"Why not? Perfect lighting, nice contrast. You're even smiling a little. Hey, there's the trolley bell. Take this sign. Get over there, quick. Be sure to stand where people can see you when they get off the trolley. Tell them to come to the van."

Anya stood for the rest of the afternoon at the trolley stop, with Corax curled up on a blanket at her feet. She panicked, at first, that some policeman might be looking for her. But people read the sign and hardly glanced at her face.

It seemed like almost everyone from the city, those who had a little money to spend, wanted a photograph of themselves in their summer finery. They would see Anya's sign as the trolley pulled in, and run to get in line at Hugh's van. Girls in their light summer dresses, children in sailor suits, men in boaters and bow ties. Hugh photographed them all.

Hugh and Anya stayed and worked in Mertensia the next day, too. It was Sunday and the crowds coming from the city were even larger. All kinds of people were photographed that day by Hugh Durant. One trolley was full to overflowing with handsome black people dressed in their Sunday best. And a truck full of brown people in work clothes drove through town that day too. A few of them even managed to scrape together ten cents to buy a photograph to send back home. Hugh had so many customers that by noon he needed Anya's help at the van.

"Just leave the sign. I can go faster if you get people posed for me while I develop prints. Remember how we did it when I took your picture?"

"Yes, I do."

"Get them to pay you, too. Wear this bag and put the money in there."

So Anya got each person seated, ready for Hugh when he came out of the van with a finished print. She felt shy at first, but as she began looking critically at her subjects, she realized there were little things she could do that really helped them look better. She straightened the men's hats or asked them to hold them on their knees. She fixed a strand of hair here, a collar there. She asked the women to hold a pretty lace hankie or a nosegay of flowers. She had the most fun with the children, giving them Tisias the crow to hold or posing them with an arm around Corax. People waiting in line laughed and applauded when Hugh's shutter snapped just as Corax licked a baby's cheek.

While they worked, Anya nearly backed into a man in the crowd. He wasn't laughing like the rest. He was looking hard at her, his hands in his pockets.

"That your father?" He gestured toward Hugh. Everyone was having fun. At the moment, the question did not strike her as personal.

"No," she replied.

"A relative?"

Anya had been enjoying the merriment and was feeling light-hearted for the first time in days. Suddenly, she was worried.

"That guy a relative of yours?" the man asked her again.

"My uncle."

He nodded, still watching her closely. Anya cursed her stupidity, but then he simply turned and walked away. She sighed with relief.

*T*hat evening, Anya and Hugh were too tired to cook supper.

"A hot meal would be nice tonight," said Hugh, "but let's not bother. How 'bout a quick sandwich and go to sleep?"

"All right."

"You were a pretty good help today."

"I'm glad," she said, eyes glowing.

"You'll help me again tomorrow?"

"Sure. I'd like to, Hugh."

"We'll leave early."

They had just cleaned up their dishes and were getting ready for bed when they heard a loud rapping on the side of the van. Hugh stuck his head out.

"Hey! What do you – " he yelled, but stopped when he saw that the person who was smacking his night stick against the wagon was a uniformed policeman. "Help you?"

"You can't stay here."

"Leaving first thing in the morning, Officer."

"You're leavin' now, is when you're leavin'."

"Sorry?"

"We don't want no tramps here. You stayed too long already."

"I'm not a tramp. I own this photography studio."

"Couldn't care less. You don't live here. Yer a tramp."

"Hey, I brought a lot of commerce to your town today. Thanks to us, I believe your local grocery did a very brisk business."

"Don't give me that! You ruin business for our locals. We already got a guy here who takes pitchers. He lives here and he runs a real store. He don't want you here. Nobody wants you here. You can just keep a-movin' on."

"Come on, you can't expect me to harness my horse in the dark. You don't have to worry. I'm really too tired to cause anybody any trouble tonight. We'll be out of here before you're even awake tomorrow."

The policeman jabbed Hugh's shoulder with his night stick. "Look, Mac. Get this straight. You head on down that road or you're sleepin' in jail tonight." The policeman looked at Anya. "That your daughter?"

Hugh hesitated. "No. My niece."

The policeman snorted. "Yeah, sure. Well you can both just take yerselves down to the hobo jungle. Thataway, down to the Four Corners by the tracks. You'll see all the weirdos camped out there."

"We're not weirdos, Officer. I run a perfectly respectable – "

The policeman snorted again. "Respectable? You're a bum, simple as that. You got no right to be here."

"Okay. I see how things are in Mertensia."

"You just move – "

"We can't get out of this village fast enough, Officer, believe me."

CHAPTER EIGHT

*I*t was almost nine o'clock at night when Hugh's wagon pulled into the hobo camp outside of Canandaigua. Anya was slumped beside him, hardly able to stay awake. Corax was asleep in her lap, as was Tisias, on the back of the seat. Hugh parked the wagon behind a couple of tumbledown shacks and Anya sat up.

"Where are we?"

"In a jungle, as they call it."

"I don't see any trees."

"It's an encampment for homeless people."

Anya, now homeless herself, looked around with new interest.

All was quiet, though there were a number of men still about. The night was warm and the crickets, sawing on their fiddles in the high grass, had abandoned themselves to atonality. A golden summer moon floated at the horizon, so heavy it could barely lift itself into the sky. Overhead, the silver dust of the Milky Way was a tiara made of shining worlds that were real only in stories. Under this glorious sky, Anya could see a few poor tumbledown shelters and several men asleep on the ground, some with a very thin bundle for a pillow, some with nothing but a folded newspaper under their heads. A couple of small campfires, earthbound stars, were still lit. Men were gathered here and there in quiet groups, and several curious faces turned to them as they drove up.

Two men wandered over, one in an old baggy suit, the other wearing a bow tie and bowler hat. Corax, still sleepy, rested his chin on Anya's arm and barked half-heartedly.

"Good evening," said the man in a bow tie.

"That animal a bone-polisher?" the other asked, pointing in genuine fear.

"What's a bone-polisher?"

"He a mean critter? He bite?"

"You needn't worry, Sailor Bill," said his buddy. "You can see he's only a pup."

"Well, you can't be too careful. Does he bite?"

"He never has," said Anya.

"See? No need to fret, dear man. Here sir," the man in the bow tie offered, "let me help you with that harness." He petted the velvet of Clodhopper's nose.

"I'd better do it. He's pretty touchy," warned Hugh. "I'm afraid he'll bite you."

"No, look. He likes me already. I have a way with horses. I used to have quite a handsome stable, back in the day. Ah, I miss them. They were wonderful friends. They had a lot more affection for me than my indifferent spouse ever did." He shrugged and grinned. "Pathetic, but true."

"Why doncha call in at our fire when you're done here," the one called Sailor Bill suggested. "Bring your little girl."

"It's late. She's pretty tired," said Hugh.

"Aw, share some grub with us. Bring a cup and spoon. We got a mulligan stew going. C'mon, we're singing some old time songs over there. Nothing rude or nothing. Nice homey songs. It's just that some of them 'bos can't carry a tune in a bushel basket and could use a little help. You sing, honey?" he asked Anya.

"Well, a little, I guess."

"C'mon over, then."

Anya looked up at Hugh. "Maybe we will," Hugh hedged.

"Do we have to go over there, Hugh?" Anya asked, after the men walked away.

"Wouldn't hurt. Looks like we'll be sleeping here for the next few nights. Might as well be friendly."

"They don't look too nice."

Hugh raised an eyebrow. "This, from that dirty little ragamuffin who recently showed up at my van?"

Anya's mouth fell open. Had she looked like that? "Should we take them the bread we bought today?"

"That's a nice idea, kid."

Anya, with Corax cradled in her arms, stood right at Hugh's elbow when they joined the men at their fire. Tisias, indignant, was left at the wagon.

"Sit down! Glad to have you!" the men said. "Hey, they brung bread! Cut this up, Frisco. There's enough for us all."

"Bread! Hey, I thank ya!"

Anya clung to Corax and sat as close to Hugh as she could get.

"Nothing for us, thanks. We've eaten," said Hugh, when they were offered stew. "We just came over to say hello."

"You sure you don't want any?" The hobos couldn't believe anyone would turn down food. "This here stew's got meat in it. Big Shorty scored some off a butcher in town, just today. Not too old, neither. And Sailor Bill nicked a coupla carrots ..."

"Did not," Bill insisted. "I traded for 'em. Most of 'em."

"... and we got 'taters, even."

"No. Thank you, though," said Hugh. "You men traveling together?"

"Well, me, I'm bound south with The Swede here. The cold'll be comin' an' I just can't take it no more."

"Frisco Kid and me just got here," said another. "Feels great to stop riding the rails, have some real grub, get boiled up for a change."

"Boiled up?" Anya looked up at Hugh. He shrugged.

"Mike means he boiled the bugs out of his clothes and took a bath," explained Windy Will, the man with the bow tie and bowler hat.

"Oh." Bugs?

Sailor Bill laughed. "Michigan Mike, he got here just today. Looked like he'd been drawn through a sick horse."

"We thought we'd all bathe today, it being Sunday," said Windy Will. "So you came at a good time. We spruced ourselves up a bit, as you can see." He gave his tie a tweak.

"Got our glad rags on."

"Then Windy Will gived us all haircuts."

" 'S good you didn't come while we was waiting for our clothes to dry. Who wants to look at a bunch of scrawny naked 'bos? Haha!"

"Lordie lord!" cackled Frisco. "Wouldn't wish that sight on my worst enemy!"

"Where you people bound?" another hobo asked Hugh.

"I'm hoping to work up some business in Canandaigua for a few days. How are things in that town?"

"You taking pitchers? Should be good business. The train brings a load of city types down from Rochester. But you gotta watch them bulls. Mighty mean."

"Bulls?"

"The cops. They'd as soon lock you up as look at you. Irish Johnny got pinched the other day, just for walking down the street. Thirty days they give him, way up in Erie."

"No, they got him here. In town."

"Irish Johnny? I heared he got thirty in Erie."

"You heared wrong, Bill."

"I sure hope so. Poor Johnny." Sailor Bill shook his head sadly. "Poor poor Johnny."

"Thirty days don't sound like much," said another hobo, "but I swear to god, in Erie you get nothing to eat but bread and water. Never so much as a cup of soup. Then you gotta load box cars all day, even though yer starving. And the joint is crawling with bugs and coughing sickness. Hardly a day goes by you don't get bashed in the head for looking cross-eyed at some stiff."

"You're not the same man when you come outa there. If you come out." All the men grunted agreement.

"My goodness! Seriously friends, there's no need to discuss this now," said Windy Will.

"Yeah Frenchie! Stop it already! We all done time. We know what it's like. Stop all this griping and get out your squeezebox! Give us a tune. The little girl here don't want to listen to our tales of woe!"

"She can sing, she says. Can't you, darlin'?"

Sailor Bill's tender gaze gave her courage. "A little, maybe."

"Sing us a tune. Here, I'll hold your doggie. What's your name, honey?"

"Anya."

Frenchie played a few chords on his concertina. "You know 'O Danny Boy', Anya?"

"Oh! That's a good one!" the men exclaimed, settling back. "Sing us a bit of it, darlin'."

When she finished, Sailor Bill wiped his eyes with the backs of his hands. "That was the prettiest thing I ever heard," he said. "I'd sure love to hear another."

The moon was high in the sky when Hugh, Anya, and Corax finally went back to the van to sleep.

*T*he next morning Hugh's van left in a foggy dawn for

Canandaigua, early enough, Hugh hoped, that they could get a parking spot close to the trolley stop. No one else was on the road yet. A little birdsong and the clopping of their horse's hoofs were the only sounds in the grey morning. Corax stood on his hind legs at the edge of the wagon, scenting the morning breezes. Hugh, hunched on his seat, was enjoying the quiet.

"Boy, I've never done anything like that before. Like last night, I mean, singing with those men," Anya said as they lumbered down the road. She paused. "I never knew people like that, did you? They were much nicer than I thought they'd be. I mean, they were shabby looking and all, but still friendly. You know what I mean?"

Hugh flicked his eyebrows in answer.

"I never would have thought," she mused. "Quite nice people, really. Didn't you think so?"

Hugh, silent.

"Yeah, that man with the bow tie was funny, wasn't he?" Anya chirped. "He actually seems quite smart." She gave Hugh a moment to answer. He didn't. "Well. To me, anyway, he seemed smart. He speaks well, doesn't he?"

"Uhh."

"I liked Sailor Bill the best, really. He seems so sweet. And he loved Corax. I felt sorry for him, though. His shoes, they're falling apart. Did you notice?"

Grunt.

"What did they mean about bugs in their clothes, Hugh?"

"Lice. Bedbugs."

"Ew. Is it all right if I have a bath and wash my clothes tonight? I have to get boiled up."

Hugh snickered the smallest of snickers.

"I'll carry the water," said Anya. "And heat it." She looked about at the fine homes they were passing. "They don't have much of anything at all, the hobos, do they, Hugh?" She stroked Corax's head affectionately. "I mean, really, it looks like they have nothing of their own. Do they?"

Hugh straightened and sighed. "How can they, on the road all the time?"

"But they share whatever they find, don't they?"

"Mostly," said Hugh.

"Where are they all going? Windy Will said none of them have homes to go to."

"Wherever the trains take them, I guess."

"But they don't buy tickets?"

"They sneak onto a boxcar, if the guards don't catch them. There are some who ride under the boxcars."

"There's no place to sit under there, is there?"

"They lie flat and wedge themselves underneath, just above the wheels. It's very dangerous. They have to hide from the railroad workers, so they squeeze in wherever they can."

"Did you ever do that, Hugh?"

"No."

"That's good. I'm glad. But where are they all going? Don't they want to have homes?"

"Maybe they've lost their jobs. Maybe they're just birds that can't stand cages."

"Like you?"

"Maybe." A pause. "You too, eh kid?"

Anya tilted her head, pondering, quiet for a moment. What had become of that Anya who used to live on Elm Street? Would she have believed, a week ago, that she'd end up here?

"Never," she said aloud.

"Huh?" asked Hugh.

Anya reached to stroke Corax's head and he answered with deep understanding in his eyes. "Right, puppy? We never ever knew we'd be here."

*H*ugh parked the van in Canandaigua and set up his tripod. Trolleys came rolling into town crowded with people taking a holiday by the lake, or people who just wanted to get away from the heat of the city for a day. Hugh had all the business he could want, and once again Anya was busy helping.

When the sun began to drop and people boarded trains bound for the city again, Anya helped Hugh pack up the equipment. Flush with the day's earnings, they bought meat and vegetables and an entire tray of the grocer's wife's cookies to take back to the camp. Several hobos had managed to scrounge scraps of cast-off lumber to make a meager fire for cooking.

"I'll get the harness off Clodhopper and get him fed, kid. Go on without me. Take the food over to the fire. I see Windy Will over there. I'll bring our plates, and that cider we bought. I'll be there in a few minutes."

"Okay. Come on, Corax."

"Hey! Our little nightingale and her pooch are back!" cried Sailor Bill, so pleased to see Anya coming.

"Here's our little philosopher-dog. Hey, you're such a good boy!" Windy Will bent to stroke Corax's head.

"Whatcha got there, Anya? Good lord! Meat!"

"Meat two nights in a row?" said Frenchie. "What happened? I died and gone to heaven? Gimme that, I'll get it ready for the pot. Thanks, Anya!" Corax danced beside him, all the way to the fire.

"Yeah, thanks Anya, and tell your daddy thanks."

"Oh, Hugh's not my father. He'll be over in a few minutes."

"He ain't your father?" asked Sailor Bill, instantly suspicious. "What, your uncle or something?"

"No. Not really."

Bill squinted at her. "How'd you meet up with him?"

"Just chance, I guess."

Sailor Bill put down the buffalo nickel he was scratching at, and spoke softly to Anya. "Honey, you ain't flown the coop or anything, is you?"

"What do you mean?"

"You a runaway?"

"Well ...." Anya sat down. "Are you going to turn me in?"

"Hell no! Oops, cursing. Sorry. But no, we would never. Still, honey, the road ain't no place for a kid."

"Geez, Bill," said Big Shortie. "What you sayin'? I seen hundreds of kids on the road, lots as young as her."

"Anya ain't that same kind of kid. Come on, honey! Ain't you got somebody to take care of you?"

"I'll be with Hugh as far as Geneva. Then, I don't know. He heads south after that."

"Look, little girl," said Sailor Bill, moving closer to Anya. "You musta come from a good home. I can tell. You got manners. Why can't you go back home, honey lamb? Huh? Why?"

"Bill, if she thinks home was a bad place for her, don't tell her to go back!"

"I worry, okay?" snapped Bill. Quietly to Anya he asked, "Was it that bad, honey?"

"They wanted to put me in reform school." Anya blurted. She folded her arms and turned away, glowering. Would the hobos think she was terrible now?

Many raised eyebrows, many sympathetic groans. Surprised by their show of support, Anya turned back.

"What? Reform school!" "Lordie lord, Anya, stay outa there!" "Sounds like she got good reason to be on the road." "She sure do!"

Windy Will touched her arm. "May I share some advice? I've been on the road for two years now and this is what I've learned, Anya." He stood up, posing like an orator. "Never forget rule number one of the Hobo Laws! Decide your own life, and don't let another person run or rule you."

"Hobo Laws?" said Anya.

"Absolutely, my dear. A set of rules issued at the 1889 Hobo Convention."

"Yessir, Will!" "This man knows his stuff!" Everyone nodded. "Yer right, Will!"

"That's pretty smart talk there, Willy," said Frenchie.

"I urge everyone to learn those laws. Frankly, I believe they outline precepts that all people should live by."

"That so, Will?"

"Absolutely."

"Like, fr'instance?"

"For instance, rule number two advises helping your fellow hobos because someday you'll be the one needing help. Number three, take only what you need and leave the rest for the next person."

"He's good, ain't he, that Will?" said Sailor Bill, nudging Anya. "Smart 's a whip."

"But that one about 'decide your own life', that's the best law, ain't it, Will?" declared Big Shortie.

"Absolutely. You must be free to make your own decisions."

"Uh huh. Of all peoples in this world, us hobos have learnt you gotta be free."

"Yeah." "Yep!" "Yessirree bob," repeated the men.

"It's all we got, really. Our freedom." "Yep. That's it." "'T'sall we got."

"Freedom is priceless," said Windy Will.

"You prob'ly done right, honey, getting away. Just run and keep running!"

Windy Will sat down next to Anya and spoke quietly. "But, to your mind, Anya dear, is every way closed before you?" he asked.

Anya nodded, her eyes brimming.

"You've thought about this? I just want you to be aware of what you're getting into. A person becomes something else on the road," Windy Will said thoughtfully, folding his hands around his knee. "You become a not-there, a not-responsible. It's addictive."

"Here, Anya. I'm going to give you this, for luck on your road." Sailor Bill dropped the nickel he was working on into Anya's hand. Whenever he came across a nickel, which was not too often, he liked to carve a face into its soft surface.

"Thank you, Bill! It's ... it's lovely." He had delicately carved and scratched at the coin and transformed the Indian on its face into a skull.

"You can trade it for something you need. It'll be worth more'n a nickel now," he told her confidently.

"Bill's an artist, see," said Frenchie.

"Save it for a rainy day," Bill advised. "So you don't plan to go south with Hugh?"

"No."

"Whyever not? He seems a good sort, and you'd be safe with him."

"He'd rather not have me hanging around, probably, eating all his food and bothering him. And I want to find my grandparents."

"And they is where?"

"I think they are in Lake Placid."

"I hope you're not thinking of riding the rails? Now I'm really gonna worry!" said Sailor Bill.

"The train?"

"You know, doncha," said Big Shortie, "that them rails is downright dangerous, even for strong growed men? Lookit Tiny Tim over there. See him there, on that little wagon? Nothing but two stumps for legs."

"What happened?"

"He fell, trying to jump on a boxcar. Got runned over."

"Well, how 'bout Pistol Pete?" said Sailor Bill mournfully. "Gawd! Eighteen years old. I saw him ridin' possum with my own eyes. Oh gawd, poor Pete." Bill wiped his cheeks.

"Riding possum means lying on top of a passenger car," Windy Will explained to Anya.

"Not very safe."

"Next thing we know'd," said Bill, sniffing loudly, "he's lyin' next to the track, his face smashed in." Bill honked into his old handkerchief and wiped his eyes again. "God rest his soul. Who knows what happened?"

"Gee," said Anya, horrified. "Well, I'll be safer walking. Besides, I've got my dog with me."

The hobos looked at little Corax and laughed. "Oh, he'll keep you safe!"

"What we gotta do, Will, is show her the codes. I know they're secret and all, but she's only a kid. And all alone."

"That's not a bad idea."

"Yes, you're right. Look Anya. Pay attention because this is important for you. You know what a town water tank looks like, right?"

"Yes, those big high round things."

"Every time you come to a new place, look for the water tank. All the news you need to know is right there."

"News?"

"Somewhere on the tank. Signs that give warnings. Advice. Here, see this sign?" Frenchie scratched a symbol in the dust. "It means this town is good for battering privates."

"She don't know what that means, Frenchie. It means knocking on doors of houses, begging for food."

"Begging?" asked Anya.

"Here's a useful sign, Anya. You'll see this on some houses." Will made a drawing. "Some hobo puts it there, right on the house, so we all know the people who live there are good for hand-outs."

"I don't want to ask for hand-outs."

"Anya, how you gonna live?" cried Frenchie. "You gotta ask, little girl! And people like to give to kids.

"I was on the road as a lad," said Big Shorty. "Three different ladies offered to adopt me." He laughed. "I was better looking back then."

"See, Anya? Folks won't be afeart of you. They probably won't let you come inside the house, but they might bring a plate out to you."

"Oh, how I loves to throw my legs under a table! I'd love to have a nice set-down about now," said Sailor Bill.

"No. Ya can't expect that. But betimes they let you set on their back porch."

"Yeah. Maybe even sleep in their barn."

"I knocked on a door once," said Frenchie. "A cop answers. Yeah, chief of police! I was so scairt I almost swallowed my head. But what does he tell me? Go to the police station, he says. They got a room in back. They let me wash and sleep there for a night."

"Well, that's sure not yer usual."

"You got that right. You can't trust them bulls! Look, this here sign is important, Anya. This here sign says the bulls are hostile – the cops, right? They don't want no hobos in town. You see this sign and you just keep right on a-walking, no matter how hungry you are. John Law will pinch you for sure, and jail is no place for a kid."

Hugh came up just then. Corax was the only one to notice him. Anya was bent over beside five hobos who were scratching with sticks in the dust.

"What's going on?" Hugh asked.

"We're showing her the codes ...."

"... so she'll be safe on the road."

"But Anya," warned Sailor Bill, "you ever see a gang of little road kids? Don't think they'll let you join them. They won't. Never! You gotta hide from them. Hide real good, fast as you can. I once seen a bunch of little eight, ten year old boys, bony as sticks, tackle a grown man and take everything he had. They stripped him naked and nearly busted his head doing it. They're like little wolves, those kids. Get away from them!"

Anya blinked. What had she gotten herself into?

"She's not going to have to worry about any of that," said Hugh. "Maybe I"ll get her passage on the canal as far as Albany."

Anya stared at him, amazed. He looked away, shrugging.

"She can get a train ticket to Massena from there, can't she?"

"I'm going to look into all that for her."

"So this grand-daddy yer visiting, Anya? He a good man? He'll take you in?" worried Bill.

"I think so."

"Grand-daddy?" asked Hugh. "In Lake Placid?"

"I hope so." She looked up at Hugh again, and he was staring at her. Had she hurt his feelings? She had shared more of her story with these hobos than she had with him.

"Hey you 'bos!" shouted Frenchie from near the fire. "This here stew's just about boiling."

"We brought some cider," said Anya.

"Pour me some of that! Yer the best! Our own little hobo princess!"

"Here's to good luck on the road, Little Tramp!"

"Just remember, Anya," advised Windy Will, his tone quiet and grave, "no one is ever really alone on the road. The wind that tramps the world is right beside you." He nodded. "Those are Jack London's very words. Have you read any of Jack London's stories, Anya?"

"Omigawd. You talking books again, Will?" groaned Sailor Bill.

"You and yer fillo-sophing! Let's stop yakking and eat!"

*A*nya was quiet, walking behind Hugh on the way back to his van that evening. He hadn't said much to her all night. Was he angry because she was always tagging along, a thorn in his side? She had to scurry to keep up with him. He was a big-framed man, though he carried no fat – hardly anyone did in those days – , and his strides were long. Corax trotted close behind.

Hugh unlocked the van and they stepped in. Anya gave Tisias the crow a crust of bread, which he tore into with gusto.

With all the talk about being on the road, Anya had a lot to think about tonight. Soon she would be on her own again. That was probably for the best. She must be a burden to Hugh. Her, and her animals. Still, just when Hugh was probably wishing she'd take her pets and go, she was changing her mind about him. She was getting to like him. She wondered what it would be like for her when he headed south. She would be all alone again, except for the dog and the crow. And the wind.

Hugh sat down on his bed. "Sit down, kid. Talk to me for a minute."

She sat, twisting her fingers in her lap.

"I'm a little worried. I've been thinking about a kid your age being on the road."

Anya slumped in the chair. She knew he was going to tell her to leave.

"Sailor Bill told me your folks wanted to put you into reform school. I didn't know that, Anya."

"He told?"

"Is it true?"

After a minute, she nodded. "Yes. My – my grandmother, yes."

"What did your father have to say about that?"

"I don't hear from him very often. He left after my mother died. He has other things to think about besides me."

"That's tough. How old were you when she died?"

"Four, I guess."

"So your father has been gone all that time?"

"I hardly remember him."

"I can't believe you did something so terrible that your grandmother would send you to reform school."

"I didn't do it! But they said I did! They were going to call the police!" Anya's voice caught in her throat. "I would never do anything to hurt Mrs. Wright, but they wouldn't believe me. I was afraid to tell you. I was so afraid you'd ...." She looked bleakly at Hugh and gathered Corax into her arms, holding him tight. "They said it was my fault. Mrs. Wright, our housekeeper, ... she ... she fell down the stairs and got really badly hurt and maybe ...." She could not say the words. She buried her face in Corax's neck.

"You were afraid. So you ran away."

"I had to, Hugh!" she sobbed.

He folded his hands between his knees and rounded his shoulders, rocking a little. "I see that, kid. I see that." He let her cry for a bit. "You did the hardest thing, running away. That takes courage."

She shook her head.

"Sure it does. I know. I had to do it too."

"When you were a kid?"

"When I was a kid, and again, after I'd grown up. Just about a year ago. And you know what?"

"What?"

"I was scared both times."

"Really?"

"Now it looks like I'll always be on the road."

"You'll find someplace, Hugh."

"No." He shook his head. "I'm too much of a curmudgeon. I put people off."

"What's a curmudgeon?"

"A sourpuss."

"Oh. Heh heh. Yeah." She thought about that. "But a grown man running away?"

"What do you think most of those hobos are doing? Sometimes we just find ourselves in a place that's bad for us, with people that are bad for us." He shrugged." And we have to get out, if we can."

"Who was bad to you?"

Hugh laughed a short laugh. "The lady I was engaged to. I made the mistake of falling in love with my boss's daughter."

"Is that who that is, that picture over there?"

"That's her. Liza."

"She's awfully pretty."

"Yes she is. But she and her father had plans for me. And I knew I couldn't live up to them."

"So you left?"

"So I left."

Anya nodded.

"I dunno." Hugh leaned his elbows on his knees. "Maybe I was a coward."

"Yeah. Me too. I was so afraid."

"Afraid to go, afraid to stay."

"Yeah."

"But here we all are." Hugh sat up. "And who would have thought?"

"What?"

"Me and a kid? A dog, a bird?"

"Do you mind, Hugh?"

He studied Anya's face for a minute, his chin on his hand. "Well, you never know what or who is around the next corner."

"But, do you mind?"

"Actually, kid, I was wondering." Anya's stomach knotted with worry. "I was thinking maybe you could come south with me. You're a pretty good helper. Then, after I finish my job down there, in maybe a month or so, I could drive you to Lake Placid. It'd be kind of fun. I've never been there. Sounds like an interesting place. They had the Olympics there last year. Maybe I could get a job, with a newspaper or something, for the winter."

"Really? Really?" Anya felt herself grinning and crying at the same time. She hid her face in Corax's fur again. "I'm not usually such a cry-baby," she sobbed. "Honest! I'm not, Hugh."

"Oh, you're one tough old lady. Of that I'm very sure! We're quite the pair, aren't we?"

"Hugh?"

"Yeah?"

"My real last name is Netherby."

"Netherby?" He scratched his head. "Wow. That's a long name to paint on the side of my van."

*T*hey went back to Canandaigua the next morning. The trolleys were as busy as before, and soon there was a crowd of people lined up to have a portrait taken. Hugh worked as quickly as he could, snapping pictures and running inside to develop the film and print the photos. While he did that, Anya helped the previous sitter choose a print. She took their money and tucked it into her bag. Then she got the next sitter posed, ready for when Hugh came out again.

Their routine was working like clockwork, which is why neither of them noticed the uniformed policeman watching them carefully. He had a small poster in his hand, which he referred to several times, looking from it to Anya and back again. A woman approached the policeman. They shook hands and both stood watching Anya for some minutes. Finally the policeman left, but the woman stayed, waiting patiently for the right moment. She had a plausible story all ready to tell Anya.

She didn't have to wait long. Hugh hung up a sign that said CLOSED FOR LUNCH. He took the money bag from Anya, fished out a few coins to give to her, and went into the van. Anya and Corax walked two blocks to the grocer's, to buy lunch.

When Anya did not return in a few minutes, Hugh got worried. He walked down the street to talk to the grocer, who said he hadn't seen the girl with the red dog since the day before. Where was she? She couldn't have run away again, could she? Hugh became frantic, searching up and down the street but not finding her. Then, seeing two uniformed policemen coming his way, he stopped to ask their assistance. They spoke for a minute, then Hugh stepped back, raising his voice.

"You'd better tell me what you've done with her, or I'm raising holy hell!" he threatened. He gesticulated, furious. One of the policemen pointed a menacing finger and shoved Hugh's flailing arms. With an oath, Hugh pushed back. As soon as he did that, hot anger flamed their cheeks and he knew instantly he had made a mistake.

"Whoa! Oh no, Buddy Boy," one of the cops said. "Don't nobody holler at us!" Which wasn't quite true. The boss's roar caused fear and trembling, and okay, yeah, their sainted mamas had tongues that could raise blisters. But no one else.

"Wha'dya think, Louie? You think we should let some unholy flea-bitten peddler give us lip?" said the other.

"Not hardly," said Louis, giving Hugh a shove. "We been

trained, Mac. We knows howta handle a balla slime like you."

Hugh resisted. They had clubs. They convinced him, very bluntly, very painfully, that they were not to be messed with, and they dragged him off, unconscious and trailing blood, to spend a few restorative nights in jail.

*I*rish Johnny was just getting out of jail as Hugh's inert body was heaved into a cell. The policemen left him where he fell, and Irish could hear them talking. He eavesdropped shamelessly but knew better than to speak. He couldn't wait to get out of there and into the open air again. He beat it out of that town as fast as he could, and hiked out to the hobo jungle beside the tracks. Windy Will welcomed him.

"Irish! You're back. Did you have a difficult time in John Law's correctional facility?"

"You didn't know, Will? It wasn't no facility. It was jail I was in all this time. But I'm out now and that's all I care about. I wasn't nothin' but a punchin' bag for them bulls, but now they got somebody else to beat up. I'm off the hook. You shoulda seen the guy they pinched today. Dragged him in, a big bloody mess. Poor guy was out like a light. They said he were a tramp but his boots sure looked wrong. Not a hole in 'em."

"Do you know who it was?"

"Never seed him before, but I heard them say he was takin' pitchers in town here."

"What? Not Hugh?"

"Dunno."

"What did they arrest him for?"

"Mouthin' off. You just can't backtalk them guys."

"Was there a child with him? A little girl?"

"Nope. Nobody. Nobody that I saw."

"Good lord! Where could she be?" Will scratched his head. "I'm going to borrow a clean jacket and go into town to look for her."

"Watch yerself, Will. I wouldn't go near that town. Them bulls is hostile!"

Windy Will hurried into Canandaigua and found Hugh's van empty, except for a lonely and pathetic one-winged crow. It was late afternoon but the sign on the van still said CLOSED FOR LUNCH. And no sign of Anya. Will was sure it was Hugh they had thrown in jail, but he didn't dare go there to inquire. Instead, he hitched Clodhopper to the wagon, turned him around, and drove him back to the hobo jungle. Tisias the crow had plenty to say about the whole situation, but not a soul was listening.

CHAPTER NINE

*N*earer the city, Officer Harvey Wallhanger was sitting on the edge of his desk, thinking. He made a mental list. Anya Netherby was still missing without a trace. A servant had hinted that her aunt might have something to do with that. This same aunt, Helen Netherby, was wearing jewelry that was very possibly stolen. How did she pay for jewelry if her family was broke? And where was she buying it?

Wasn't it strange that there was a missing child and stolen jewelry in the same house? Had the girl seen or heard something that put her in danger? If so, he was frightened for the child. He was also very worried for her aunt. It rattled him, how worried he was for Helen Netherby.

Harvey got up to pace, then threw himself into his chair. These burglaries in their county now – he needed to know more about them. Homes of wealthy people had been robbed. Jewelry and small valuable items were stolen by a man so stealthy that he never left a shred of evidence. The press called him the Cat Burglar. The police investigated each crime, investigations headed up by Harvey's immediate superior, Cesare Toda. But when Harvey asked to see the files on the Cat Burglar robberies, Toda had been outraged, telling him to back off.

Thick-bodied, loud-mouthed, Toda was the man who had nicknamed Harvey "Smallwanger". Harvey didn't care about the name-calling. It did bother him that he was being pushed aside. A few days ago, he had interrupted a discussion about the Cat Burglar in Toda's office. When Harvey walked in, Toda had quickly stuffed a folder of photographs into a drawer. He locked that drawer with a key that he kept on his key ring. What was the big secret?

Okay, Harvey decided. Take the bull by the horns.

The next day was Sunday. Late that night, when he knew Toda had gone out to a poker game, and when the only other officer on duty was three sheets to the wind, Harvey walked into Toda's office. Skillfully, he picked the lock on Toda's drawer and took what he needed back to his own desk. By the light of one small lamp, Harvey pored over a folder of photos and insurance claims.

Here it was. Exactly what he had most feared.

A diamond and pearl ring stolen in 1931. Its setting – identical to the one worn by Helen Netherby in a family photo of that same year.

And another photo, a diamond ring he had seen her wearing just this week.

A strand of pearls and tiny sapphires. She wore one just like it.

Oh Miss Netherby, thought Harvey Wallhanger. My lovely lady. Where are you buying these jewels?

Then Harvey came across something he wasn't really looking

for, and rather wished he hadn't found. Sick with dread, a film of sweat broke on his brow. He pulled the photo from the bottom of the pile. It was a candid photo of an elegant gentleman, dated 1930. The man was wearing a very handsome gold stick pin in his tie. At its end, four small emeralds were set in a clover shape. One year later, that pin had been stolen. The photo was apparently submitted after the robbery, maybe for insurance purposes, but hidden away in this file instead.

Numb with shock, Harvey realized that he saw that tie pin all the time. Here, in the office. The exact same pin, he was sure, because the gold bezel setting on one stone had a deep nick in it. Harvey saw it every day, that emerald stick pin, on the necktie that rippled over the bulging belly of Cesare Toda.

Helen Netherby's stolen rings. A stolen emerald stick pin worn by a police officer. Two people, somehow connected? It seemed so unlikely. Big blustery Cesare Toda and the delicately lovely Miss Helen Netherby? What kind of relationship could they have? Was Miss Netherby buying stolen jewels from a police officer? Or was Cesare Toda something else to her? More than just a policeman? A lover, maybe? The hackles went up on Harvey Wallhanger's perspiring neck.

Harvey didn't know who to tell about what he had found. Cesare Toda was very chummy with the chief of police, and it was always dangerous to point a finger at a fellow officer. As for Miss Netherby – Harvey's thoughts stalled there.

Why did I have to be the one to find this? he wondered. What should he do now? Should he keep the photos of the jewelry, or leave them in the file? In the end he slipped four of them into his briefcase. Then he went directly to the train station, and put them in a rented locker so he could quiet his fears until he figured out what to do.

I am a coward, Harvey thought, a complete coward. Oddly, that turned out to be a good thing. It made him very cautious, and Harvey needed to be cautious.

*P*revious to this, Harvey had gone to visit the housekeeper, Mrs. Wright, every day for the last four days. She suffered a broken arm, a broken leg, and had dislocated her jaw when she fell. Now it was Monday, a week after the accident, and the bandages had just been removed from her head. Though the swelling prevented her from speaking, she could eat pureed foods now. And her back was a little less painful. She could sit up partway.

Mrs. Wright had just woken from a nap. She was so grateful to this stranger who was helping her. Some nice woman. Her name was Betty. Apparently, Betty was someone's cook. Mrs. Wright couldn't figure out whose. Betty was now plumping the pillow behind Mrs. Wright's head, trying to make her more comfortable. And, here at the end of her bed, was that man again. That quiet, well-mannered man, dark-haired, rather nice-looking, with sympathetic dark eyes. She liked his eyes. Mrs. Wright could only dimly remember having seen him before. Was it earlier today? Was it yesterday? He held a white straw fedora in his hand.

"Hello, Mrs. Wright," he said to her.

She gave a small nod.

"I'm Officer Wallhanger. I've been asked to look into the disappearance of Anya Netherby." He told her the same thing every day.

Mrs. Wright, as always when he spoke to her, looked confused.

"Do you remember Anya? I was hoping you could tell us where she might have gone."

Mrs. Wright's eyes flashed a look at Betty.

Betty leaned over the bed. "Remember, Petunia? Remember I told you that Anya is missing?"

Mrs. Wright was visibly upset. She tried to speak.

"She can't really talk yet, Officer," explained Betty. She looked fondly at Mrs. Wright. "I tell her every day that Anya is missing. Honestly, I'm not sure she remembers from one day to the next. Do you remember, Petunia, that I told you yesterday about Anya?"

Anya? Mrs. Wright made a small movement of her head. "Nnn," she said.

Betty looked at Officer Wallhanger. "Maybe tomorrow she'll be able to tell us something."

*O*fficer Wallhanger was losing sleep, not to mention his appetite, over this case. Today he stood by the front door of the Netherby residence again, preparing himself mentally to confront Helen with two of the photos he had found in the police files. She answered the door and, looking at her, Harvey was assailed by doubts. It was so difficult to imagine a woman like this being involved with a thug like Cesare Toda. She was lovely, and was as always, tastefully dressed. Apparently there was no such thing as a humble house dress in her closet. Today, she was wearing a softly draped afternoon dress in a subdued print. It slid over her slim hips and fell to below her knees, without hiding her ankles. Harvey tore his eyes from those ankles and gazed at the strand of pearls and tiny sapphires at her neck, and ...

... but he was getting distracted. He put it down to fatigue and tried to rouse himself to accomplish what he had come to do.

"May I come in for a moment, Miss Netherby?"

"Yes. Certainly." She gestured him to the hall chair he had sat in before.

"I came to return the family photos you so graciously lent me."

"Oh. Yes. Thank you."

"I'm sure you're anxious for news of your niece."

"Of course."

"Unfortunately we have had no word as yet. I had copies of her photo mailed to police stations in several towns. Eventually, with any luck, someone will spot her. Now, I must ask – I don't want to worry you because we have no reason to expect foul play. But you would tell me, wouldn't you, if you had received any phone calls?"

"No, she hasn't phoned, Mr. Wallhanger."

"I meant calls from kidnappers asking for ransom. Or notes from such people? Anything of that nature?"

"Oh. No, no." Helen touched her forehead, the diamond on her finger catching the light. "Oh my goodness. I hadn't considered that."

"I would have thought that the threat of kidnapping would be a great concern for her family."

"Fortunately, we have not been contacted in any way." Helen rose. "But thank you for coming. You'll alert us as soon as you hear anything?"

"I certainly will." Officer Wallhanger remained seated. "There's another thing. I have a photograph I'd like you to look at." Harvey held two photos. He handed her one. He kept the other in his hand. No need to upset her, he figured. He ignored the Voice of Reason in his head. "This photo" he told her, "was taken for insurance purposes. Do you recognize any of that jewelry, Miss Netherby?"

Helen sat down. "No, I don't. No." She handed the photo back, and leaned to see the one that he still held. Quickly, her left hand covered the ring on her right.

"I'm surprised you don't recognize the pearl ring in this photograph," he said, "as it is identical to the one you are wearing in your family photo." He pointed.

"What? Oh my, yes. You are so observant, Mr. Wallhanger! That old ring. I forgot about it. I sold it some time ago."

"Where did you sell it, may I ask?"

"I – I pawned it. Desperate times, you know, call for desperate measures. It wasn't really of any great value, unfortunately. Just paste. I had forgotten all about it. Where did you get this photo?"

He didn't want her to know he had looked at Toda's files. "The ring was stolen."

"Stolen. Ah. I see. Probably after I sold it."

"Ah, yes. Probably. Yes." Harvey felt inexplicably relieved. Still, he had to follow up. "Can you give me the name of the pawn shop you used? And the date? Just so I can close this file."

"Well, let's see. It was a shop in the city." She pressed her left hand to her head and kept her right hand in her lap. "You know, I think I've probably forgotten the name of the shop. What do they – you know – what do they call it? When your mind purposefully forgets things that are unpleasant?"

Harvey looked at her with sympathy.

"It was such a difficult time in our lives, Officer. I'm sorry. You'll have to excuse my bad memory."

Wallhanger stood up and Helen rose immediately. She was so touched by the look of concern in his face.

"Well," she said with a smile, "that's that, I guess."

"Yes. Thank you." He gave an awkward short bow. "Have a most –" he had to stop to clear his throat, "have a pleasant day, Miss Netherby."

*W*allhanger spent some of the next morning trying to contact Anya's father. Cornell University had returned his phone call with nothing to report, but suggested he contact Columbia University. That call had borne fruit. He now knew Jackson Netherby's approximate whereabouts in New Mexico, but had not been able to reach him by phone. He sent a telegram, without much hope.

*M*eanwhile, Helen Netherby was steeling herself to visit Mrs. Wright at the hospital. It had to be done. That Wallhanger man had scared the daylights out of her with those photos of her rings. She had to keep up appearances, and she absolutely must speak privately with Mrs. Wright. That lady had seen things. Helen must convince her that she hadn't seen what she thought she saw.

Everything is going wrong at once, thought Helen. Threats were coming at her from all sides. Mr. Wallhanger and his photos. Mrs. Wright, coming upon her in the middle of the night. And always in the background, a third person. Giancarlo, her biggest problem. Why had she gone to him? She had been upset, yes, but why had she told him about Mrs. Wright? It had only made things worse.

Helen bought a bouquet of flowers and a box of chocolates to take to the hospital, and was relieved to see that the police guard was not outside Mrs. Wright's door anymore. Betty the cook, unfortunately, was there.

When Helen entered, Mrs. Wright looked at her uncertainly. She seemed vague about who Helen was. Betty, sitting beside the bed, was not vague at all.

"Miss Netherby," she said in clipped tones. "I'm surprised to see you here."

"I'm surprised you're still here." Helen bowed her head. That sounded mean. Everything she said came out sounding mean these days. "It's kind of you, Betty ...."

"Neil and I take turns sitting with Petunia. Just so you know. We're always here."

"Very kind." Helen turned her back. She set her flowers on the table. "Has she ...?" She could feel Betty looking daggers at her.

"You're wondering if she has said anything?"

"Well ... I wondered if ...." Helen bit her lip and rearranged a couple of blossoms. "Poor lady," she murmured. She faced Betty again, gripping the table behind her.

Betty said nothing. She didn't even try to hide her contempt.

Helen felt it, and Betty was glad to see that she did. Betty also noticed that the big diamond ring was gone from Helen's finger. She was tempted to comment, then restrained herself.

They stared at each other until Helen looked away, trying to gather her thoughts. Confrontations – oh, after all of the arguing she endured at home, she should be better at confrontations.

"You haven't found a new job, Betty?" Helen asked.

"Pardon?" Betty asked, sharply incredulous.

"I was wondering if you or Neil have found new jobs?"

"We're looking around. We'll find something."

"Oh. I was just wondering because ...." Helen looked down. She couldn't finish her sentence. Betty's eyes were so angry, she couldn't even think straight. "I was just wondering if you needed ...."

"No. We don't. We don't need anything."

Helen took a step toward Mrs. Wright's bed. "Maybe I'll come back tomorrow, Mrs. Wright." She had lost her nerve. She turned and left quickly, miserably unable to bear the look on Betty's face.

*O*n Tuesday morning, Harvey Wallhanger looked up from his desk when a massive presence made itself felt in his doorway.

"Officer Toda. Good morning." For the first time that Harvey could remember, Toda was not wearing his emerald tie pin.

"You are one stupid Canuck, you know that, Smallwanger?" He leaned over Harvey's desk, speaking low.

Harvey slid back in his chair. "It's not nice to deride someone because of their place of birth."

"Yeah, well maybe you are gonna have to go back to that place cuz you are in trouble here." Toda's thick forefinger jabbed the desk.

"Canada is a nice country. Maybe I should go back. What's the problem, Toda?"

"The problem is I didn't give you no leave to go through my files. That's the problem."

"Someone has accessed your files?"

"Don't play innocent with me, Smallwanger! Whadjoo do? Pick the lock?"

"How could you possibly think I would go through your files, Cesare?"

Toda backed up and looked over his shoulder. "You thought I wouldn't know?" he hissed. "You crud! You been asking about my files and all of a sudden there's stuff missing from them. You think I can't put two and two together? You stepped over the line, you little turd. I swear you are dogmeat! You screw with me and you are DOGMEAT!'"

Much to Wallhanger's relief, the chief passed his door just then. Toda's beefy hand gave the door jamb a loud slap as a warning and he backed, smoking mad, out of the room.

This was grim news. Harvey had hoped that it would take Cesare Toda some time to figure out that there were photos missing. Later in the day, though, Harvey received some good news. His phone rang. A police officer in Canandaigua had intercepted Anya Netherby and she was now in the care of the local Ladies' Aid Society. Harvey was jubilant. The child had been found! Finally, a breakthrough!

He immediately called Miss Netherby, but got her mother instead. Anya's grandmother told him she had a lot of packing to do for a trip, and couldn't waste a day driving down to Canandaigua to pick up her grand-daughter. Couldn't Mr. Wallhanger send one of his men down there instead? Harvey Wallhanger had no authority to send anyone. He would have to take the train down there himself.

So that piece of the puzzle was solved, he thought. But now that the child had been found, what was he to do with this other information in his possession? Dread settled over him again. Stolen jewelry turning up in strange places. When this information got out, heads were going to roll. He didn't want his to be one of them. He would have to figure something out.

When Harvey got back to his apartment that evening, he hung his hat on the coat tree, turned and froze. The entire place had been ransacked. Someone had violated his home, had come in searching for something, destroying as he went. His books had been ripped and flung all over the floor. He owned very little furniture, but the cushions on his only armchair had been knifed open and gutted. Shaking, he gathered up the stuffing and managed to get most of it back inside the cushion cover. Thank God he had hidden the key to the train station locker in his hat brim. If that key had been found ....

A knock at his door startled him. As soon as he opened it, a hard blow to his abdomen nearly took his breath away.

"Evening, Smallwanger."

"What do you want?" grunted Harvey, doubled over.

"Yer about ta find out, ain't ya, ya little weasel?" A muscle-bound thug dragged him to a car waiting in an alley. When Harvey refused to admit that he had stolen any photos, a couple of goons beat him senseless, dumped him in a heap behind some garbage cans, and drove away.

It wasn't until the next morning that he was found.

He didn't show up for work that day. It was two days after that before the swelling on his mouth and face subsided enough so he could speak intelligibly. He phoned the Netherby residence. The new maid told him that no little girl called Anya had appeared at the house. She must still be at the orphanage, he realized. He boarded the trolley himself, swollen black and blue though he was, and went to Canandaigua to bring Anya Netherby home. He limped into the institution maintained by the Ladies' Aid Society and showed them his badge. The child Anya, however, had disappeared without a trace.

CHAPTER TEN

*T*he Ladies' Aid Society did important work. They kept a house for children who had no parents, or whose parents could not care for them properly. The job wasn't easy but they ran a good clean establishment, and efficient, very efficient. The house had been donated by a wealthy woman, and had been a lovely home at one time. Now the once-elegant gardens had been scalped to make a bare playground, and had been made safe from intruders by a brick wall. As if anyone wanted to intrude. The first floor of the house was mostly offices and classrooms, and also included a parlor and a small formal dining room. A large kitchen and the children's dining hall were in the basement. The top floor had been made into dormitories, one for boys and one for girls, walled off from each other and accessible by separate staircases.

If you enter that house through the big front door, what strikes you first is the quiet. A house for children, quiet as a tomb. There is a parlor to the left of the grand foyer, with chairs and a cold fireplace. The walls and sparse furnishings wear paint in dull and faded shades, no loud or jarring colors. No piano or houseplants or books, as in the old days. No occupants either.

Upstairs, in the girls' ward are two rows of five beds. No loud or jarring colors here. The sheets and blankets are grey and the walls are grey and the room is grey. And neat. All the toys are put away in the toy box – the rags that had once been stuffed animals, a jumble of naked dolls with matted hair and staring eyes. The bookshelf holds a few tilted books, each one minus a cover or with sections of pages coming unglued from their bindings. Between every pair of beds is a small open cupboard for clothes, every single article neatly folded inside. One or two girls lie curled on their beds this afternoon, their arms wrapped around themselves. Like the dolls, they stare. You wonder what they see. The sheets smell strongly of bleach because a couple of the children wet their beds at night. The whole room, in fact, smells of something strong, but not of home.

See what a nice house we have made for you, say the ladies of the Society. Here you don't have to worry about food, or where to sleep. Here we will take care of you, as though you were little birds, our little pet birds. Here we will keep the doors locked and guard them for you, so no one can get in to hurt you. You will be safe here.

Safety is necessary to troubled children, to be sure.

But the eyes of the children are vacant, their skin dull. Like flower buds on a frosty morning, their faces are closed tightly. They seem like empty shells, but no, they are not empty, not really. There is someone hidden inside, waiting. Waiting and watching, day after day, for the touch of a warm and kindly hand.

This is the house, belonging to the Ladies Aid Society, to which Anya was taken. No pets were allowed in this establishment. So it required two strong young women to drag Anya, screaming in protest, through the grand front door. The dog Corax was beside himself. First barking, then lunging at the women's legs with sharp teeth, all he wanted was to stay with Anya. They had to kick him to make him back away. Still Anya shrieked his name, and still he came at them. One of the policemen got out of his car to help the women. He kicked Corax so hard that he sent the dog rolling across the gravel. By the time Corax regained his feet, they had all gone inside and slammed the door in his face. The policeman chased him away, but he crept back later and sat on a church lawn across the street, never taking his eyes off the front door of the orphanage.

Inside, the women insisted on filling out their paper forms. Name, date, the time and location of Anya's "rescue". Anya didn't want to give her real name. But what would happen when Hugh came to get her, as he surely would, and they told him they had no one named Anya? Reluctantly, she told them.

They took her upstairs. Dulled by disbelief, she undressed as ordered. Her clothes were taken away and disposed of. She was instructed in how to bathe and wash her hair with bad-smelling shampoo. She was given a dress to wear that was identical to every other girl's dress, no-color, long-sleeved, two buttons at the throat, shapeless, smelling of bleach. They let her keep her own boots. She was shown to a bed, told to sit there and wait for Matron. She wasn't waiting for Matron, she was waiting for Hugh to come and get her. She sat and stared.

The rows of beds were empty now. She didn't know where the

other girls were. The room had two windows facing the street, closed on a summer day. Outside, the sun shone on maple leaves that rocked soundlessly. Anya realized it had been days, a week maybe, since she had been in a house. It felt so strange. She went to the window. Across the street was the Presbyterian church. Sitting next to the steps of the church, looking up and down the street and carefully examining everyone who went by, was a red and white dog. Her Corax! Sitting on the steps next to the dog was a man, clean-shaven, dressed in his glad rags and decent shoes that he borrowed because they only had holes in the bottom where they didn't show. Sailor Bill! He was there because he had found Corax there, and the dog refused to leave. Bill sat down and waited with him, hoping to find out where Anya had gone.

But Anya thought he had come to get her out. A surge of joy lit her. She rapped on the window.

"Bill! Bill!" Hugh must have asked Bill to come to get her.

Neither Bill nor Corax heard her. She rapped on the glass and called. She tugged at the handles to open the window but it was nailed shut. She ran to the other window. It too had been nailed closed. She ran downstairs and pulled frantically on the front door. It needed a key to open it, even from the inside. The parlor had windows facing the church. She slapped desperately against the glass. For a girl who was never allowed to raise her voice, she was making a lot of noise.

"Bill!"

Corax raised his head. His ears perked up.

"Corax! Corax!"

Heavy footsteps stomped up behind her. The two women were back again, and Matron too, this time. They dragged Anya kicking and flailing into Matron's office and pushed her onto a hard wooden chair.

Wellmygoodness! She would have to sitbyherself for the restoftheday, Matron sputtered, until she learned to be morecooperative! Behave. Act like a young lady, forheavenssake. This wild behavior simply wouldnotdo. They had a closet. A few hours in there by herself would give her time to think about how to be agoodgirl, anicegirl.

The matron turned the key in the closet door and went immediately to put in a call to the police, complaining about the vagrant who sat with his wild dog on the church steps across the street.

*I*t was dark outside when the closet door was unlocked. Hugh had still not come for her. He would be finished working, now that it was dark. Soon he would come. Soon.

Anya was marched upstairs, given a thin nightgown, and told not to go near the windows. One of the care-givers would stay in the room until everyone had fallen asleep.

An hour later, Anya was still wide awake. She could hardly believe that Hugh had not come. He had said, hadn't he, that he liked having her with him, helping him? Not in so many words, but he'd sort of said it.

The woman who was guarding them slipped out of the room. Anya rolled onto her side and felt a warm hand on her wrist. She raised up onto her elbow.

"What do you want?" she demanded. There was a girl kneeling beside her bed.

"Shh! You're new here. What's your name?" the girl whispered.

"Anya."

"I'm Hattie. You didn't have a very good day, did you?"

"I hate this place."

"Most of us hate it. I'm getting out as soon as I can."

"Really?"

"I'm not saying when."

"Take me with you!"

"Sorry, no. I can't take anyone with me. It's too hard. Besides, I don't even know you. I don't know what you're like. You know what I mean?"

"I have money. I'll pay you." She had the nickel that Sailor Bill had carved, and Hugh had given her money to buy lunch that morning. She had hidden it in her sock, then transferred it to her boot when she was undressing for the bath that afternoon.

"You have money?"

"A dollar and fifteen cents."

"Hmm."

"Please, Hattie. I'll die in here."

"No! You won't die, Anya. Never say that. You can't let yourself think like that."

"I'd sooner die than stay here."

"Stop it! Talk like that makes you weaker than you are."

"Fine. I'll get out, even without your help."

"A dollar and fifteen cents, really?"

"You can have all of it."

"Look, I'll have to see. Talk to me tomorrow?"

"Okay."

"But don't let them see us."

"We can't even talk to each other?"

"They watch me. They know they can't trust me."

*H*attie Fish, she was called. She was eleven years old, a good two years older than Anya. Her Onondagan name meant Dancing Brook Fish. All the children in her tribe had been taken from their homes and placed in a boarding school, to teach them to read and write English and to forget their native customs. This was the third time Hattie had run away. She had been caught again by the police, and placed in the orphanage here until someone from her school could come to take her back. They would be coming soon. Hattie didn't have much time to prepare an escape. She wanted to go home. She knew she wouldn't be allowed to live on the reservation with her parents, but she hoped she could live in the forest near by and visit them secretly until she was finally too old to go to school.

*F*or breakfast the next morning, porridge was served. The heads of nineteen silent children bobbed rhythmically over their bowls, boys at one table, girls at another. Then they lined up and filed out to do their chores before classes. They had to go to the schoolroom even though it was summer. On their way there, Hattie put a hand on Anya's arm and steered her toward the bathroom so they could talk.

Worried that they were spending too long washing their hands, Hattie spoke softly and quickly.

"I've been thinking about --"

"Are you going to take me with you?" Anya whispered.

"I have thought about it. Really, I have. But I just can't."

"You can trust me."

"I'm sorry, Anya. It's just too risky."

Anya scowled. She had been thinking about this too, all night long. "Look," she hissed. "I could tell Matron on you, if I wanted to."

"See?" said Hattie, slapping her hand on her leg. "I was afraid you were a little rat."

"Don't you dare call me a rat!"

"If you tell on me –"

"I said I could tell on you. I didn't say I would. Please, Hattie, take me! You won't be sorry, I promise."

Hattie sighed and crossed her arms.

"I'll give you all my money," Anya said.

"You'll give me all of it?"

"Yes, I will."

"One wrong move and I'm leaving without you. I swear, you do one stupid thing and you're not coming with me."

"All right."

"And I won't give you your money back."

"I won't do anything stupid."

"If you give me one bit of trouble," Hattie hissed, "I will put such a curse on you that you will wish you'd never been born. An Onondagan curse!"

"I promise. I *promise* you, Hattie. Here." She slipped off her boot. "Take this." She dropped her coins into Hattie's palm, except for the carved nickel that Sailor Bill had given her.

"Okay. Talk to me before supper. Til then, stay away from me." Hattie turned away to hide the coins. "Go ahead. Leave. You go first. We can't be seen together."

Anya slipped out of the bathroom without another word.

At the end of the afternoon, the girls sat on the floor in the hall, waiting to line up for supper. Hattie Fish only glanced at Anya on her way to the bathroom. After a minute, Anya got up and followed her.

"Listen." Hattie spoke in a whisper. "We learned something as children," she told Anya. "An undergrounder does not need to hide. She can depend on the misperceptions of her opponents."

"I don't know what that means."

"What it means is, we'll let them think everything is normal because it looks normal. But looks can fool you."

"They can?"

"They'll think we are here, but it won't be us."

"What are you saying?"

Hattie pulled up her dress. Under it, she had a sash wrapped tight around her waist. In that sash, among other things, she had hidden a tiny pair of stolen manicure scissors. She gathered a long hank of her lustrous black hair in her hands. "I'm saying that in two days, this all has to come off," she said. "Yours too."

*T*he children had finished their chores for the morning and were all in class. The women in the kitchen were cleaning up after breakfast. Eveline, one of the cooks, bundled up the garbage and took it out to the metal garbage can. She took a moment to savor the beautiful summer morning, then turned to go back inside.

"Lula, for crissake! You scairt me! What you doin' out here?"

"Lookit here, Eveline. Lookit this little guy! Ain't he sweet? But I can't get him to come to me."

"Ohh, loooo-kit him! Where'd he come from?"

"I don't know. He was just nosin' around. But I wanna take him home."

"Maybe he belongs to someone."

"I don't care. Jimbo needs a good hunting dog."

"C'mere, little one," warbled Eveline. "C'mere!"

The red and white dog lowered his head and just looked at the women.

"He's hungry, that's what he is. Go get that piece of bacon I saved out."

"Get it yerself, Lula."

"I'm afraid he'll run away. Get it, Ev. Come on."

Eveline brought the bacon. "He won't take it."

"Throw it to him."

The dog took the bacon and ran.

"Tomorrow I'm gonna bring a rope. I hope he comes back. My Jimbo will just love him."

*I*n the afternoon, Anya managed a glance out a window that overlooked the street. Sitting next to the church steps was a very watchful red and white dog. Sailor Bill lounged at the top of the steps, under the porch roof. The police, in response to Matron's complaint, had attempted to drag Sailor Bill away, but were stopped by Reverend Young. The Presbyterian minister claimed he had asked Bill to sit on the steps. They were expecting a delivery of flowers for a funeral, and Bill was waiting to help carry them into the church. Anya watched them for as long as she dared, but now she knew better than to knock on the window. Still, she passed it as often as she could. Bill wasn't always there, but Corax was.

The next morning, while the children were again at their chores, Corax trotted around to the back of the house and squeezed through the gate. Lula spotted him. She didn't have access to the gate key, but she tried to get him to come to her. He wouldn't come close enough and she had forgotten to bring her rope. She tossed the dog a piece of cheese. He snatched it up and ran off with it, but she knew he'd be back.

*O*n Anya's third day at the orphanage, Hattie motioned her urgently to one side of the room.

"I'm leaving soon," she announced, not looking at Anya, and barely moving her lips. "I'm not telling you when."

"You better take me with you, Hattie."

"On one condition. Only if you don't mess up. You hear me?"

Anya could barely conceal her excitement. "Will it be soon?" she squealed softly.

"Stop that!" Hattie Fish scowled and stalked off.

She passed Anya again later, and whispered to her. "Don't look at me. You're going to give us away with that stupid grin."

"Sorry."

"Are you ready to be serious now?"

"Yes I am."

"Good. Now listen. There will be a ball game in the evening tomorrow. I've got a plan, but I have to pay three boys."

"Pay them for what?"

"Trust me. Shh! Shut up!" Hattie hissed. "Matron!" She walked away.

Passing the window later, Anya saw Corax still waiting by the church steps. How long would he stay there? He would get hungry, she was sure, and need to eat. When she got out, how would she ever find him? Stay there, puppy, stay there and wait for me. I'm coming.

The next morning, Lula had her piece of rope ready and was determined to catch the red and white dog. Jimbo had tied a noose on one end of the rope, and had told her to lure the dog close, slip the noose over his head and pull. If the dog fought, just pull tighter and keep pulling.

"What on earth you doing, Lu?" whispered Eveline in the kitchen that morning.

"Cuttin' a piece of beef for that dog. Jimbo wants him bad, and I promised him."

"Yeah but that meat is for the big fancy dinner tonight."

"Plenty here. Don't worry."

The minister from the Presbyterian church and his wife had been invited to have dinner that evening with Matron and the director. Several times a year, on summer evenings, Reverend Young liked to play ball with the boys for an hour or so, while Mrs. Young taught a Bible study group for the girls. On some evenings, that meant that the Youngs had to endure dinner with the Matron as well, but they took on the task cheerfully so they could spend time with the children.

This morning, the kitchen help were busy sweeping the good dining room, preparing a special dinner for their guests, and even placing small vases of flowers on the children's tables downstairs. Lula was taking advantage of a minute alone in the kitchen to cut a slice off the roast. She knew that a hunk of raw meat would be irresistible to the red and white puppy. She took the meat outside and, just as she had expected, there sat the dog by the gate.

She held the meat close to the ground and slid her hand into her pocket.

"C'mere boy," she called.

Corax came forward cautiously.

"Geez, his ribs are showing," Eveline said. "Poor little guy."

"We'll fatten him up, soon's I can get my hands on him. C'mere little fella."

Corax crept closer. He squeezed under the locked gate.

"Lookit. He's gettin' to like me now."

Closer, closer.

Slowly, Lula pulled the noose from her pocket. "C'mon, c'mon."

Rope! The one thing Corax had learned to fear. He took one look at it, lunged for the meat and fled. Lula chased him. He struggled to get under the gate. His head was through. She pulled his tail. Yelping, he dropped the meat outside the gate and snapped hard at her hand.

"Ouch!" she screamed. "You stupid – " Well, Lula called the dog something pretty vile and not really repeatable. The important thing is, Corax got away with his piece of meat and Lula ran inside to wash the blood off her hand before Matron saw it.

*U*pstairs, Hattie whispered to Anya.

"Everything is just about ready. I've got kids all lined up to help. I paid Jim and Frankie each a quarter."

"A quarter!"

"I had to. If they get caught, they'll be in such trouble. And Lyle wanted fifteen cents."

"That leaves us only fifty cents, Hattie."

"Also five cents to Linda."

"For what?"

"Her barrettes."

"What?"

"I needed barettes! Let me see you figure out how to get our hair to stick on boys' heads!"

What in the world was Hattie Fish planning? "I'm getting scared, Hattie. You're sure this is going to work?"

"If any of those kids rat on us, we're sunk. And you. I still don't know about you."

Anya sagged and felt her stomach turn over. If Hattie left her behind ... or if Matron found out ....

Hattie was silently ticking off the points of her plan. Aloud she said, "We have to braid our hair. But I haven't figured out where we can hide to cut it."

"Cut what?"

"Our braids."

Anya gaped at her.

"The bathroom's no good. We've been seen in there together too many times. There's nowhere private in this place."

"Hattie! What are we going to do?" Anya snapped her fingers. "Wait! I know a room!"

"An empty room?"

"It should be, unless someone else is being punished."

That evening, the children were lined up behind their chairs in the dining hall, waiting to greet Reverend and Mrs. Young when they came in. Matron was upstairs in the small formal dining room, flitting around, fussing over place settings. The staff who supervised the children's dining hall were not very attentive today. They were more interested in some bit of gossip that was going around. They counted heads, nine girls and ten boys, and were immediately swept back into a discussion about some quaint drama of their own. They didn't notice a small girl with uneven braids whose dress hung like a sack off her skinny shoulders, nor the tall girl with the heavy legs whose sleeves were so short they couldn't be buttoned. At the other table was a tall boy with his trousers bunched around his waist, while the trousers of the boy next to him didn't reach his ankles.

"Be seated," ordered one of the staff, after the Reverend and his wife had greeted them and passed through. "Girls, no hats at the table! You know that!"

Jim and Frankie, at the girls' table, obediently removed their hats. Jim noticed the girl across the table staring wide-eyed. He looked down at Frankie. Anya's braid was safely clipped over one ear, but over the other, the braid and its barrette hung by only a strand of hair.

"Yer hair's comin' off," he whispered. Frankie found this pretty funny and started to giggle. Jim pulled him down behind the table and re-attached the other braid. When Frankie sat up again, his face had turned red and his eyes leaked tears of silent laughter. Jim nudged him hard in the ribs. This brought on a guffaw of giggling, and got the girls across the table laughing. The girls at the ends of the table looked at each other with perplexed smiles, and they too started to titter. The staff looked up. The whole table of girls was giggling like demented chickens.

But then dinner came. All laughter ended.

Lima beans. Plain, boiled lima beans. Tasting like pebbles of dried dog vomit.

No one found lima beans even remotely amusing. Since the rule was that they eat everything on their plates, the next half hour would be sheer torture.

Frankie and Jim knew just how to handle this. Under the boys' table was a hole in the floor. All the boys knew it was there, and through this hole, over the years, had passed serving after serving of lima beans. If it weren't for the mice of this establishment, the floor would stink of decomposing food. But word had gone out all the way to the rafters tonight and there was a fair bit of activity beneath the floor on the boys' side.

Frankie peeked under the girls' table. Solid unblemished floor.

He looked at the ceramic flower vase in front of him, pulled the zinnias out, inserted all his lima beans, and put the flowers back. He mopped up the puddle of water with his napkin. Up and down the table, the girls took notice, and up and down the table, little vases were quickly stuffed with lima beans. Napkins were filled with beans, folded neatly beside plates and squashed flat. Beans hid in bread baskets, and the few stray beans that remained had to be mashed underfoot. The girls were so involved in hiding their lima beans, they didn't have time to wonder about the two strange and highly suspect newcomers at their table. Which leads logically, does it not, to the conclusion that lima beans are good, or at least useful, if you don't want anyone to notice you're disguised as a girl?

The staff came in. They stalked up and down behind the chairs."You've all cleaned your plates tonight!" they exclaimed. "Dessert for everyone!"

After dinner, the Presbyterian minister took the boys outside for a ball game. They usually played until dusk, and the boys really enjoyed it. While they played, the girls met Mrs. Young in the seldom-used parlor for Bible study. Mrs. Young was a lovely lady. The girls all fought to sit near her. For the entire hour, they absorbed every detail of her clothes, her hair, her every move. No one remembered a word she said.

When they walked with the girls to the parlor, Jim looked at Frankie in panic. What? They would have to sit here and listen to

Bible study? Hattie, that birdbrain, had never mentioned Bible study! They should have demanded more money.

Outdoors, as the ball game got underway on the playground, the boys looked curiously at the two strangers. Where had these guys come from? Wait a minute. Was that –? Hattie shut them up with a murderous look. Several of the boys had run afoul of that look before. Aww, phooey. So now they had to put up with a stupid girl on their ball team. And what in the world had she done to her hair?

It was Hattie's turn to bat. The pitcher wiped his nose on the back of his hand, spit on the ball, and grinned malevolently. On her first swing, Hattie blasted the ball all the way to the back wall and made it to third base. Okay, okay. She wasn't one of the guys, but they had to admit she could swing a bat. That other one, though, Hattie's small friend? He played ball like a pathetic girl.

When Hattie and Anya's team took the field, Hattie pulled Anya to the outfield, back beside the wall. "Stay here, near me."

Anya's heart galloped like crazy.

Lyle stepped up to the plate and thumped the bat on the ground. Hattie braced her hands on her knees and stared hard at him. She threw a bleak look at Anya, pale as a ghost beside her. Oh, look at her, Hattie groaned to herself. She's in great shape. And I'm going to have her dragging after me? Eww boy, Lyle had better not blow this.

Lyle swung at the ball and missed. Hattie straightened abruptly, a murderous frown on her face. He looked at her and smirked.

Incredible! She had paid him good money! She would beat him to a pulp, that feeble pinhead! A gooey pulp!

He swung again. A spectacular miss. He looked at Hattie and shrugged and smirked.

She could hardly breathe. She glared daggers at him. Beat him? No. She would kill him with her bare hands! Horrible fears of having to spend the night in the boys' dormitory ran through her head.

The last ball. Lyle wound up. He swung. Crack! The ball sailed over the wall.

The boys groaned. "Lyle, you pisser! Sorry, Reverend."

Anya wanted to scream with joy. So this was Hattie's plan!

"I'll get the ball!" Anya offered. One of the boys boosted her to the top of the wall. "I can't see it!"

"Climb down and look for it, stupid!"

"How will I get back in? Someone come with me."

"What a – !"

Hattie grinned. The little twerp was playing her part perfectly. "I'll go with her – him," she offered. "Help me up."

Hattie and Anya dropped over the wall. The boys waited. They milled around. They turned cartwheels and jostled and shoved. Foul words that they dared not use in front of the minister stuttered accidentally off their tongues. Somebody boosted one of the little kids to the top of the wall. He hung there on his elbows.

"I can't even see them!" he declared.

Reverend Young got worried and went to get the key to the gate. This took some time. He finally got the gate unlocked. He tramped around outside the wall. He called and got no answer.

He found the baseball not far from the wall, but the two boys? Something terrible must have happened to the two boys.

The girls in the parlor were suddenly aware of a commotion in the street outside, noisy enough to interrupt the Bible study. They ran to the windows in time to see a Model T automobile come roaring down the street, blasting its siren. It was full – it was *bulging* with cops. It was coming here! The girls were chattering with excitement. Jim and Frankie pushed their way to the window.

The car pulled up in front of the orphanage. The driver yanked so hard on the brake that three of the cops nearly fell off the back.

Seven of them, like big black ants, scrambled over each other, trying to get themselves and their big clumsy feet out of the car.

What could be happening? A gaggle of little girls, flocking to the front door, were elbowed aside by Matron and told to stand back.

Seven cops, all in a line, pounded through the front door of the orphanage.

Seven of them, all in a line, ran right out the back door, led by Matron, followed by the minister's wife, the staff, and by all but two of the girls.

Jim and Frankie stayed behind. They just had time to change back into their own clothes. Hiding the two pairs of braids presented a problem, though. Hattie had warned them that, if ever that hair was found, their skins would erupt with monstrously hideous running sores – the itchy kind – an Onondagan curse for all of eternity. It probably wouldn't take Matron long to realize that it was

Hattie and Anya who were missing, but it must not become known that they were disguised as boys.

At the last minute, Jim found the perfect place to hide the hair. Simple, close at hand, it was a good choice. Those braids only came to light when the parlor sofa was donated to the Elks Club, ten years later.

CHAPTER ELEVEN

*F*rom the time he received Wallhanger's telegram, it took Jackson Netherby, Anya's father, a day to hike out to a train station, and another two and a half days to reach Rochester, New York. He didn't fraternize with the other train passengers. He sat by himself, looking out the window for hours at a time. After living for years with the soft pastels of the arid southwest, these green plains, the rolling meadows, the wooded hills seemed impossibly lush to him. He hadn't realized until now how much he missed the verdant landscape. There were other things in the east, though, that he had not missed, which is why he had been putting off going home for all this time.

Sitting on the train for so long gave him lots of time to think, and to worry about his missing daughter. He had been considering returning to the east for the last few months. He knew he had been selfish, staying away. The child must wonder why her father cared so little about her. Working in New Mexico, he had come to know people from the Navajo Nation, and he was fascinated with the way they raised their children. Up to that time, he had felt a twinge of guilt whenever he thought about leaving his daughter to be raised by her grandparents. But he learned that this was common behavior among the Navajo. If such an arrangement made things better for the child, no one had a problem with it. He liked a lot of things about the Navajo people – the way they took special care to prepare children to be worthy adults, and the skillful way parents taught their children to respect and sympathize with others.

He had postponed a return to his family for long enough. This was not going to be easy, Jack told himself gloomily, as he walked to Elm Street from the train station. First of all, he wasn't the same man who had left four, almost five years ago. Then too, there were certain things that would never change: the painful memories, the associations – he had been standing on his parents' front steps when he found out his wife had been killed – not to mention his guilty conscience, the little girl he had left behind. She was no longer the toddler he pictured, but could she possibly be old enough to run away? Had his family considered that she might have been kidnapped? That was his nagging fear. These were his depressing thoughts.

He hadn't heard a word of Anya's disappearance from his parents, and he didn't know if that boded well or ill. His mother had his address. Why hadn't she contacted him? His dad had written to him no more than once a year in the entire time he'd been gone, but he could certainly have made an effort to reach Jack now, unless Dad had sunk even further under Mother's thumb. His father was the only person in the family with whom he felt close. Jack and his sister Helen had fought every day of their lives, and his mother was so excitable that she had practically driven Jack to a nervous breakdown when he was younger.

Now here he was, standing on the porch of the Elm Street house at last. He dreaded knocking. He just stood there, wavering. It was strange to be coming back. At the same time, he felt as though he had never left. If he had indeed changed, why did he still feel like the same naughty little troublesome Jack?

Finally he lifted the knocker and let it fall. Like a judge's gavel, the rap of that knocker was sentencing him to days, maybe weeks, of angst.

"*Jack?*"

"Hello, Helen." His sister looked flustered, he thought. Anxious, unhappy.

"My god, Jack! Why didn't you let us know you were coming?"

He stepped into the hall, the old familiar hall, the same as ever, smelling the same as ever. "Have you heard from Anya?" he asked.

"So you know? About Anya?"

"Helen, tell me. What news?"

"They found her, they found her. Don't worry. The police are picking her up in Canandaigua."

What a relief! He dropped his bags to the floor. "So she wasn't kidnapped? She ran away?"

"Apparently. How did you even know she disappeared?"

"The police department contacted me. They apparently felt I, as the child's father, might be slightly interested in her welfare." Jack threw himself down onto a sofa in the parlor and reminded himself to hold back the sarcasm.

"If you were that interested in your daughter, you would have been here for the last four years."

"Okay. Let's not start fighting right away, Helen. Tell me how Mother and Dad are doing."

"Well, they are hiding out, literally, at Aunt Ida's for a couple of weeks. Trying to avoid all their nosy friends, all the negativity that's been flying around, what with Anya running out on us and all. Of course, who is left to clean up the whole mess? Me, as usual."

"But how are they?"

"Mother and Daddy? Same as ever. Maybe they've been at each other's throats somewhat more than usual. Daddy lost everything in the market a couple of years ago. Well, you know all that, and Mother ...."

"Yes, Mother wrote more than one scathing letter about that."

"... well, she's rather a wreck. She can't manage without money. She just can't. It's been very difficult, Jack. Awful, really! I hate you for abandoning us like you did. You left me to handle everything by myself. I'm about ready to crack with all the stress."

"I'm sure you are handling things more than capably, Helen. How is Anya? It must not be easy for a child in this house. I'm not sure I blame her for running away, if that is what happened."

"It's not as if she is the only child here. I have Robert to worry about, too."

"Has he been troublesome?"

"Well, there are his bills to pay. His school is expensive. I have no husband to lean on. We can't afford the servants. It's been one thing after another."

"He does well at school?"

"Oh, you know. Fairly well."

"And Anya?"

"At school?"

"Yes. How does she do?"

"She's fine." Helen bit her lip and searched desperately for a change of subject, but not quickly enough.

"She wasn't at school when she ran away, was she?"

"No. She was here."

"Does she like Harley?"

Helen made fists in her lap. "I might as well tell you. Anya doesn't go to Harley. She goes to the local public school."

Jack reared forward in his seat. "What? I left money for – "

"I know. I know." She opened her hands, pleading. "But we have been desperate here. You have no idea! And my son's schooling – "

"Are you telling me – "

"We had to, Jack! We had to! Daddy's income just wouldn't cover running this house and sending Robert to school, so we had to – "

"Don't tell me you sent Robert to school with Anya's money. Don't you dare tell me that!"

They were yelling now.

"Don't you dare tell me I haven't done a good job raising your child for you!"

"I never wanted you to raise her! I wanted Elizabeth's parents to do that!"

"We needed her money, you idiot! We are broke, Jack! We can't even make ends meet as it is! The things I have to do for money, I can't even tell you."

"Like what things, Helen? Like getting a job? Like working for a living? You're thirty years old and you've never worked a day in your life!" Oh good, thought Jack. Now she's crying.

"I have been working! I have to do things that I hate myself for. You can't know how much I hate myself, Jack! You have no idea!"

"What? What things do you have to do, Helen?"

"Forget it. You wouldn't understand."

"I think I would."

"You would not! You – you always had everything. Always the star! Our Jackson, so smart! Our Jackson, so great! A great job, a good marriage."

"Well – "

"I know. Your marriage ended tragically. But you have no idea what it's like for me, a woman alone, helpless."

"You're hardly helpless."

"I had no choice, Jack. No choice."

"No choice in what? You had the same benefits growing up that I did. You had choices. Maybe you just made the wrong choices."

"I did. I did. I know I did. Oh, Jack! If you only knew." Tears spilled through her fingers.

Jack got up and crossed to the sofa where Helen sat. He put his arm around her and she threw herself onto his chest, gripping the front of his shirt and sobbing. He had never seen her like this.

"Hey, we'll work something out, Sis." He made her sit up. "Don't cry. We'll get everything ironed out." He stood again. "Sit there a minute. I'll get Mrs. Wright to make us some tea."

Helen took his hand, shaking her head.

"What? You didn't let Mrs. Wright go?"

"No." She pressed the back of her hand to her mouth. "She – she – "

"She what?"

"She's been hurt. A little bit hurt."

Jack sat down again. "What happened?"

"She fell. She's in the hospital."

"Oh no. The hospital! That's terrible!"

"That's not the worst part, though."

"What's the worst part?"

"Mrs. Wright slipped on a marble that your daughter left on the stairs."

"Oh my god."

"I told Anya to pick them up, but – "

"She didn't do it on purpose, did she?"

"Mother thinks she did."

Jack rubbed his forehead. He had only been home a few minutes. It seemed like hours. He needed to get out, for a while at least. "I'll tell you what. Why don't you go take a nice bath and relax.

I'll visit Mrs. Wright at the hospital, and when I come back we can sort things out. Okay?"

"Sort things out? That's not likely to happen."

"When are Mother and Dad coming back?"

"In a week or so. She can't talk very well, you know. Hardly at all."

"Mother?" Jack asked, incredulous. Maybe even hopeful.

"Not Mother. Mrs. Wright."

"Oh. Still, I should go visit her. When I get back, I'll take you to dinner."

"Really?" Helen's face lit up. "No one has taken me to dinner in ever so long."

When Jack finally laid eyes on Mrs. Wright, he felt as though he had come home to his real family. After her fall, she had had trouble remembering people, remembering anything, but she knew Jack Netherby instantly. She threw open her one good arm and hugged him like a son.

"Jackie, Jackie. I'm so happy to see you! Oh, goodness! You brought these for me?"

"Nothing but the best for my favorite lady."

"Oh, Jackie! Yellow roses! So many! You shouldn't have."

"Helen told me you couldn't talk after your injury."

"I'm much better now, especially now that you're here. You haven't met Betty."

"No. Hello."

Betty the cook, amazed that Petunia suddenly remembered her, said, "You've come to look for your daughter, Mr. Netherby?"

"I thought they found her."

"They traced her to Canandaigua. She was safe in the orphanage there, but when that policeman went down there to get her today, she was gone again. Look here's the telegram he sent Petunia. I guess he tried phoning the house, but no one answered."

"Gone again? I don't believe it. Oh man. I'm going to have to go down there tomorrow to search. Well, she's only a kid. She can't have gotten far."

"You'll find her, Jackie, if anyone can."

"I hear she's been quite a problem."

"Anya? Oh no, Jackie. She's a wonderful girl, isn't she, Betty?"

"She's lovely. She ran away the day Petunia got hurt. Something went wrong." Betty bit her lip, not sure what Mr. Netherby had been told. "I don't know what happened."

"What could have come over her?" Mrs. Wright shook her head. "What made her do that? Why, Betty, why?"

"I'm not entirely sure," Betty hedged, glancing at Jack. "Maybe I'll go get a cup of coffee while you two chat."

Jack took Mrs. Wright's hand. "I'll go to Canandaigua tomorrow. I'll find her," he said. "Don't you worry. Just get yourself well." He perched on the edge of her bed. "So look at you! Here you are, covered in bandages and casts. I'm so sorry this had to happen."

"Well, my knee gave out and – and ...." Mrs. Wright's eyes slid back and forth. "Wait!" She blinked in thought. She gasped. "No!" Then she dropped her face onto her one good hand.

"What's the matter? Are you all right?"

"Oh Lord Jesus Lord Jesus Lord Jesus!"

"What is it?"

She grasped his hand. "It's you, Jackie! You! You made me remember!"

"What did you forget?"

"I forgot everything from before. But now, oh lordie lord, I remember. I remember it all!"

She looked so upset, Jack was afraid she was going to cry.

"Mrs. Wright, I just had Helen crying all over my shirt. What do I do that upsets people so?"

Mrs. Wright gripped his arm in distress. She was almost crying. "Jackie, I have something bad to tell you. And I don't want to. It's very bad. But it's got to be told. It's got to!"

"Tell me. Go ahead. I'm a big tough guy. It's about Anya, isn't it?"

"Anya? No."

"About Anya leaving a marble on the stairs? You stepped on it and —"

"No. No! There was no marble. That wasn't it. My bad knee gave out at the top of the stairs. That's why I fell."

Jack just stared.

"I'm not talking about my accident. It's what I saw one night. Oh lord! I saw Helen late one night." She looked up at him, trembling.

Her voice sank to a whisper. "She was emptying a bag, about this big, onto the table. Diamonds, Jackie. Diamonds and pearls. And jewels. Jewelry, all over the table! Where did she get all that stuff? I've seen her wearing beautiful things. Who gave them to her? What is she up to? Is she selling jewels? Is she doing something wicked, and somebody is paying her with jewelry? The trouble is, she knows I saw it all. That's what scares me. She knows I saw it."

*G*one was any hope of a pleasant dinner. Back at home, Jack found Helen dressed in a lovely summer dress, ready to go out. An hour ago, he would have wondered where she found the money to buy a dress like that. But he didn't wonder now. She had a shawl draped over her arm and a telegram in her hand. She shook it in her brother's face.

"She's gone again, Jack!"

"So I heard. The police notified Mrs. Wright when they couldn't reach you."

"I am absolutely disgusted with that child!"

"Before we talk about Anya, Helen, I want to know – "

"You're blaming me? Just explain to me, will you please, exactly what that girl is up to. What the devil is she trying to do?"

"Sit down. It seems that you are the one with the explaining to do. So tell me. Let's have it, Helen."

Helen stiffened. She stuck her chin out. She felt sick all of a sudden. "We're not going to dinner?"

"Not until you tell me what's been going on here."

"What do you mean?"

"Helen."

"I don't know what you're – " Her voice shook.

"Helen!"

"What!"

"Tell me what is going on."

"I don't ... Stop it! I ... I can't."

"The cat's out of the bag. You have to."

"What ...?"

"I just spoke with Mrs. Wright."

"Oh my god."

Jack sat down. "Sit here. Come on. Let's hear it."

"No! Okay wait. No! Well. Maybe I did some things. But I had to, Jack. I had to!"

"What things?"

"It's none of your business. Just shut up. Leave me alone." Her face crumpled. "I never meant to hurt anyone."

"Sit down, Helen. Tell me about it."

"I can't. No, I can't! I was only trying to help. Honest, Jack. I was."

"I want to hear this."

"No! Stop pestering me!" She sank onto the sofa. "I can't! But I – it's just – I need ...."

They talked for almost three hours.

*H*elen sat bent almost double on the sofa, her arms cradling her body. Jack rose and crossed the room to stand at the window. It was dark outside, too dark to see. He jingled some coins in his pocket. "Have you sold my Chrysler?" he finally asked Helen.

"Your car?"

Jack turned and nodded.

"No, of course not. It's in the garage."

"Does it have gas in it?"

"Probably. Neil used to take pretty good care of it, when he was here. Why?" Her voice sharpened. "Where are you going?"

"The whole reason I came back east was to look for Anya. I'm going to find her."

"But what about me?"

Jack turned and looked at his sister. "What about you?"

"What am I supposed to do now?"

"That is for you to figure out, I would say."

"Thank you so much! You know, it would just be nice if you were here to help out once in a while. You can't just run out on me now, Jack. You're making me feel like I'm some kind of evil person."

"I imagine Anya is feeling like an evil person too, right now."

"Who knows what she's feeling. Why would a child who had everything ever want to run away, anyway?"

"She must have thought something was not right. Something was missing."

"It's not my fault she's gone! Stop saying – "

"I know. If I had been here, none of this ever would have happened."

"That is right, Jack!" Helen stood up abruptly and jabbed a finger at him. "You're absolutely right. You never should have left us."

"I know." He rubbed his chin. "I can't imagine what she must think of me."

"Who?"

"Anya."

"Oh. Pfft. She never even knew you."

"I'll have to try to make things right with her. First, I have to find her. I wonder – which room is her bedroom?"

"It's – upstairs."

"Which one? Maybe there's something there, some clue – "

"We've looked. There's nothing."

"Still. Which one?"

"The attic."

"What?"

"She sleeps in the attic. Why are you looking at me like that? She likes it up there."

"For crying out loud, Helen! How could you do this to her?" He ran upstairs to Anya's shabby little room.

When he came down, he could hardly look at his sister. He went into the hall and picked up his bags. "I'm not coming back til I find her." Even though it was late, he threw the luggage into his red Chrysler Imperial, backed out of the garage and headed south for Canandaigua.

CHAPTER TWELVE

*T*he population of the hobo jungle of Canandaigua was shrinking. Cold weather was coming and many of the hobos were bent on catching trains to warmer places. But there were some new additions. Two families of Hispanic migrant workers had stopped for the night. They had arrived in one truck, the two fathers and one of the older boys riding in the cab, and their wives and other children riding in the back of the stake truck. The two fathers were now bending over the front of the truck. The hood was up, and as dusk fell, one man brought out a lantern, lit it and held it high.

"You find 'im?" he asked the other.

"Think so."

"Is that 'im?"

"*Si.*"

"He loose?"

"*Si.* Loose gas line. We got any those – *como se dice?* Yeah okay, I hold him, you ...." He twirled a finger.

They both looked up as a Model T came roaring into the camp. It was driven by two policemen from town, Chick Mancino and Burtley Brown. Chick, short, wiry, and agile, jumped out and threw a large wooden chock behind a wheel of the car. Burtley was slower. He was taller, with wide pink cheeks and a soft belly. Grunting a bit, he extracted his barge-shaped feet from under the steering wheel.

Sailor Bill and Windy Will were still in camp. They stood up.

"Oh great!" whined Bill. "Brown and Mancino."

"What's up, gentlemen?" Windy Will asked the officers when they swaggered over.

Chick twirled his stick. "Looking fer a coupla girls. Runaways. From the orphanage. Seen 'em, either a' youz?"

The two hobos shook their heads. "Why are you out here asking us?"

Chick bristled and prodded Sailor Bill's ribs with his stick. "Shut yer trap. We kin ask who we feels like askin'."

Burt, the big cop, set his hand on his fellow officer's arm. "S'okay, Chick. Don't excite yourself. Look boys, you know we in the Department keep a pretty close eye on the doings out here. One of these girls was seen at your fire one night. Just this past week." He stopped and looked closely at their faces.

Bill and Will, from long practice, knew how to keep their faces empty. Just stay focused on one thing, like the wart on the cop's right eyebrow.

"You seen her this evening?" Burt asked.

Bill and Will shook their heads.

"Mind if we look around?"

"Nothing here," insisted Sailor Bill. "That girl's been gone now for quite a bit."

"But look all you want," said Windy Will. Sailor Bill frowned at him. "She's not here, Bill, so let them look all they want."

Chick smacked his stick against his hand and surveyed the scene. "That there van over there," he said. "I'm havin' me a look inside there."

"It's locked," said Windy Will.

"Well gimme the damn key."

"We don't have it. We think the owner's in jail. You'll have to get it from him."

"Oh yeah," said Burt. "You know. That guy. They're letting him out soon. Maybe tomorrow."

Chick laughed his mean little laugh. "Oh him! Had to wait til his bruises mended. Captain doesn't want the whole town seein' a prisoner looking so beat up. Me, I think it's a good warning to guys like you."

"C'mon, Chickie. That's enough," said Burt. Chick was making the men of the Department look mean and cruel, and Burt didn't like that. " 'F you don't mind, we'll just have a look around, boys."

"We gotta get into that van, Burt. That's where they is, them girls. I betcha anything." He strode off, elbows pumping, his stick pounding the air with each step. He went straight to the door of the van and beat on the lock. Clodhopper the horse, tethered nearby, bugled in terror and Tisias the crow added his raucous voice to the clamor. Chick continued to beat uselessly against the door. Burt came up, followed by Bill and Will.

Burt gave a loud whistle. "Chick, we'll go back to town and get

– Hey! Chick!" Chick turned around with crazed eyes. "C'mon, man. Leave it be. We'll get the key and come back. Get down."

Reluctantly Chick jumped from the wagon. But he didn't like the look on Sailor Bill's face. He scowled. That hobo looked just a bit too smug. Like lightning, Chick's stick hit on one side of Bill's head, then the other. That would teach him to look down on officers of the law.

Chick bared his sharp little teeth and looked around. Everyone in the camp was staring at him, tense, wary. Sailor Bill was doubled over in pain. Chick's chin jutted forward. He twirled his stick.

"Okay, Chickie, stay calm. Let's go. Ya ready?" Burt asked him, a warning note in his voice.

That tramp with the bow tie – Chick didn't like his face at all, either. When Burt looked away, he managed to give Windy Will a sharp jab in the ribs, just for good measure. "We'll be back, scum buckets," he snarled. "Just you watch yerselfs."

*A*nya and Hattie were not in the hobo camp at the edge of town, but that was certainly their destination. Anya couldn't wait to see her friends the hobos. Maybe they would know where Hugh had gone. Had he left town already? He would have come for her otherwise, wouldn't he?

But at least she had her dog now. After escaping over the back wall of the orphanage, she and Hattie had run to the front of the building. Corax was lying on the lawn of the church across the street, his head on his paws, his eyes riveted to the front door where he had last seen Anya. He saw some movement in the shrubbery. Two figures scooted across the lawn. He raised his head. He stood up and barked, then ran like the wind into the street.

A car blared its horn, once, twice. Corax stopped and shrank close to the pavement. Anya screamed. The car never slowed for a moment, and whizzed past within inches of his nose.

Then Corax was running. There she was! His girl! He launched himself through the air and into her arms. The dog wriggled and yipped and couldn't stop licking Anya's laughing face. They were both so overcome with joy that Hattie had a hard time moving them off the street and into the bushes alongside the church.

Crouched in the shrubbery, Hattie took a minute to let Anya cuddle her dog. Then she took firm hold of her arm. "Anya, come on! We have to get going! Which way?"

"I think we go along that street to the edge of town."

"You *think*?"

"That's the best I can remember." She had been so upset when that lady had brought her here, that she wasn't really sure how to get back to the hobo camp. "I think the jungle is that way."

"Jungle?"

"We'll be safe there, you'll see."

They heard, in the distance, the blare of a police siren.

"Come on, then. Let's stay in back of these houses. Don't go out onto the street."

Corax danced, crazy with joy, around their ankles. "Find Bill,

Corax! Can you find Bill?"

It was useless, Anya knew, to expect a puppy to lead them, but Corax ran beside them with great sense of purpose. She just hoped and prayed they were going in the right direction.

It was almost fully dark now. Dodging through gardens and over fences, Hattie, Anya, and Corax ran till they were breathless. They were thankful that backyards were mostly empty, now that night was falling. Children had been called inside to get ready for bed. They passed one boy who was still galloping his toy horses around his sandbox, but they passed him so silently, so swiftly, that they were gone before he could look up.

Then they came to a garden that was completely overgrown. They had to crawl through bushes and weeds to get through. Hattie crouched and clambered through the shrubbery, getting scratched to bits. Anya followed her, holding aside a bush so Corax could crawl through. She glanced back the way they had come. A lantern bobbed back there. A tall figure passed a lighted window.

"Cops!" she hissed at Hattie. They looked frantically for a place to hide.

"We can crawl under these bushes."

"Too risky," said Hattie

"Where's Corax?" Anya panicked.

"There he goes, up those steps." A cat, standing against a screened door with its back arched, jumped up to the railing. "Follow him. We can duck inside there for a minute."

"It's someone's house! We can't!" whispered Anya.

Hattie clamped a hand on her arm and dragged her up the steps after the dog. She opened the screened door, stepped into the house, and stopped abruptly. Anya and Corax halted beside her, all three of them with eyes wide with amazement.

They gaped and looked around. They were in a kitchen. There was hardly room to walk, and so much stuff everywhere, there was not a single bare surface. Books with pencils stuck in them, in piles atop tilting sheaves of paper. Shelves overflowing with plates and saucers, creamers stacked on teacups, pitchers and jugs and crocks and bowls, ladles, cookie jars, and copper molds.

And cats. Two sleeping on the windowsill, one on a bookshelf, a yellow cat sound asleep on the bread box, a white cat nestled in the egg basket and swishing a languorous tail. This is what the girls saw.

Corax, completely flabbergasted, saw only the backsides of two orange cats as they ran from the room. He was seized by an inexplicably strong impulse to chase them but he didn't want to leave Anya's side. He sat down and gave his ears a good hard shake, trying to figure out what had brought on such a strange urge. Chasing a cat? Whatever for?

It took the two girls and Corax a moment to notice there was also a person in the room, a woman who sat at the kitchen table. She looked out from behind a tower of thick books on medieval history, dipping her spoon into a bowl of Cream of Wheat cereal, as though it were breakfast time instead of after eight o'clock in the evening.

"Well, finally!" the woman exclaimed, putting her spoon down and beaming at them.

Hattie and Anya stared, speechless. Anya looked nervously at the screened door behind her. Slowly she pushed the wooden inner door closed, so if anyone passed through the back yard and managed to work their way through all those bushes, they would not be able to see inside.

"I was expecting you boys yesterday!" exclaimed the lady, rising. A cat fell from her lap to the floor. Corax hid behind Anya's legs. "I must have gotten the days mixed up."

"Yesterday?" Mystified, Anya looked at Hattie.

Hattie snapped her mouth closed. She hesitated, but only for a moment. "You told us – I thought you told us to come today," she stuttered. "I think it was supposed to be today."

"Did I say that? O my soul! Silly me! Well, at any rate, come in, boys, come in. The dog, too. Sure! Come in. Sit down. Just throw those old towels and things on the floor."

The woman bent to clear a space on the book-strewn kitchen table and swept another cat to the floor. Corax didn't know what to make of him, but neither cat gave him long to think about it. They jumped to the top of a cupboard where a family of mice had congregated behind a teapot. The mice weren't intimidated. They were well aware that these feline sluggards presented no threat.

"Now," said the lady briskly, "have you had breakfast, boys? I can make you some runny eggs. And toast. How about some eggs?" She had a wide smile. It was painted a fire-red and somehow did not clash with her enormous bush of frizzy orange hair. Her cheeks were rouged with pink spots that seemed of a piece, surprisingly, with her old-fashioned orange shirtwaist.

Eggs? Eggs sounded very good to Hattie and Anya. Cautiously, they pulled chairs out from the table, slid the stacks of linens to the floor, and sat down. Corax sat expectantly beside Anya's chair. The audience of mice vied for advantageous positions on the cupboard shelf.

"No, you know what?" The lady tapped one finger on her temple. "I changed my mind. Let's have soup. Now I just picked this okra yesterday. Or maybe the day before. Straight from my garden!"

Okra soup.

Even the mice wilted from disappointment.

"Oh! No need to bother with soup, Ma'am," said Hattie. Anya hunched mute in her chair, her eyes sliding from bold Hattie to the outrageous woman.

"No soup? But I don't have much else to offer you, I'm afraid."

"That's all right. We just stopped in for a visit."

"I have a few chocolate chip cookies left over. That's about it. I'm sorry, boys."

"Well, chocolate chip cookies would taste very good about now," said Hattie.

"Really? You're not just being polite?"

"We like cookies, Ma'am."

The flame-haired lady studied her collection of Aunt Jemima cookie jars and only thought she saw a long pinkish tail. It was quickly withdrawn. She found the jar that actually contained cookies on her third try. She set it on the table and arranged two large piles of cookies on plates. "All right. I'm sorry these are not store-bought. Just plain old home-made. I really must do some shopping this morning. Oh well. Prune juice to drink?" she asked.

"Oh no," said Hattie quickly. "Don't trouble yourself."

"What about milk instead? That's all I've got."

The girls nodded. "Yes, please."

"And your doggie! Cookies for him?"

Anya finally spoke. "Could he have a drink of water?"

"But of course." The lady set a bowl at Corax's feet and petted him tenderly while he slurped. "And what do you call him?"

"Corax," said Anya.

"Corax! Now wasn't he a most brilliant man? I think we should study the ancients this year, when school starts again. Oh me oh my, I will surely miss having you two in my class this year."

"We'll miss you too. You were our favorite," improvised Hattie. Anya could only nod.

The lady sat down. "Now tell me, boys," she said conversationally, "where are you off to this morning. Doing some fishing?"

"Not today. We're ...." Even the intrepid Hattie could not immediately think of what to say.

"We're looking for the train station," Anya piped up. If they could find the train station, the hobo camp was nearby.

"Don't be silly! The train station? You pass it every day on your way to school."

"Do we?" Caught, both girls looked blank. Their eyes met.

"Of course you do. Oh!" The lady inhaled sharply. "Wait! I'm so sorry! I'm mixing you up with the Shadwaladder boys."

"Right," said Hattie. "It's the Shadwaladders who live near the station."

"Yes yes. You're right. Well from here, you just keep on a-going." The lady waved her hand. "Straight down the street. Where are you off to on the train?"

"Uh, my grandmother's."

"How lovely. And where is she located?"

Hattie jumped up. She had no idea what towns the train went to. "I'm sorry to rush out, but we don't want to miss our train. Thank you for the cookies, Ma'am."

"You'll come tomorrow, won't you? Okra soup tomorrow."

"We'll try, Ma'am."

"Oh fiddle! That won't work. You'll be at your grandmother's. Well, be sure to come see me on the first day of school. I'll be looking for you."

"We will. Yes, yes. The first day of school. Thank you for the cookies."

The lady stood in her kitchen doorway, orange hair orange clothes all aglow. "Tootles! Tootle-ooo! Bye-bye, boys!" she chirruped, waving gaily. Anya and Hattie turned and waved and hurried off into the dark, with Corax galloping behind.

The lady, deep in thought, turned back to her kitchen and her laconic cats. Two of these lolled on the top of the cupboard, looking cross-eyed at the mice who were stuffing their cheeks with cookie crumbs.

I swear, sighed the black kitty, examining her claws, I'm fed up with these mice. There are so many, we're over-run.

Yeah, aren't we supposed to be eating them or something? asked the blonde.

They don't look very appetizing, said the black one. Do you really want to pick mouse fur from your teeth all day?

I got enough problems with my own furballs. You know, I think tomorrow we should make every one of these rodents light out for the territories.

Yeah. The black cat stretched and rolled onto her back. I'm all for that. Cats is cats and mice is mice, and never the twain should meet.

Wish I'd said that, yawned the blonde cat.

The lady, preoccupied, scooped the white cat from the egg basket. You know, it's funny, she confided to him. I can't figure out if those kids were boys pretending to be girls, or girls pretending to be boys.

A few hobos still sat around the fire, one smoking the butt of a cigarette he had found, the others picking their teeth with splinters of wood. Tisias the crow dozed on Sailor Bill's shoulder. Suddenly the bird sat up and squawked long and loud.

"Look!" said Windy Will, peering into the dark. "It's the red dog."

"He's here?" Sailor Bill stood up and squinted with his uninjured eye. "Corax!" he yelled.

The dog ran at full speed, leapt into Sailor Bill's arms, and smothered him with dog kisses. The old hobo laughed with joy. Tisias the crow scrabbled to keep a foothold on Bill's shoulder. Bill turned at the sound of running footsteps and everyone around the fire stood up, looking nervously into the darkness. Relieved that it was only a pair of boys and not policemen again, they relaxed.

"Will! Bill!" called Anya.

"What in tarnation? That you, Anya?"

"Yes, it's me!"

"Well good to see you, lassie!" "Anya! We was worried!" "What happened to your hair? And who's this with you?" The men crowded around Anya. They felt almost like family to her and she smiled happily.

"This is Hattie Fish. She looks like a boy but she's a girl, too. Bill, what happened to your eye?"

"Aw, just some of them bulls. They come over to --"

Windy Will interrupted. "You needn't worry about why they were here. Are you girls hungry? We haven't much, I'm afraid."

"Thanks, but no." Anya peered beyond the fire. "Hugh? Is Hugh here?" She started eagerly toward his van. He *was* here! Why hadn't he come for her?

"Wait. He's not here."

"But his wagon --"

"He got pinched, Anya."

"He's in jail? What for?"

"Sassing an officer, I guess."

"Since when is that illegal?" asked Hattie. "They can't put you in jail for that."

"They purty much do what they want in this town, son – or Miss, rather. That's why most of us is moving out soon. Our luck's about up here."

Anya turned to Sailor Bill. "Where will you go?"

"Me? I ain't goin' nowhere. I can't ride the rails no more. These old legs ain't fast enough to catch a train."

"But," Anya protested, looking at the crazy-built shacks and tents of the hobo jungle, "you can't stay here all winter."

"There's a lady down the road. She's very generous," offered Hattie. "Maybe she'll help you out, once in a while. Look for the garden that's all overgrown."

"Oh oh. Speakin' of bulls," said one of the men. "Lookit this. Here comes them two devils again." The black Model T Ford was careening through the darkness. It braked sharply and two men got out. Because the car had no parking brake, they put wooden blocks under the wheels again.

"Girls, quick. It's you they're looking for. C'mon!"

Windy Will hurried them over to the migrant workers' truck. There was a gang of women and children sleeping, or trying to sleep, in the back, piled together for warmth.

"Hey Raoul. *Que pasa?*" Softly, Will greeted the man who sat on the tailgate.

"Hey Will."

"Listen. Can you take these two kids aboard? The bulls are here, searching for them."

"Mariana! Mariana!" Raoul jostled the shoulder of the woman nearest him. She sat up. "Got to fit two more in here, quick." She looked sleepily at him and shook her head. He spoke rapidly in Spanish and she understood. Raoul offered a hand. "Get in, boys."

Hattie jumped onto the truck and hid herself quickly behind two girls. Anya swept Corax up and followed her, embarrassed to be making trouble. Mariana jostled the children to make space for her. Speaking in Spanish, she shook a child sleeping near and made him move over. She gestured for Anya to lie down.

They were just in time, because Chick Mancino was prowling near. He and his partner Burt came up to the truck. They had unlocked Hugh's van but found nothing.

"Evening," Burt said cordially.

Raoul nodded. "*Buenas noches.*"

"We're looking for a couple of girls. They're runaways. Seen 'em?"

Raoul shook his head, shrugged and gestured that he didn't understand English.

"Chick! Bring the light!" Burt turned back to Raoul. "Sorry." He pointed to his eyes. "Got to look." He spoke loudly, as if people who did not speak English were also hard of hearing. "Got to look."

Chick stood to his full five feet three inches of height, and slapped his stick against his palm belligerently. Yep, got us some foreigners here, he deduced shrewdly.

"Go check on our car, Chick," said Burt. "Make sure nobody touches it. I won't be a minute here." Chick strutted over to the car and Burt raised the lantern. Sleepy children whined softly and shielded their eyes. The two women looked impassively at the cop, trying to keep the hate off their faces. Corax's lips curled like window shades and he growled low in his throat. Anya held him tight and tried to quiet him. The light passed back and forth. Brown-skinned Hattie blended perfectly with the Mexican folks, her ill-cut hair looking tousled with sleep. The light settled on Anya's white face. She did look out-of-place. Mariana put her arm around Anya in a motherly gesture. Corax's growl grew louder.

The dog recognized a cop's uniform. Burt recognized that dog. Anya recognized the policeman she had spoken to a few days ago while she worked alongside Hugh. The light didn't move from her face. Her eyes locked fiercely with Burt's. Her heart stopped beating. No one in the back of the truck moved a muscle.

No white girl here, but this boy, now, what's he running from? thought Burt. Something so bad, he'd rather be with Mexicans? Musta been pretty bad. Poor kid.

Corax had reached the end of his patience. Someone in uniform had once kicked him, kicked him hard, and he hadn't forgotten. He stood stiff-legged and barked ferociously. Anya, now the center of attention, was in a panic.

Finally, Burt lowered the light. "Looks like your little doggie doesn't much care for officers of the law."

Chick came back and surveyed them with slit eyes.

"All right," said Burt. "Sorry to wake you all. Good night." Burt nodded to Raoul and looked at Anya once more, gesturing to her with a small motion of his chin. Then he called to Chick, who still raked his eyes back and forth over the people in the truck. Corax, his body tight as a coiled spring, didn't stop growling, didn't take his eyes off the cop.

"C'mon, Chick."

"That there is a mad dog. He should be put away."

"C'mon. There's nothing here. Let's move on."

Chick banged his stick hard on the side of the truck, sneering when he saw that it made the children jump. The dog lunged angrily and Chick leapt away and hurried after Burt.

Hattie breathed, relieved. Once again, she and Anya, instead of hiding, had been saved by someone's misperceptions.

Anya was thinking about the hobos. What have I brought on these people, she wondered? I'll bet Sailor Bill was struck by that policeman's stick, and it's my fault that it happened. She decided that she had done enough to endanger the hobo camp. Maybe she was even the reason Hugh had gone to jail. She knew there would be more searching in the morning. She would have to leave this place, even without Hugh. She had no choice.

At first light, after several attempts at getting the truck started, Raoul managed to coax the motor to life, and Anya, Hattie, and Corax moved out with the Mexican people. The girls tried to ask Mariana where they were going, but she could not understand them.

Later that afternoon, the police finally decided that Hugh's bruises had faded, enough anyway that they could let him out of jail without having to explain anything. He walked back to the hobo jungle and heard that Anya had come and gone.

"You don't know where the Mexicans were headed?" he asked the hobos.

"No. We didn't none of us think they'd be going anywhere this morning. That old truck of theirs, they couldn't even get it started. They was surprised as we was when it finally run. Then off they went. Sorry, Hugh."

"I just feel a little guilty, that's all. I made some promises to the kid."

"You done yer best for her, Hugh. She'll be okay with Raoul. Don't worry."

So Hugh harnessed Clodhopper the horse, set Tisias the crow on the back of the wagon seat, and trundled off to Geneva, hoping to work the last day of the town fair.

*O*n the shore of Keuka Lake, the vines of Rocky Stream Vineyard basked on south-facing slopes. Bathed all day in sunlight and refreshed by lake breezes, it was a choice spot for growing grapes. Three generations of Aumory Couteau's family had lived there, building additions onto the old farmhouse that crowned the hill, improving the extensive flower gardens and a pond, and reveling in views of the glittering blue lake. Now that Prohibition was over, the vineyards below the house were once again being harvested. A couple of the larger vegetable fields, which had seen the family through tough times, had recently been put to other, less utilitarian uses. And hidden in a fold of hills, because they rather tarnished the aura of prosperity, were two long rows of old ramshackle cabins, uninsulated, unpainted, without plumbing. This was where the migrant families stayed, those workers so necessary to a successful harvest on such a large property.

It was the last Saturday of August. The weather had been warm and dry at Rocky Stream and Aumory Couteau needed workers desperately. His fields were full of ripening vegetables, and, unusually early, his vines were already heavy with grapes. So he was happy to see Raoul's truck come trundling up his road, filled as it was with laborers. He motioned them toward a row of empty cabins and put them to work immediately. He had checked the ripeness of the chardonnay grapes that morning. The berries pulled off easily. They were ready for picking, and with any luck, he would have several crates for his own use, plus a couple dozen more to take to the train by Monday morning.

Raoul helped everyone off the truck and immediately steered them all toward the fields. Anya and Hattie trouped out to the vineyard with the other children. Corax, thinking this all a delightful romp, bounded at their heels. Raoul handed everyone buckets and knives. While the rest of the family scattered to work among the vines, he gave Hattie and Anya a lesson in picking grapes.

"Okay, boys. You wanna make some money? You pick for me. Eat Mariana's food, sleep here, pay me when Boss pays you."

Anya and Hattie nodded. Picking grapes – that would be an easy way to earn money so they could finish their journey.

"Boss pays, you pay me half," Raoul repeated, making sure they understood.

They nodded.

"Okay. *Andale, andale.* We pick grapes. Do like so." He showed them the stem of a large bunch of grapes. "Reach under. Cut him here on stem. See here, big part? Cut knife away, push away, like so. No cutting hands." He lifted grape leaves and peered underneath. "Look under. Get all berries. Put in." He pointed to the bucket. "On vine, no berries. *Nada.* Put all in." He pointed to the bucket. "Porter, he come, he take grape. Okay?"

He squashed a grape in his fingers, chewed the seeds, and spit them out.

"Yeah, these good. But these, no." He picked some withered grapes and held them under the girls' noses. They pulled back with sour faces. "No good, see? Rot – rotter?"

"Rotten?" Hattie suggested.

"Rotten." Raoul kicked the earth with the toe of his boot. "Put him in ground, not in – " He pointed again to the bucket. "Okay? Good." He pointed to Corax and wagged a finger. "Dog, him no make trouble. Okay? Okay good. *Trabajen.*"

They worked until sundown, emptying bucket after bucket into the porter's baskets. It was not the easy job that Anya expected. The muscles in their shoulders were burning. Raoul came by every once in a while. He looked at their buckets, clicked his tongue and shook his head. He motioned with his hands for them to work faster, and he moved on down the row.

They were up at first light the next day, even though it was Sunday, and again picked until sundown.

CHAPTER THIRTEEN

On the same Saturday that the girls began working in the vineyard near Hammondsport, Jack Netherby arrived in Canandaigua to look for his daughter. The police station caught his eye as he drove into town, and he remembered that Helen had received a telegram that mentioned the Canandaigua police. They should be able to give him some helpful information. Chick Mancino was on duty, lolling in a chair with his feet up on the desk while he pored over a girlie magazine. A vintage toothpick hung on his lip.

Chick looked up when the door opened. A man came in. Chick didn't like piece of popcorn that, you know, gets stuck between your teeth. He frowned, with one eyebrow raised. "Eh?" he grunted.

"Anya Netherby? The missing girl. You sent us word that she had been found."

"Nope," replied Chick. Sometimes he just felt like pretending to be ignorant.

"I'm sure the message came from here. She was placed with a local orphanage, but has disappeared again."

"Not our fault, you know."

"I'm not accusing you. I'm just trying to get some details."

"Don't got any idea 'bout that."

"Look, is there someone else I can speak to?" Jack saw the policeman frown. "Come on, help me out, here. She's been gone a long time and we're very worried about her." his looks, his sport jacket, or his crisp open-necked shirt.

"Good morning," Jack said. "I've come to inquire about a missing child. I believe your people had custody of her for a while?"

Inquire? Custody? Chick snorted. Tricky words pained him, like a little

"Not our job to take care of people's kids for them."

"I know it's not your job," replied Jack, exasperated, "but if you could tell me ...."

"Can I help you?"

Jack looked up, hopeful.

"Officer Burtley Brown," said the policeman, extending a big soft paw. "What is it you're looking for?"

"My daughter, Anya Netherby. She's been missing for some time and we were told ...."

"Oh yeah, her. Sorry for the confusion." Burt gave Chick an admonishing look. Chick put his feet on the floor. "That girl ran away again. She and another girl, an Indian. Tell you what you'd best do. Go out past the train station. The jungle, they call it. A settlement of, uh, wha'dya call 'em? Uuh, what's that word?" He snapped his fingers. "Uh, transients out there. Those guys spent some time with her and her uncle. They can maybe tell you more."

"Uncle?" Jack coughed out the word.

"Oh? Not her uncle? Well, they was traveling together. He's, you know, one of them traveling pitcher-taking guys."

"A tramp," interjected Chick, his feet back on the desk so he could fiddle with his socks. Two of the things that really annoyed him. Socks sliding down inside his boots. And tramps. He hated lowlifes.

"He's not really a tramp, I wouldn't guess," explained Burt. "But we did have to lock him up for a few days."

"Lock him up?" Jack sputtered. His daughter was getting dragged around by a criminal? Maybe she had been kidnapped after all. "Okay, tell me how to find this ... this settlement. Are these guys hobos?"

"Oh yeah!" exclaimed Chick. "They sure is! And watch yerself out there. Them jungle buzzards'll rob ya blind."

"Oh, come on now, Chickie. There's a coupla guys out there that ain't too bad."

"You don't have a photograph of Anya, do you?" Jack asked.

Chick, demonstrating sly intelligence, took the toothpick out of his mouth and pointed with it. He gave Jack a discerning squint. "I thought you was her old man. What d'ya need her pitcher for?"

"I am her father, but I've been away. I haven't seen her for several years."

Jack saw Chick and Burt exchange glances. Fed up with trying to pry information out of them, he took out his wallet, and slid two five-dollar bills across the desk. Chick's eyes bugged. He held the bills up to the light. He had that feeling like when you finally poke that nasty piece of popcorn out from between your teeth.

Burt shrugged. "Oo- kay. Where'd that poster with her pitcher go, Chick?"

"That? I tossed it."

"Oh gee. Sorry," said Burt.

"Ah. Gee. I'm sorry too. Okay. Well, really, Officers. Thanks a million for all your help."

Jack started to fold his wallet, then plucked the two fives from Chick's fingers and pocketed them. Burt's mouth hung open. When Chick lurched from his chair, Burt had to put a restraining hand on his shoulder.

*J*ack jumped into his car and sped out to the train station. Across the tracks he saw a few ramshackle shelters held together, from the looks of them, with little more than chewing gum and spit. There was a general mess of junk everywhere, and a few ragged bums hanging around a cold fire. He could not picture his daughter, still not even nine years old, fraternizing with these men.

Windy Will looked up in alarm when he saw the red convertible come roaring up and brake in a cloud of dust. A slim, deeply-tanned man leapt out and came running over.

"Morning. How're you doing?" said Jack.

"Good morning," Windy Will answered.

"I"m looking for someone. A little girl. I was told she was here for a time."

"Really?"

"Can you tell me anything about her? Where she might be?"

"No I can't."

Sailor Bill came limping up and listened to the conversation. He leaned heavily on a stick, his chin thrust out and his eyes narrow with suspicion.

"But they said she was here." Jack took out his wallet again and extracted a few bills. "Here. Anything you can tell me would help. Who was this man she was with?"

"Who's asking?" said Windy Will, ignoring the offered money.

"I'm her father. Please, I'm desperate. That man who was here posing as her uncle – he's not her uncle. He's a criminal, I'm told."

"Who told you that?"

"The police."

"Oh," laughed Windy Will. "With whom did you speak? Officer Mancino?"

"I don't know. The point is, I've got to find her and I was told she was here. Or you might know where she's gone."

"I don't."

Sailor Bill gave Will an imploring look.

"When was she last here?" Jack tried again to thrust money into Will's hand.

"Thank you. I don't want your money. How do I know you're really her father?"

Jack blinked. "I …." He had absolutely no proof.

"Are you from the reform school, by any chance?"

Jack's face paled under his tan. "What are you talking about?"

Will turned away. "Yes, just as I thought. I'm sorry. We have nothing to tell you." He strolled away.

Jack stood there in disbelief. Anya traveling with a criminal who claimed to be her uncle, and now, what was this about reform school? He ran his hands through his hair, sick with worry. Then he stopped and looked up. One old hobo stood near, bent over a stout stick that he used as a cane. The man was looking at him with sad eyes, one of them swollen and bruised.

"Have you seen my daughter?" Jack asked softly.

Sailor Bill loved sweet little girls with pretty singing voices and cute red dogs and stories with happy endings. He studied Jack's face carefully, noting similarities. Then he nodded slowly. "Yes, I seen her."

"Please, I beg you. Is there anything you can tell me?"

Sailor Bill thought for a minute. He had a feeling about this guy. "She left early yesterday morning."

"Oh my god, thank you."

Bill could sense that the man's gratitude was heartfelt. "She thought she was bringing too much trouble to us here, them bulls so hostile to us and all. She left with a truckload of Mexicans."

"Mexicans?"

"Migrants."

"Do you know where they were going?"

"South. Down to lake country. Heading for a farm, or maybe a vineyard. I don't know any more than that."

"Thank you, thank you. You can't know how grateful I am.

Thank you so much." Jack held out the money that the other hobo had refused, though the policemen hadn't. "Please take this."

Sailor Bill shook his head. "Good luck finding her. Tell her Bill's sure missing her and her red pooch."

Jack looked at him, dumbfounded. "I will."

"She's a sweet little girl. Be sure to mention me." He tapped his chest. "Bill." He touched his finger to his forehead and limped away.

Jack went back to his car and drove out to the road. He stopped at a grocery, bought apples, bread, and cheese. He went back to the camp, waved to the men who had turned to watch him, and left the food sitting on a crate.

As the red convertible disappeared, Sailor Bill realized that he had forgotten to mention that Anya had cut her hair short to look like a boy.

Jack spent the next two days driving all the way around three of the Finger Lakes, up one side of a lake and down another, going from farm to farm, looking in vain for his daughter. On Monday, he was at Rocky Stream Vineyard, inquiring about a little white girl. No one had seen a white girl.

At that very moment, Anya and Hattie were at the Penn Yan station, lugging crates of Rocky Stream grapes from Raoul's truck to the train.

On the same Monday, Hugh Durant was trying to drum up a

little more work in Geneva, even though the fair was over. He was about to pack up his equipment and posters, when a well-dressed man came over to his wagon.

"You have some nice work here," the man told him. "Very nice. I'm looking for a photographer for a one-day job. You interested? I'm willing to make you an offer you can't refuse."

"Sure," said Hugh.

"I've got a girl flying in on Wednesday. Cute little gal. Only eighteen years old and she pilots a plane like she was born with wings. Elinor Smith. You've heard of her, right?"

"No, I haven't."

"Come on! She's been all over the news."

"Yeah, I don't get much news."

"What she did this spring was fly under four bridges in New York City. Under four bridges over the East River, all on the same day! Eighteen years old. Did it on a dare. I myself am a pilot, and I know that's not something you undertake lightly. Most pilots wouldn't try it at all. Too dangerous, what with so much boat traffic, freaky winds under the bridges. Well, really, it isn't even legal, but she's so cute, she got away with it. She's broken some altitude records too. Flies better than most men."

"Wow," Hugh managed to insert.

"Yeah, so anyway, she's delivering a new plane for me to try. I'm giving her a welcome party, a luncheon, and I want some photographs. It'll be good publicity for me. And for my business too." He offered Hugh a handshake. "Aumory Couteau is the name. I run a vineyard down near Hammondsport."

"Hammondsport. Good, I'm traveling down that way anyway."

"I'll pay you good money. Just be there by Wednesday morning."

"I'll need to be paid up front."

"Before I see the photos?"

"That's the way I work."

"Well, okay. Soon as you get there, I'll pay you in full."

"All right, Mr. Couteau."

"We're at Rocky Stream Vineyard. Come straight south along Keuka Lake, and drive right up to the house. Got it?"

"Sure. Thank you, sir."

On Tuesday morning, Hugh had the van ready to head down toward Hammondsport, but was reluctant to leave. He had once told Anya he would be working in Geneva, and he thought just maybe she'd turn up. He could wait, but he didn't want to be late for the job at Rocky Stream Vineyard on Wednesday. That afternoon he set Tisias the crow on his perch on the wagon seat and turned Clodhopper onto the road south, abandoning all hope of finding Anya.

As it happened, as Hugh drove south, Jack Netherby was driving north on the same road. He stopped in a small town to telephone his sister, as he had promised.

"Helen. It's Jack. How's it going?"

"Pretty well, I guess."

"Did you make any progress?"

"We're having dinner tonight."

"Dinner? That sounds promising."

"I guess."

"Keep your spirits up. If anyone can convince this guy, it's you."

"I don't know."

"Come on, now. This is your only chance. Don't blow it."

"I'm scared, Jack. Really scared. I don't want to go to jail."

"Just remember what we talked about."

"When are you coming home?"

"As soon as I find my daughter."

"I wish you were here."

"You'll be fine. You've got to make it work. You've got to."

"I know."

"And Mrs. Wright? You've been to see her?"

"Yes."

"Good girl. How's she doing?"

"She may come home this weekend."

"Wonderful. I'll call again tomorrow."

"Promise?"

"I promise. You can tell me all about your dinner."

He hung up and got back in the car. Not even sure where to go next, he continued his aimless way north, deep in thought, so deep he didn't see the horse and wagon until he had almost blasted past them. At the very last moment, his eye was caught by the sign on the side of the van: HUGH DURANT, PHOTOGRAPHER. It took another minute to sink in. Anya had been traveling with an itinerant photographer. Maybe that was his wagon! That criminal! Maybe she was with him still. Even if she wasn't, at the very least he could wrap his hands around this child-snatcher's neck and throttle the living daylights out of him!

Jack braked and pulled a U-turn so fast that the car fish-tailed in the dust. He roared after the van, pounding on the horn as he came alongside. He gestured frantically at the driver, who gaped at him with open-mouthed amazement.

Of course, to old Clodhopper the horse, the little red car with its horn blazing right at his shoulder could just as easily have been Satan incarnate, astride his pitchfork. The horse screamed in panic and swerved off the road. Into a field he went, only to find other terrors there that were just as frightening – tall cornstalks waving in the wind! A flock of fluttering jabbering creepy black birds! The tornado sound of a hundred wings as they rose into the sky!

Hugh stood up on the bouncing wagon, pulling with all his might on the reins. Tisias the crow flapped his wings madly, trying to keep his balance on the wagon seat while his bones were nearly shaken out of his body. In the midst of all this, out of the corner of his eye, Hugh saw Tisias suddenly take to the air! Flying! Anya's broken-winged bird was following the black birds that rose from the cornfield. Still Clodhopper galloped on, the van careering behind. Along the edge of the cornfield they went, lurching across ruts, bucking rocks, while Hugh tried to stay upright, yelling at the top of his voice. Clodhopper had a full head of steam up and was doing his best to flee from this nightmare. But he was suddenly stopped, not by cornstalks or birds, but by mechanical failure. A back wheel jolted off its axle and went rolling through the rows of corn.

The wagon tilted. Clodhopper strained. He struggled to keep moving. Hugh leapt from the wagon, cursing like a trapeze artist with imperfect timing.

Meanwhile, Jack Netherby had pulled his car to the side of the road. He jumped out, ran into the field, and caught at the horse's reins on the opposite side. It took two men to wrestle Clodhopper, quivering and tossing his head wildly, to a standstill.

Cautiously, Jack crossed in front the horse, whose hot breath blew in snorts down the back of his neck. The kidnapper! He made a lunge for Hugh.

Hugh was swearing furiously and could hardly wait to paste this playboy with the fancy red car. He swung a wild punch at Jack, but missed. "You trying to kill me, you stupid son of a gnarly fat (pig)?", "pig" being a far more cordial word than the one he actually used.

"Yeah, you're damn right I'm gonna kill you!" Jack aimed a fist at his nose but Hugh fended it off.

"You freaking idiot!" Hugh's fist almost thumped Jack's ear.

"You're as good as dead unless you tell me where she is! Is she in there? Huh? What'd you do with her?" Jack yelled back, fists jabbing the air.

"Who the – ?" Hugh stopped for a minute, and just managed to dance away from an uppercut.

"Aww!" Jack nearly dislocated his arm with that punch. "If you hurt a hair of that girl's — !"

"What?" Hugh shrieked. He heard the word "girl", thought Jack was talking about women, and exploded again, spewing swear words like hot lava. "I never laid a finger on your woman!" He wound up for a real stunner.

"I'm not talking about women, you debauched imbecile!" Jack side-stepped.

Raging mad, Hugh swung wildly, stumbled, and reamed Jack out with a torrent of oaths.

Jack could not get a word in edgewise. "I'm not — ! Wait! Stop!" He grabbed Hugh's forearms and held tight.

Hugh struggled. Grunted. Pushed. Glared.

Clenched together, arms locked, Jack noticed the bruises covering Hugh's face. This guy is a real degenerate! Of course Anya would be forced to run away! She was running from him! Jack vowed to kill him. No, wait. He'd get no information from a dead body. Talk first, murder after.

"Stop!" With a bulldog look, Jack slackened his grip. "Hold it! Just listen to me!"

Hugh pushed Jack's hands away. "Get off me, you brute!" He aimed another knock-out punch that connected with air. He ducked away from Jack's swing, and came at him again.

"Stop it, you jerk! Listen! I'm not looking for a woman. I'm looking for my daughter. I'm Jack Netherby."

"Netherby?" Hugh stopped cold. He gaped.

They stared daggers at each other. They huffed and panted.

Jack held his hands up, defensive. "Look." He stopped to catch his breath. "Just tell me what you did with her."

"I didn't do anything with her!"

"I don't care what kind of weirdo you are. I won't kill you. But you will tell me what you did with Anya, if I have to wring it out of you."

Hugh backed out of reach, put his hands on his hips and bent over, panting heavily. "How do I know – ?" He coughed.

"What?"

"How do I know you're her father?"

"What the hell do you care?"

"Prove you're who you say you are."

Frustrated, Jack groaned and punched his palm with his fist. "Crap on a stick!" he shouted. "Give me a break! I've got no proof! I am her father! What can I tell you?"

Hugh wiped his sweating brow and pulled the back of his hand across his mouth. "Wait here a minute." He climbed into the wagon, brought out two items, and stood looking down at Jack. He held up a small worn leather bag.

Jack's jaw dropped. "My marbles! How did *you* get them?"

"What about this?" He held up Anya's book.

"Robert Louis Stevenson! My name is inside the cover."

Hugh opened the book. It said "JAC KS ONN ET H ERB Y" in large childish letters. Hugh closed the book and looked at the man who had sworn to kill him. Finally, he climbed down from the wagon. Approaching cautiously, he stuck out a hand. "All right, a truce. I believe you. Hugh Durant's the name."

Jack refused his hand. "Wait. So she was with you? Voluntarily? Or do I throttle you right this second?"

Hugh gave him an exasperated look. "Now just hang on to your britches! I resent that!"

"Then tell me what happened."

"Yes, she was with me. And yes, it was her choice. Holy mother! What did I want with an nine year old kid? But she's gone again. Gad, you didn't have to run me off the road to find that out." He wiped his brow again. "I was hoping she'd turn up in Geneva, but I haven't seen her for almost a week."

"A week?" Jack's shoulders drooped. He leaned against the sweating horse, his hopes dashed.

"Whoa," said Hugh. "Hey! Sit down, why don't you?" He took Jack's arm, trying to keep him from toppling over. "You okay?"

"Yeah. Just disappointed. What – hey," he mumbled. "I really am sorry about your wagon, man."

Hugh scratched his head. "Yeah. This is not good. I've got to be somewhere."

"Where do you have to get to? I'll drive you."

"Hammondsport, for a job. But not till tomorrow morning."

"Look, there's a barn over there. Let's see if we can get some help for your wagon. Then I'll drive you to your job."

Gingerly, they unhitched the still-distressed horse and coaxed him across the field. Jack paid the grudging farmer to give Clodhopper a stall, repair the wagon wheel, and bring the wagon back to the barn.

"There goes my afternoon," said the farmer woefully.

"If you can get the wagon ready by, say, six o'clock, there'll be something extra for you."

The farmer belched in discontent but took Clodhopper's reins, and pulled him into the barn. Just inside, Clodhopper perked up visibly. Sensitive soul that he was, he immediately detected an intriguing presence. A *ladyhorse.* Pleased, much more so than one might expect for a horse of his age, he lifted his head, batted his eyes at her, and followed the farmer willingly into the stall next to hers.

"Well that's a first. I never saw that horse so docile," exclaimed Hugh.

"You don't know the secret ingredient, man." Jack gestured to the mare. "She does. Hey, I wonder if there is somewhere we can get something to eat. You hungry?"

"Starved."

"There's so much I want to ask you. Let's go get my car."

"Wait." Hugh stopped Jack with a hand on his arm. He shaded his eyes to watch a flock of crows circling over the barn. He could not spot any that had an injured wing. The birds swung off toward the south and were gone. Hugh shrugged. "Okay. Let's go."

They found a roadside inn. Over fat sandwiches on good country bread, the two men sat in the inn almost all afternoon. They had a lot to talk about.

CHAPTER FOURTEEN

*T*hat same evening, Harvey Wallhanger was also at an inn. He took a round booth in a dark corner of the old Fairport Village Inn. He looked around. Pick a restaurant in another town, she had said to him. I don't want to be recognized. Harvey shook his head. He wasn't sure what was going on.

He worried the knot of his tie, his thoughts a jumble. This lady he was meeting, he was pretty sure she had lied to him at least once. What was she covering up? He brushed a bit of nothing from his lapels. He had purchased a new tie today, and spent more than he should have. He tightened the knot. He looked up.

Here she was. Standing here, next to his table. Smiling. A cool mountain mist blew in from somewhere. Harvey breathed deeply. Birdsong and the scent of pine – Geez, he was forgetting his manners. He stood.

"Miss Netherby!"

"Mr. Wallhanger. Thank you for arranging this."

"I'm sorry to bring you to such a – " He gestured at the room.

"No no, this is perfect." She slid into the booth, keeping a space between them that was big enough for another person. Good. He must be wary of appearing too friendly.

The waiter came and they ordered drinks.

"Have you heard anything more about your niece?" Harvey asked.

"Well, her father came home."

"He did? Your brother? Jackson, isn't it?"

"Yes, and that was thanks to you, apparently. He's someplace in the Finger Lakes tonight, looking for his daughter."

"I feel very badly that I wasn't able to be of much help. I was put out of commission for a couple of days. A bit of an accident."

"Yes, I see. Your poor face is all cut up."

"You should have seen the other guy," Harvey lied.

"You brought Jack home to us. That was a tremendous help. I appreciate that so much."

Harvey loosened his tie a little. You're grinning like an absolute idiot, said the Voice of Reason in his head.

"I'm hungry! Shall we order?" she asked.

Harvey ordered chicken, the cheapest dinner on the menu.

"A green salad and the roast for me," Helen told the waiter.

"Mr. Wallhanger – " Helen stopped and sighed.

"Miss Netherby?"

"Mr. Wallhanger, I called you because I have some information for you." She bit her lip, playing with her spoon. "And I would like to offer a trade."

"What kind of a trade?"

"Some information I have, in exchange for immunity."

"Immunity? From what?"

"I don't want to go to jail." She raised sad eyes to his.

Jail? Buying stolen jewelry is an offense, but jail? She's exaggerating, angling for sympathy. Well, she wouldn't get it. Keep your distance, said that Voice in his head. "What is the nature of your information?" he asked.

"I need your promise first."

Harvey frowned. He wondered what she knew, or thought she knew, that could possibly interest him.

"I suspect that what you probably need is a lawyer, Miss Netherby."

"I can't afford a lawyer."

"If this is about buying stolen jewelry – "

"Well, no. No. It isn't. Not exactly."

"I'm sorry," he said, watching her carefully. "I honestly don't know how much help I can be." He didn't need any more secrets. He had his own secret. His boss was a thief and he didn't know who to tell.

"I was hoping we could work something out. You and I." Her grey eyes held his. "Couldn't we, Mr. Wallhanger?"

You're getting sucked in, taunted the Voice of Reason. Why don't you just get up and walk away?

No, stay! protested a contradictory voice. You have a chicken dinner coming, Harve.

"Well." He hedged. He scratched his head. "I would have to know more and –"

She moved a little closer to him. Harvey loosened his already loose tie.

"This information I have," she whispered, forcing him to lean closer, "it's very – I have something to tell you that would be worth knowing."

"But I'm probably not the person you should be telling."

"I just feel that you are, for some reason."

"Well. Let me think about it. Okay?"

Helen nodded. Their food arrived. She picked up her fork and smiled at her plate. Like a tiny light at the end of a long tunnel, she felt hope for the first time in two years.

Harvey just looked at his food. He had lost his appetite.

He should not get mixed up with this lady. She lied. She could not be trusted. He was sure of that.

Yeah well, you're pretty slippery yourself, Harve, argued that new voice that was not the Voice of Reason. You, picking locks, stealing photos? You're some kind of saint?

"We'll have to arrange to meet again, don't you think, Mr. Wallhanger?" suggested Helen.

He had gotten distracted. "Meet again?"

"Are you free tomorrow night? We should go somewhere different."

"Tomorrow?"

"I just want to get this off my chest, you know what I mean?"

Inspired by a sudden willingness to help with that, his mouth said, "We could try the Clematis Inn in Penfield."

You *imbecile*! the Voice of Reason protested, loud and clear.

"Penfield would be perfect," said Helen.

"You're sure?"

"It sounds lovely. May I treat next time?" she asked, her face alight.

Harvey looked at her. What had just happened? He unlocked his eyes from hers and sliced recklessly into his chicken. Was Harvey Wallhanger, once the most upright of men, willing to sell his soul to the devil? For the promise of a free dinner?

Yes, apparently he was.

CHAPTER FIFTEEN

*U*nder a burning September sun, the entire countryside along the Finger Lakes was heavy with the sickening smell of Concord grapes. Anya was glad that the dark purple grapes were not ready to be picked. That smell! She thought that if she had to be close enough to handle them, she would surely be ill. All week, she and Hattie and Raoul's family had been picking the green Chardonnay grapes. The overseers were constantly entreating them to work quickly, before the fall rains came to swell the grapes until they split their skins. Each day, the workers were allowed only two short breaks and a quick lunch and then they were back in the fields, bent over the vines again, picking and cutting, and straightening now and then to ease the kinks in their backs and arms. Even the toddlers worked, given the task of chasing marauding birds from the vines, and Corax was thrilled to assist them.

Anya wiped her eyes with a soaked bandanna. Unlike the bronzed faces of the Mexicans, her face had sunburned on her very first day in the vineyard. Hattie took one look at her and asked Mariana if Anya could borrow a hat. But the hat did nothing for the ache in her shoulders from reaching up to cut the grapes hiding in the lower vines. The adults left the low bunches to the children while they cut from the tops of the vines.

Anya could not pick as fast as Hattie. Several times a day, though, Hattie would drop a bunch of grapes into Anya's bucket so the porters wouldn't reprimand Anya for being slow. When a bucket was full and the porter came to empty it, they were given a drink of water from an earthen jug. A few minutes later, Anya would feel thirsty again. The sun was hot and the work was hard.

After the sun finally dropped in the evening, after they had washed hands and faces in buckets of cold water, after they had gathered around the fire, waiting to be handed a delicious tortilla made by Raoul's wife Mariana, they fell onto hard wooden beds and barely moved until dawn kissed the vineyard. Then, in the first cool light of a lavender morning, they would take up their buckets again and start working their way down the rows of pearly green grapes. Through dawn's dusky violet, the burning azure of noon, the last gold of sunset – until the sky turned to black night, they labored on.

Anya was forced to work as long and as hard as the Mexican children, but her face grew red with the effort. The shirt of her orphanage uniform became drenched with sweat. Raoul and his family never complained about the long days. They never spoke disrespectfully to porters and overseers. They worked quickly and without ceasing because this job meant everything to them, and to their families back home in Mexico. They were trapped in this life, made hostages by necessity, but glad to be able to earn a living.

When their work in the vineyard was done for the season, when the vegetable farms were finished harvesting, the family would move south to pick oranges. And if orchards were ruined by weather and there was little fruit to pick, they would be forced to move on again, to pile into the truck and try to find other work, to beg for work if they had to, else the family would go hungry.

Anya and Hattie were working here because they needed money for the rest of their journey. They had promised part of their wages to Raoul to pay for their food, but when the grapes were finished, they would walk away with something the Mexicans did not have. Anya and Hattie had hopes of better times ahead.

Summer weather lingered and one noon burned into the next. Anya and Hattie were no longer sure how long they had been working in the vineyard. The day they saw a little red plane buzz low over the property, Anya wasn't even sure what day of the week it was. All hands stopped picking and shaded their eyes to look up. The biplane circled the Rocky Stream estate and landed on a new airstrip that used to be Mr. Couteau's potato field. Elinor Smith, the famous girl pilot, was helped out of her plane by a party of admirers and the laborers bent to their work again.

Mr. Couteau spent the morning posing for photographs beside the red Waco 9 plane with his arm around Miss Smith. They had never met but she tolerated his over-friendliness, willing to cooperate with him until she extracted his down payment for a new Waco 9 biplane of his own. Hugh Durant had them pose for shots of

Mr. Couteau climbing aboard as Miss Smith showed him the controls. He took photos of them taking off, of the plane circling above the vineyard, and of the rather perilous landing mishandled by Mr. Couteau (but secretly rescued by Miss Smith).

Then Elinor Smith was whisked into the house to change from her heavy leather flight jacket into a pretty summer frock and dainty slippers, ready for the gala luncheon on the lawn above the vineyard. Several dignitaries from town had been invited, and some of Mr. Couteau's family had come to rub elbows and get themselves photographed with the eighteen year old ace pilot.

Champagne corks popped at the party up by the house. In the fields, the laborers crowded beneath a scrap of canvas to get out of the sun while they ate their meager lunch. Anya and Hattie sat back-to-back on the ground, and Corax waited politely for his crust of bread before wandering down to the pond for a drink and a chance to sniff around.

Up the hill, at the party, Mr. Couteau's adult son had been charged with the care of his eleven month old baby while his wife helped the other children to food. Unfortunately, the baby's father was a little distracted today. He had been beguiled out of his senses by the wide smile and laughing blue eyes of the adorable girl pilot, Elinor Smith. He wasn't even aware he had let go of his little son's hand. He didn't realize that the child, free at last to explore, had set off down the hill. The baby spotted a red and white dog down by the pond and stumbled that way on fat wobbly legs. The slope proved too much for him. He got going so fast, he could not stop. He plunged over the bank of the pond and, much to the dog's surprise, he landed face down in the water, floating there, too stunned to move at first.

Corax knew the dangers of water. The child did not respond to his barking. When he saw the baby begin to struggle, he had no choice but to plunge in. He sank his teeth into the baby's diaper and dragged the child, choking for air, onto the muddy bank. Corax left him there and ran barking up the hill to Anya's side. She dropped her sandwich and jumped up. The dog turned and ran toward the stream, barking at her over his shoulder.

"What's wrong?" asked Hattie, rising also.

"He sees something!" Anya began to run after Corax and Hattie followed.

They found the child lying among the rocks and mud, gasping and blue. Hattie scooped him up, held him upside down and slapped his back. Water coughed from the child's mouth. His color returned and he started to wail. Hattie hugged him in relief, Anya patted and cooed to him, and Corax danced on his hind legs. Raoul's wife Mariana had seen the commotion and had run up the hill to find Mr. Couteau. In half a minute, the whole lunch party was down beside the pond.

"This dog found him," Hattie explained, as Mr. Couteau's daughter-in-law snatched her baby from Hattie's arms.

After the child's cuts and scratches had been attended to, after the baby's father had been banished in shame, Mr. Couteau turned to Anya and Hattie.

"Boys! You're my little heroes! Come with us, come up to the party! Bring the dog! We have to make sure we get your pictures in the newspaper. Where's that photographer?" he yelled, as he led the girls up the hill.

"He left half an hour ago," said Mrs. Couteau. "I'll call the paper and see if they can send someone out. Now Aumory, give those boys a piece of cake, for heaven's sake! And that little dog – cut him a slice of turkey."

Corax was petted and given way too many treats, and Anya and Hattie were handed huge slabs of three-layer cake and ice cream.

"Come and meet Elinor, boys! Where is she?"

Miss Smith had gone in to change back to her flying clothes. Hattie and Anya stared when she came out. She had looked so pretty in her sundress. Now she was dressed like a man. She wore trousers tucked into heavy leather boots, a fleece-lined leather jacket and silk scarf, a man's shirt, and even a tie. Her curls were tucked into a tight-fitting leather helmet. She came right over to shake hands with the heroes who had rescued the baby, and to stroke Corax's head.

"Boys! Well done!" She ruffled their short haircuts and bent to see their smiles. She didn't have to bend far. She was only an inch taller than Hattie. "And this is your heroic dog? Tell me your names."

Grinning from ear to ear, they mumbled through mouths full of icing.

Miss Smith seemed taken aback. "Anya? Hattie? I'm sorry, girls, really I am. I was told you were boys."

Raoul, just leaving the party to go back to work, turned and looked at them curiously. "Girls?" he said to his wife in Spanish.

"Si!" she said. *"Ciertamente!"*

Ha, thought Raoul. No wonder I could hardly get a decent day's work out of them.

Elinor put her arms around the girls. "You know what? Hattie, Anya, I'm going to give you a ride in my plane. Would you like that?"

The girls nodded, thrilled speechless.

"Aumory, can you spare these two for half an hour?"

"Uh, certainly, Elinor. Whatever you wish."

"They deserve a treat, don't they?"

"They saved my grandson's life. Yes, indeed they do deserve a treat."

"Good. Your man has refueled my plane?"

"Yes he has, Elinor."

"I can lend them goggles, but they'll need jackets. You must have something they could wear, don't you, Aumory?"

"Of course, Elinor. I'll get something from the hangar."

Elinor led them toward the field. "Let's go, then. You're going to love flying. I know you will." She glanced over her shoulder as they walked out to the airstrip. "Now," she said confidentially, "can you tell me something? I'm just curious to know why everyone thought you were boys."

"Well, we let them think that, ma'am," said Hattie softly.

"What's the matter? Aren't you proud to be female?"

"Oh, it's not that! It's just that we were – " Hattie looked questioningly at Anya.

"Running away," said Anya.

"Please don't tell on us! She'll be put in reform school and I'll have to go back to boarding school!"

"Reform school! May I ask, uh – ?"

"What I did wrong? I got blamed for something I didn't do."

"So she ran away. Like me," said Hattie.

"Did you? So how did you get here?"

"It's a long story," said Hattie.

"Raoul helped us get away from the cops," Anya added.

"Raoul? He is one of the migrant workers?"

"Yes, ma'am."

Elinor picked up one of Anya's hands. She turned it over. "All these cuts are from picking grapes?"

Anya nodded.

"What's your plan, girls? You aren't going to pick grapes for the rest of your lives, are you?"

"We're trying to earn money. I want to go to Lake Placid to find my grandparents."

"And I want to get back to the Onondaga reservation."

"Onondaga? That's near Syracuse, isn't it?"

"Yes, ma'am. Very close. My uncle Eddie is a mechanic at the Syracuse airport now."

"Really? Eddie who?"

"Eddie Fish. Do you know him?"

"Eddie! Of course I do. Listen, you're trying to get home? I'm going back to Syracuse this afternoon." Elinor squinted her blue eyes thoughtfully. "Did you sign any kind of contract, or promise to work here?"

"We told Raoul he could have half our pay."

"Which, as you are children, is probably a pittance. Hmm. Let me think."

They stood next to the little red plane now. Anya was suddenly afraid. This airplane was awfully ... skimpy. Elinor put a fond hand on its wing.

"Okay. Here comes Mr. Couteau with jackets for you. It's going to be a cold ride. A *long* cold ride, if you want to come all the way to Syracuse with me. Would you like that? If you do, you would both be closer to your destinations."

Hattie's eyes widened. Anya's mouth fell open.

"Is that a 'yes'? My plane has room for two passengers. It's got a beautiful Curtis OX-5 engine, 90 horsepower. I think you'll agree she's a pretty impressive machine." She laughed. "Maybe I can make pilots of you both one day."

"Yes Ma'am!" said Hattie eagerly. Anya kept silent, afraid to admit she was terrified to go up in the air in such a flimsy machine.

"We can arrange something about your farm pay with Mr. Couteau."

"But wait – " stammered Anya. "I don't want to – "

"You don't want to give up the money? Or – you're not afraid of flying, are you, honey?"

Looking into Miss Smith's eager, confident face, Anya couldn't bring herself to confess the truth. "Well, see, it's my dog. I can't leave him behind!"

"Oh, the *dog*! I forgot about him!" Elinor lifted Corax into her arms and planted a kiss on his head. "Of course we'll take the littlest hero! You'll have to hold him tight."

"I will, I will!" Comfort for her terror.

"Aumory," said Elinor, stretching out a hand as Mr. Couteau came up, "thank you for a wonderful luncheon. I'm off now, so I'll say good-bye. I'll pass your check on to the company, and many thanks. I'm sure you'll enjoy your new Waco when it comes."

"You're leaving already? No ride for the boys?"

"These boys are girls, my dear Aumory, and I'm taking them with me to Syracuse."

"My workers? No, you can't do that! I need them. Hold it. What did you say? Girls?"

The girls panicked. He simply had to let them go with Elinor!

Elinor put a confidential hand on Mr. Couteau's arm. "Aumory honey, there are such things as child labor laws, are there not?"

"But not for Mexicans."

Elinor raised the girls' faces with a finger under their chins. "Look at these faces, honey. Neither of these girls is Mexican."

"Oh."

"Would you be kind enough to tell – " Elinor looked at the girls.

"Raoul."

"Yes, give Raoul their pay. Is that all right, girls? There is really no other way to handle this."

"Yes. All right," they said. It seemed a good trade-off.

"We'd better get going. Dusk comes early now. Hold the dog

under your coat, honey, to keep him warm."

Elinor strapped the girls in, adjusted their goggles for them, and flipped a switch. Her engine roared alarmingly. They bumped and trundled clumsily down the runway, nearly shattering Anya's fragile confidence, until the heart-stopping moment that their wheels lifted from the earth. They rose, high high higher. They buzzed the vineyard, circling it at a frightening angle, and watched the fields and house grow small. Elinor tilted her wings in a final salute and up they soared, higher than the cloudpuffs that blew like milkweed stars across the autumn breeze. For the first time, Anya felt the electricity of both fears and thrills charging her veins at the same time.

Stretched below was the world in miniature. They could see five of the Finger Lakes all at once, slim shards of shining silver in their green velvet beds. Over their heads, the endlessly wide blue vastness. Nothing else aloft but their little red biplane, alone in the azure deep, surrounded by the great empty sky world.

And so far below he was barely a speck, an old horse plodded down the road toward an inn in Hammondsport. Hugh Durant recognized the little red plane as it passed overhead. Thanks to its famous girl pilot, he now had a pocket full of new bills. He planned to sleep under a roof tonight for a change, before heading south to Maryland. He was looking forward to a long deep soak in a real bathtub. And his friend Jack had promised him a full dinner at the inn. It had been a rough week, one of the worst ever. He had been beaten up, had spent four nights in jail, and he had let Anya down.

She was just a kid. He hated that he wasn't there to help her when she needed it most. And now where was she? Somewhere safe, he hoped. Oh, and there was another thing that had happened this week. Call it good fortune or bad, he had lost the kid's crow.

Hugh unhitched the horse and saw to his needs, then went out to buy himself a new shirt and tie. He hadn't thought much about his appearance since he'd taken to the road last spring, and his glad rags, to use the hobos' words, were in a pretty sorry state. No wonder Jack Netherby thought he was a criminal. He took a bath and had a shave. By then, it was time for dinner. He found Jack already seated at a table.

"How did the job at the vineyard go?" Jack asked him.

"The girl was very charming. Name of Elinor Smith. She's a famous pilot, apparently."

"I've never heard of her, but then, I haven't heard much news at all for four years."

"Supposed to be an ace pilot, and still only a teen-ager. Spunky gal."

"Did you get some good photos?"

"I hope so. She's very photogenic. Lots of freckles, but she wears them well. All in all, I got to work with a good model, I was well-paid, and we finished early. What more could I ask for?"

"How about a steak dinner?"

"That would be wonderful, Jack."

"I ordered for both of us."

"Thank you. And I brought you something." He handed Jack an envelope.

Jack opened it and held the photos it contained for a long minute. "Wow. This is hard to believe. She's so grown up."

"She's a good kid."

Jack still said nothing.

Hugh pointed. "That's her dog. They are inseparable."

Jack nodded.

"Corax, he's called."

"Can I pay you for these?"

"They're yours."

"Thank you, Hugh." Jack shook his head. "I hope, when I find her, she doesn't hate me."

"At least you're searching for her. That's more than anyone in my family did when I ran away."

Jack nodded again. He looked for another long moment at his daughter's photos.

"Anya," Hugh finally said, "she looks like you, doesn't she?"

"She looks a lot like my sister. Geez, remind me to phone Helen later. I almost forgot. She's single, my sister, by the way. If you're interested. Actually, forget that. That's a bad idea. Helen's a handful on the best of days, and right now she is definitely not having her best days."

"Thanks anyway, but no thanks. I'm probably a bit too rough around the edges for any sister of yours."

"You don't seem so bad," laughed Jack, "now that I've finished beating you to a pulp."

"Hey! You never –"

They both looked up as someone came to their table.

The man tapped Hugh on the shoulder. "Mr. Durant?"

Hugh jumped up to shake hands with the vineyard owner. "Hello, Mr. Couteau. You're out on the town tonight?"

"Well, not exactly. Just dinner with my wife. Not quite up to the nightlife anymore. Back in the day, I was quite the party boy, as you can probably imagine. Not so much, anymore, though. Too many aches and pains. But I wanted to thank you for your work today. I didn't get a chance to say anything before you left this afternoon."

"You're very welcome. I'll be bringing the finished photos up to you tomorrow."

"We'll look forward to that. It's actually too bad you left early today. You weren't around for the excitement. We almost had a disaster. You missed an opportunity for some good shots." He back-handed Hugh's shoulder. "Your work could have been in the newspaper tonight."

"Oh? What happened?"

"My little grandson almost drowned. Fell into the pond when his daddy wasn't looking. If it weren't for a little dog that belongs to one of my field hands, I don't know what would have happened."

"That's too bad. I hope the boy's all right."

"Just a few scratches. He's a tough kid. Just like his grand-daddy, I might add. The baby's father is in big trouble though. I don't know if his wife will ever forgive him. The look on her face would have made quite a picture." Mr. Couteau laughed, which gave him a chance to draw a breath. Hugh stood there, trying to look interested. "And after that," Mr. Couteau prattled on, "Elinor Smith, you know, the pilot? She made off with two of my boys – you should have seen the looks on their faces. Their first time in the air. You missed a good shot there, too."

"Made off with – ?"

"Somebody from the paper tried to get a photo. I still say that if Elinor weren't such a persuasive little minx, I never would have let her take them. Now I'm going to be short-handed. 'Course they were only kids but I need all the field hands I can find. No wonder Elinor's famous, eh? She knows how to get what she wants. Yep, she flew right off with two of my boys before I could stop her. Girls, I should say – two girls and their dog. They looked like boys. I thought they were boys. They weren't Mexicans either. Don't ask me what that was all about."

"Huh. Well, sorry I missed it all." Hugh, thinking about the steak dinner that was on its way, tried to focus.

"Yes, you could have gotten some great pictures. Cute dog too – hey!" Mr. Couteau picked up a photo from the table. "This kind of dog. Looked exactly like this very dog. Red and white, he was. Interesting color."

Hugh snapped back to life. "A red and white dog?"

Jack looked from Hugh to this man standing next to their table.

"In fact, that boy today – " Mr. Couteau put his finger on the image of Anya's face and cocked his head. "That boy – no, he was a girl. He sort of looked like, hmm maybe, with her hair chopped off – could have been, I don't know – "

"It could have been this girl?"

"Maybe. I think so."

Jack stood up. "Where is that girl now?"

Couteau noticed Jack for the first time.

"This girl." Excited, Jack tapped the photo. "I'm looking for this girl. She's my daughter."

Couteau's mouth fell open. "Well, bless me."

Hugh butted in. "I'm sorry, Mr. Couteau. I didn't introduce my friend, Jack Netherby."

They shook hands. "What was the girl's name, Mr. Couteau?"

"I don't know. There were two girls. I thought they were both boys. I didn't get the name of either one. I'm sorry."

"Are they at your vineyard now?" Jack pressed.

"No, that's what I was saying. Elinor flew off with them."

"Flew off? Where?"

"To Syracuse. Back to that new airstrip in Syracuse."

CHAPTER SIXTEEN

*W*hile Hugh and Jack had dinner in Hammondsport, Helen Netherby was waiting for Harvey Wallhanger at an inn in Penfield. She looked up and there he was, standing next to her table with a smile as sweet as all the flowers of spring.

"I'm sorry I'm late."

She smiled back. This man was always so polite. "I took the liberty of ordering a drink for you, Mr. Wallhanger."

"Thank you." Harvey Wallhanger leaned confidentially over the table. "I've been trying to figure out a way to handle this information you have."

"Well, I've already decided on a solution, after all," Helen Netherby said with evident pride.

"Have you?" Harvey sat down. He had spent all night worrying. What had this lady come up with now?

"I figured this out all by myself, I want you to know. I haven't told a soul, but it's a pretty good plan. I think. I'm going to leave the country."

"You're leaving? The country?" Harvey, Harvey, said the Voice of Reason. It's for the best.

"They can't arrest me if I'm in Canada. So I'm going to tell you what I know. Then I'm getting on the ferry to Toronto tonight. I'll catch the first train to Montreal, find a place to live, and take another name."

"Montreal? Huh. I was born in Montreal."

"You're Canadian?"

"I have dual citizenship."

"You are very fortunate."

"How will you make a living, though? You won't be allowed to work in Canada."

"I have means. I have some things I can sell. Valuable things. I should be fine for a couple of years. That will give me time to find something to do, somewhere." Helen twirled her glass. "I've decided to tell you my story tonight, Mr. Wallhanger, and you can do whatever you want with it. I hope you can use it to your advantage. The only thing I ask is that you don't stop me from getting on that ferry."

Sure, of course. Leaving was the smart thing for her to do. "But what about your son? You can't leave him behind. Can you?"

"He's back at school now. I'll get him into a school in Quebec, if I can. He could stay here and live with his father, but I'd rather die than see that happen."

Harvey gripped his knees under the table. "So you are married?"

"Thirteen years ago, I was. Daddy paid to have my marriage annulled. It didn't last two weeks."

"Ah." Harvey expelled a long breath. Hey! said the Voice. Get down to business. Enough chitchat.

"So," Harvey said, trying to sound brusque. "You said you had information for me."

"Yes." Helen sighed. "All right." She was reluctant to begin. This would change everything. "What I'm about to say – I've never told anyone. Only my brother."

Harvey nodded.

She smoothed the tablecloth and started talking without looking up. "I got myself into trouble two years ago. My parents were having a huge fight one night. I went in to try to calm them down. Just as I went in, my father came running out, very upset. Mother was throwing things, first at him, then at me – a hairbrush, a powder box. She was furious. So I got out of there and went looking for my father. I found him ...." She paused, her hands clutched together. "Daddy was crying. Sobbing. I had never in my life seen him cry before. I was so frightened." She looked up quickly. "That was the day he lost a lot of money in the stock market. He was shattered. It was terrible to see him like that. I was actually afraid to leave him alone."

"Yes, understandable."

"His income plummeted. My mother was furious. There was nothing, absolutely nothing I could do to help. I didn't know a thing about earning money. I'd never even had a job. But I wanted desperately to do something to help Daddy. So, I made my first mistake. I went to my ex-husband to ask for a loan."

"Your ex-husband?"

"I absolutely hated to turn to him, but I was that desperate. I knew he had money. He doesn't earn it legally, but he always has money."

"What line of work?"

"He was a bootlegger, among other things. What I didn't know was that, when Prohibition ended, he turned to even worse crimes."

"Was he willing to help you?"

"He was willing to use me, to take advantage of me. To manipulate me."

"What do you mean?"

"He would help us, he said, but I'd have to do some work for him."

"What did he have in mind?"

"Stealing from my friends."

"You mean – "

"It was his idea, but stupidly I –"

"You robbed …?"

"Yes, Mr. Wallhanger. I am ashamed to say that for the last two years I have been stealing from my friends. Well, not friends, but acquaintances."

"You …. Wait. Don't tell me …."

She nodded.

"You aren't …?"

"I am."

"You!"

"I am the Cat Burglar."

Harvey was speechless.

Helen put her elbow on the table and rested her cheek on her hand.

"No," said Harvey. "No. No."

Helen sighed again. She nodded. Her finger traced the tablecloth.

"I don't believe it, Miss Netherby."

I warned you about her, said the Voice.

"It's true. It sounds even worse when I say it out loud."

"Phew. Wow. Yeah."

"My first mistake was to ask my husband for help. My second mistake was to agree to what he wanted. At first I was terrified, a total wreck. After a few months though, it became easy, and when that happened, I knew I was in trouble. I knew I had become a really awful person. But when I told my husband I wanted to stop, he threatened me. He threatened our son. You can see the mess I'm in, can't you?"

"Your husband knew you were acquainted with a lot of wealthy people."

"He knew I was invited to their parties, into their homes. He taught me how to copy their house keys. How to unlock their windows while a party was going on, and sneak in later. I learned how to crack a safe. Sometimes I even left their parties carrying their valuables under my clothes. And I got away with it, every time."

"How did you sell the stuff?"

"I never had to sell it. All I did was give it to Giancarlo. My ex-husband. He sold it and paid me."

"You trusted him to be fair?"

"What choice did I have? Besides, I had learned long before that you don't question anything that Giancarlo Toda does. He does not like to be backed into a corner."

"You – you were married to Giancarlo Toda?"

"Actually, that was really my first mistake. The worst in my life, except that he gave me my son."

"That man is a gangster."

"Yes, he is."

"I work for his brother Cesare."

"I know. I must admit that Cesare is the real reason I was never caught. It wasn't because I was a clever thief. Well," she smiled at Harvey with doe eyes, "I am pretty sneaky. But the reason I didn't get caught was because Cesare made sure that no one was looking for me."

Oh boy, said the Voice. Even I didn't see this coming.

Harvey Wallhanger rubbed his hand over his forehead. "Miss Netherby, I ...."

"You think I'm a monster, don't you?" This was the awful moment. Mr. Wallhanger would never think well of her again.

"No no, I don't think you're a monster." He stopped to look at her, and shifted closer in the booth. "It's – I have a secret, too. Maybe I should share it with you."

"What is it, Mr. Wallhanger?"

"I can confirm that Cesare Toda is involved in these illegal operations. I have evidence. I have a photo of a piece of stolen jewelry, an emerald tie pin. Toda wears it every day."

Helen gasped. "Have you told anyone?"

"That's just it. I wasn't supposed to know that photograph even existed. When Cesare Toda discovered it was gone, he sent his men beat me up. They tore my apartment to pieces, looking for it."

"What are you going to do?"

"Well, finally I contacted a reporter. Just today I gave him my story and the photos. Now I have only one choice. I have to get out of town as quickly as I can. If I hadn't agreed to meet you tonight, I'd be gone already."

"Oh, Mr. Wallhanger."

They sat, heads bowed.

Helen leaned toward him a little and spoke softly. "When that story comes out, your life won't be worth a plug nickel. You're as good as dead."

"I know."

"I'll be dead too, if I stay. And Giancarlo is going to be really furious when he finds he's not going to get the jewels from my last job. I'm going to sell them in Canada. That's why I have to leave tonight."

Silence again. Harvey stared at Helen's hands, her slim fingernails as fragile as seashells. The Cat Burglar. Wow.

"We are both in very big trouble, Miss Netherby."

"I know."

"I see now why you have to get away as soon as possible."

"So should you, Mr. Wallhanger."

They sat still, mired in their troubles.

The Voice of Reason in Harvey's head was silent as the grave.

Finally, Harvey rubbed his hands together. He bit his lip. He crossed his arms and sat back in his chair.

Go ahead, Harve, said that other voice in his head, that rascal voice. Go on. Say what you have to say. What do you have to lose?

He spoke. "Here's – well, – I – I have an idea, Miss Netherby. Would you like to hear it?"

"Certainly. Anything."

Harvey squinted at the ceiling. He looked soberly at Helen. "I'd like to make you a proposal, if you'd allow me. Maybe one that would benefit us both."

Helen looked at Harvey. "You have a plan?"

"I'd like to propose one."

"I'm all ears." She leaned close to him and whispered. "Go ahead, Mr. Wallhanger."

CHAPTER SEVENTEEN

When Elinor Smith's plane finally managed to land in Syracuse, Anya clutched her dog and clambered down off the wing. Their landing had been rough, but her feet were finally on the ground. She was weak with relief. Bad weather, a bank of cloud moving inland from Lake Ontario, had given Miss Smith quite a bit of trouble as they approached Syracuse. Anya wanted to scream right along with the wind that keened in the plane's wires on their descent. They had barely touched down when a crosswind lifted them and they were airborne again. After four or five terrifying jolts, Miss Smith managed to wrestle them to the ground and they taxied to a hangar. Elinor Smith and Hattie jumped out, full of enthusiasm, chattering away, but Anya straggled behind, wondering if she would ever grow to be as brave as Hattie.

Miss Smith led them to an office and introduced them to her friend Red, the airport manager.

"Red, this girl is Eddie's niece," Elinor said. "Eddie Fish, your mechanic. I hope he's still around. Hattie needs a ride back to the reservation."

"He was in Hanger Two but he may have gone home already.

You'll have to hurry if you want to catch him."

"Come on. I'll take you over there, Hattie. That's where my car is parked."

Hattie turned quickly and looked down at Anya. She wanted to speak but no words came. She pursed her lips, then finally blurted, "I guess I won't see you again."

"You're going?" Anya shook her head. Her chin was quivering. This was so sudden. How could she let Hattie go?

"We won't even be able to write to each other. We don't know where we'll be. Either of us."

"I guess not," mumbled Anya. She would never see Hattie again?

"We'd better go, Hattie," Miss Smith warned.

"So, well, bye now, Anya."

Anya blinked. She hadn't thought even once about Hattie leaving her.

"Good-bye, Corax." Hattie hid her face in the dog's fur. "Bye, Anya," she said hoarsely.

"Bye. Good-bye, Hattie." She watched Miss Smith put her arm around Hattie's shoulder. "Thank you for bringing us here, Miss Smith."

"You're very welcome. Take care, and good luck, Anya!" The lady waved and Anya watched the two of them go. They weren't even through the door and Miss Smith was already talking to Hattie about airplanes.

Hattie had forgotten her. She was alone again. If only she could go with them. If only she had someone waiting for her. Behind her, Red was putting on his jacket, getting ready to leave for the night.

"Where are you off to?" he asked her.

She looked at him solemnly. "Lake Placid."

"Oh? How are you getting there?"

"Walking."

"Walking? To Lake Placid? Where are you staying tonight?"

"I don't know."

"You don't know? You don't have any place to stay?" He pulled his collar up. "It's not very nice out there. Do you have money?"

"Fifteen cents. We'll be okay."

"Oh no. No, no. That's no good. Listen, wait a minute. Why don't you come home with me until we get you sorted out. Let me call my wife. She'll put another potato in the pot and make up a bed for you."

"Really?"

"You can't be wandering around by yourself. We'll find a way to get you where you're going."

Anya felt a little better. At least she'd be able to throw her legs under a table for one night.

"That would be wonderful. Thank you very much," she said. Maybe the hobos were right, she thought. Maybe people did like to help kids.

*T*he next morning, Red left for work early and his wife

Marion was getting ready for her classes at the university. Anya sat at the breakfast table stuffing herself with eggs and toast. Corax sat nearby, attentive and hungry. He was always a hungry dog, and growing bigger and hungrier. The phone rang and Marion grabbed it.

"Hi honey," she said. "I'm in a rush. Oh, okay." Marion put the phone on the table and called to Anya over her shoulder. "Anya, Red wants to talk to you."

Anya felt a surge of hope. Maybe he had found some way to help her get to Lake Placid. "Hello?" she said.

"Hi, it's Red. Listen, there was a guy here this morning, first thing, asking for you. He said he was your father."

Anya stiffened. "No!" she barked. They had found her? "No! He was lying! My father is out west. Did you tell him – ?"

"Don't worry! Don't worry, sweetie. I told him nothing. He gave me his card with a number to call. I can give it to you, if you want to follow this up."

"No! I don't want it! Throw it away! I don't want to talk to anybody."

"Who else would he be, if not your father?"

"A policeman. I told you. My grandmother wants to put me in reform school."

"I'm pretty sure this guy was not a policeman. Cops don't drive expensive red convertibles. Maybe you should give him a call. I know we talked about this last night, but maybe – "

"It wasn't my father! It wasn't! My father doesn't even know where I am, or anything about me!"

"Okay. Don't get upset. We'll let it drop for now. I felt badly for this guy, that's all. He seemed so worried. I thought maybe he was the real deal."

"No! He's not. He can't be."

"Okay, then. Hey kiddo, why don't you just take it easy today? You can lounge around the house until Marion gets back from school, right?"

"Sure. I – Thank you, Red."

"We'll figure something out tonight. See you later."

Marion came back, fastening an earring. "What's up?"

Anya looked at her with a grave face. "They're still after me! They knew I was at the airport."

"Oh Anya!"

"I've got to go," Anya said desperately. "I can't let them get me! Thank you for letting me stay here and everything. But I have to leave right now." Her voice was trembling. If only Hattie were with her. She missed her so much.

Marion set her briefcase down. "Honey, where will you go? You can't leave now. It's pouring rain out there. You can't brave that storm all alone."

"We'll be okay. Do you know the way to Lake Placid?"

"Anya, I can't let you leave. You have to have someone to take care of you."

"As soon as I get to Lake Placid – "

"You can't walk to Lake Placid! You're too young to be wandering all over the countryside by yourself. Listen, when Red gets home tonight, we'll figure some way to get you to your grandparents, I promise. Maybe Red can fly you there. Meanwhile, I have to get to school. There's a meeting this morning. You'll be all right here by yourself?"

"Yes." She tried to breathe. "Thank you, Marion."

"Stop worrying. You're safe here. Help yourself to anything you find that looks good. I'll see you this afternoon, if I don't blow away in this wind. What did I do with my umbrella? Bye-bye. Lock this door behind me."

Anya went to the window to watch Marion splashing down the street, fighting the storm and struggling to hang on to her umbrella. It was nasty out there, blowing and raining. She knew it would not be smart to start walking today. Maybe tomorrow. Yes, she'd leave tomorrow. She had to, no matter what anyone said. Red's phone call had upset her. How had they traced her all the way to Syracuse? She couldn't let them get her. She wasn't safe anywhere, it seemed.

She was still standing by the window, moodily considering her options, when a red car came crawling down the street. Hadn't Red said that a man driving a red car was asking for her? She peered through sheets of rain, horrified when the car did a u-turn and parked right in front of Red and Marion's house.

She dashed a note to Marion, and ran into the other room to get her boots and her last fifteen cents. She didn't even take time to put her boots on. Someone knocked on the front door just as she and Corax slipped out the back.

*J*ack couldn't believe his bad luck that morning. He had come so far, had gotten so close to finding his daughter, and now he had hit another dead end. The man he talked to, apparently in charge of the entire airport, was no help at all. That man monitored all air traffic in and out. He would have seen two girls fly in. Maybe they had landed at another airport? Still, Jack couldn't aimlessly drive from one airport to another. He'd been driving aimlessly for four full days now.

According to the vineyard owner back in Hammondsport, a famous pilot had flown two girls to Syracuse. How could they have landed here and not be seen by anyone? Maybe he should question some of the other people. He drove past Hangar Two. People were at work there. Way in the back, one man bent over a table, taking a motor apart. Another man was crouched under a plane, apparently explaining to a young boy the inner secrets of flying machines.

Eddie Fish saw a man come through the wide front door, running to get out of the rain.

"Hang on a second, Hattie." Eddie ducked out from under the plane he was working on. Hattie Fish stood up too, so she could straighten her back for a minute.

"Hello?" called Eddie.

"Hello," said Jack, shaking the wet off his jacket.

"You picked a fine day to be out."

"I know. I'm crazy to be driving around in this storm, but it's very important that I find someone."

Hattie heard him say he was looking for someone. She took a step closer to her uncle.

"I wonder if you could help me," Jack went on. "I'm sorry to interrupt your work."

"What do you need to know?"

"Two girls landed at this airport yesterday afternoon. I wondered if you saw them."

There was a deafening clang and clatter. Hattie had suddenly let go of the large wrench she was holding. Eddie Fish looked down at her. "Sorry!" she said. Her eyes were wide, staring into her uncle's.

Eddie got the hint. "No, I didn't see them." He turned back to Hattie. "You see any girls yesterday?"

Hattie shook her head.

"They flew in with a girl pilot, someone famous. You don't know anything about them? Heard anybody say anything? One of the girls was called Anya."

Eddie shook his head. "Nope. Sorry."

"Okay." Jack had a sudden thought, remembering something the vineyard owner had said last night. "These girls might be mistaken for boys. Short hair, boy's clothes."

Hattie ducked down to pick up a drill and crawled back under the plane.

"Uh, nope," said Eddie. "Maybe they came in after I left."

"Yeah, okay. Thanks. Sorry to bother you." Jack went back out into the rain and stood for a moment, surveying the scene, wondering if Anya was close by.

"Hey!"

Jack could hardly hear a man calling to him from a back door of the hangar. Eddie Fish was running a drill and the man could hardly make himself heard. He gestured to Jack.

Jack loped over and they stood in the doorway. He cupped his hand to his ear to hear what the man said.

"I tried to get your attention. You obviously didn't hear me call you over that noise," he yelled. "Ah, that's better." The drill had shut off. "I was working back here. I couldn't help but overhear you talking to Ed a minute ago. You said the name Anya and I couldn't think where I heard it. Then it dawned on me."

"You know where she is? She's my daughter and she's been missing for two weeks."

"Wow, that's a shame. Well you can stop worrying. My boss took her home with him last night. Far as I know, the kid is still at his house."

"Your boss? What kind of a guy is he?"

"Don't worry. He's got a heart of gold and a very nice wife. Your daughter couldn't be in better hands."

"Oh, that is fantastic news! Do you know their address?"

"Sure. It's 125 Comstock Place. Not Comstock Street, now. Comstock Place. Here, I can draw you a quick map."

CHAPTER EIGHTEEN

Anya and Corax ran out of Marion and Red's house, through the downpour, and up onto a neighbor's back porch. Anya tried to dry her feet. She jammed them into socks and tied on her boots. Then they crept along the side of the house and she sneaked a look at the street. She pulled back quickly. A man was running back to the red car. He started the motor and drove slowly away.

She took another look. She could just make out, through the rain, a red car turning the corner. She ran down the street and out onto a busy thoroughfare. At the corner, she noticed a peddler's van. Thinking of Hugh Durant's kindness to her, she went up to the van and looked in. She saw heaps of willow baskets, but there seemed to be no one inside. If Hattie were with her, she would think nothing of climbing into this wagon to get out of the rain. Anya picked up the dog and climbed up to the seat to wait for the owner.

A man came shambling toward the wagon from the porch of a house. Arms outstretched, he carried three big willow baskets. His clothes flapped madly in the wind. He was having trouble holding onto the baskets while keeping his old felt fedora crushed to his head. He wore two overcoats and a scarf, and a pair of very baggy trousers.

His shoes, far too large for his feet, flapped on the wet pavement.

He threw his baskets into the back and didn't notice Anya and Corax until he started to climb into the driver's seat.

"Oy!" he yelled, and stumbled backwards, nearly falling.

"I'm sorry!" cried Anya.

"Thief! Get away! Get off this wagon. There is no money here for stealing."

"I'm not stealing anything. I just wanted to sit here to get out of the rain."

"As if a little rain ever hurt anybody. It's stopping soon, God willing. Get down from there. Take that nasty animal with you."

The man heaved once, twice, three times before he got himself up to the seat of the wagon.

Anya was about to obey his order when she saw the red car turn onto Comstock Place again, cruising slowly in the downpour. She shrank back under the canopy of the van and watched him pass, glad for the rain after all.

"Mister, would you let us ride with you for a little while?" she begged. "We'll be no trouble, I promise."

"What, I'm a chauffeur? I should drive a perfect stranger all over town? No, get out of my wagon!" He flapped his outer coat to shed some rain and made shooing motions with his hands.

"Just a few blocks, maybe?"

"Do I look like a city bus to you, sonny? Do I look like I can afford to do favors for people? I am not a rich man. Has anyone bought my wares today? No. Yet some boy without a name comes, expecting favors. What? You want I should give you the shirt off my back? My pants and shoes, too, yes? Then where would poor Ephraim be? Will you tell me?"

"I don't know."

"Always it's the beggars who come. The beggars, hands outstretched." He stopped, squinting at the coins in her palm. Ah, the boy had money.

She had twenty cents, including the buffalo nickel that Sailor Bill had carved for her, but that coin she would never spend. "I can pay you fifteen cents," she offered the peddler.

"Fifteen cents. Fifteen cents, the boy tells me. That's all you got? Then fifteen cents I'll take. It's better than a kick in the pants. But it won't get you far. Give it here."

"I'll go as far as you can take me. Thank you."

"Ach, sit there and be quiet already."

The man flicked the reins. His decrepit horse twitched as though possessed but did not move a step. The man yelled at the bony old thing in some foreign language. The horse swayed right and he swayed left before finally picking up one foot, another, two more, until all his parts fell into alignment and he began to walk. He plodded slowly down the street, his head bobbing with every step.

"What language were you speaking just then?" Anya asked.

"In Yiddish I say to him 'soft words for the good horse but a whip for the stubborn horse'. Of course, this the animal knows already. This he hears every day, but always he must torture me with his disobedience. I, who feed him even when I go hungry. And still he tortures me."

The man sawed on the reins until he managed to get the horse to cross a busy street and turn left. A car swooped around them, blaring its horn.

"You got problems?" the peddlar screeched in response. "You think I am the cause?" He stood up, gesturing at the car as it sped by. "You cannot wait for my old horse? Leeches should drink you dry, and do the world a favor!" The peddler sat down again, muttering furiously. "Did I ask for this life? A poor peddler, out in rain and snow? Driving this god-forsaken horse instead of a big shiny machine? Such, such is my fate." He stood up again and yelled to no one in particular. "May all the enemies of Israel become peddlers! Then you would all know what I suffer." He slumped back down.

Anya tried to slip a question into his rampage. "I was wondering if you are heading north, Mister."

"North? North? And now he tells me which direction? I give him a ride out of the kindness of my heart and he tells me which way to go? What? Fifteen cents puts me at your beck and call, sonny?"

"No, but I was wondering if you're heading that way."

"Don't bother me with questions. We stop here. I must sell my baskets." The man's dark eyes slid over to Anya. "It rains still. You! You take these three baskets up to that door."

"Me?"

He glowered at her. "No. I'm talking to your dog."

"But I don't know how to sell anything."

"You go. You knock. You put on sad face. You say fifty cents for this wonderful basket. You bring the money to me."

"Well, I'll try."

"You better come back with that money, sonny, or I bring the plague of Pharoah to your head! No running away on poor old Ephraim."

Anya nodded and went up to a house. A lady answered her knock.

"Would you like to buy a nice basket, ma'am? It's just right for marketing but you could also use it for the flowers you cut from your garden. And what a beautiful garden you have, ma'am, even on a rainy day."

The lady looked the basket over critically. "How much, son?"

"Fifty cents. Or three for a dollar forty."

"Well, I could give these two to my daughters. A dollar forty?"

"Yes, ma'am."

"Wait right here." The lady came back and handed Anya some money. "You owe me a dime change." She looked at the boy on her doorstep, soaking wet, pants too short, and dirty at the knees. "Never mind, son. You can keep the dime."

"Thank you, ma'am!"

Anya returned to the wagon. Ephraim looked amazed.

"Three baskets sold? You got the money?"

"I told her three for a dollar forty."

"You what?" Ephraim squawked. *"Oy gevalt.* Why did I bother to get up alive this morning?"

"She gave me a dollar fifty and said I could keep the extra

dime."

"No, you owe me that dime. Three baskets, a dollar fifty."

"But she said –"

Ephraim snatched the money. "You sell more, maybe we can talk." He flicked the reins and got the old horse moving down the wet street. They stopped at the next house. Anya sat still.

"What, you maybe wait for the messiah? You want I should go hungry today? Go! Get some baskets out of the back."

They went on like this, Anya running through the rain, knocking on doors, selling baskets, and Ephraim becoming more excitable as the morning wore on.

"My baskets! You see how excellent they are, sonny boy? Every one sold! No one else can make such baskets!" He flapped the reins to move the horse out onto a busier street.

"Such skill I have. And me, I could have been a Hebrew scholar, you know, but here I am, a poor peddler. Things should have been different, if God had only once smiled upon me. Why do you look so?"

"I'm not looking so."

"You do not believe that I have deep knowledge of the word of God?"

"I believe you."

"I see you looking down your snoot. I tell you, I am so getting tired of you, sonny boy."

"No sir. There's no snoot. I believe you."

"Oh, I see it all. I know what I know. Look. Long enough you have bothered me. It's time you get off my wagon."

"But what about my money?"

"What?"

"My fifteen cents. Are you going to give it back to me?"

"Are you out of your mind, *shaygats*?" Ephraim yelled.

"I sold all your baskets for you. You should at least –"

"What are you talking? My baskets sold themselves! *Oy vey,* ungrateful boy. May the palm of my hand grow feathers if you can persuade me to take you one step farther!" He pulled over to the side of the street. "All along I knew you for a thief! Get out!" he yelled. "Take your mangy dog with you!"

"Will you at least give me the dime that lady gave me?"

Ephraim tossed his head. "So you would cheat me, ugly boy. And after I help you. Get out! Go laugh with lizards. This is my last word to you."

"It's only fair, Mr. Ephraim."

"May your tongue turn to wood if you speak one more word!"

"But –"

"OUT!"

Anya gathered Corax in her arms and climbed down to the sidewalk. She was furious. That man had cheated her! She was grateful that the rain had stopped, at least. She glared darkly as the old horse pulled the van away from the curb. Then she spotted a sheriff's office, right across the street. Sitting in front of the building was a red car. Was it the same one? She wasn't sure, it had been raining so hard when she first saw it. She signaled to Corax to follow and they hurried past, heading on down a busy city street.

A block later they came to a large cathedral with beautiful gardens in front. A narrow street, Onondaga Street, angled away from it. With its row of trees, it seemed a little more sheltering than the wide open avenue she was on, and besides, its name reminded her of Hattie. She headed that way.

As she passed the cathedral, she saw that a group of older kids, hanging around near the gardens, were taking notice of her. The group, all boys except for one girl, were suddenly alert.

"Hey. That boy over there," commented one to another, gesturing in Anya's direction. "Whaddya wanna bet his mommy just gave him a little pocket change and he's off to the store?"

"Let's grab him. He'll be good for a few cents."

"He's good for more than that. Father Cremiano gave me a dollar for the kid I took to him last week."

"A buck?"

"He wants to get little kids off the street. He paid me when I told him the kid was an orphan."

"Was the kid an orphan?"

The boy giggled. "How should I know?"

"A buck! Let's get him!" "Susie, go get that kid." "Yeah, Susie. Get him talking."

"Hey! Hey you!" called the girl. She trotted toward Anya and the boys ambled nonchalantly after her.

"Hey! Wait up!"

Anya paused.

"Do you have a nickel I can borrow? My mamma sent me out to buy bread but a man stole my money. She's going to kill me if I don't come home with bread."

"Sorry. I don't have any money." Anya put her head down and walked on.

"You don't have money? Yeah, I just bet. I say you do. C'mon. All's I want is a nickel."

Anya hurried faster.

"Wait! Kid! I wanna talk to you! Let me pet your dog."

Anya started to run and Corax followed at her heels. She nipped across the street just ahead of a line of cars whose drivers were stewing impatiently, trying to get around a horse-drawn dairy wagon. The gang of teenagers slowed to thread their way through the traffic. Anya fled down the street. To her left was an alley, running alongside another church. She turned. There was a row of garbage cans in a small enclosure. She yanked off one lid. The can was full of fireplace ashes. She opened the next. A few vegetable peelings swam on the bottom but there was plenty of room for her. She put one leg in, turned to grab Corax, and saw he was nowhere near. Where was her dog? The gang of teenagers came to the end of the alley. She ducked into the garbage can and pulled the lid over.

She heard them run past. Then a few came back. "Where's the little rat?" "He can't be far." "Go that way. We gotta nab him!" "Hey! Watch out! A cop! Let's get out of here!"

After a while, the sound of their voices disappeared. Very carefully, Anya lifted the garbage can lid just a crack. She looked up and down the alley. There was no one about. Quickly she hopped out of the can but stayed inside the enclosure. Still she saw no gang of kids.

And no Corax.

What had happened to him? Those kids, those hoodlums! Did they have him? Wary, she came out of the trash can enclosure. She passed quickly down the alley, looking frantically. He was nowhere to be seen. Afraid to go out onto the street again, she ran to the other end of the alley. It opened onto a busy street. No dog!

Once more she traversed the alley, thinking he might have found some little nook or cranny to hide in. She called, she looked everywhere. She ran out onto a street. He wasn't used to city streets. He could get run over! She panicked now. She turned right and took her courage in hand. She would have to go back up Onondaga Street to see if he was there. Even if she had to confront that gang of kids again, she would do it. And if they had her dog ... she made herself put that fear aside.

She turned the corner. Onondaga Street was ahead. There was a small garden at the corner, with a wrought iron fence. Maybe he had squeezed in there. No, no Corax.

But there on Onondaga Street was the red car, parked at the curb.

Now she knew it was the same car. A man was leaning nonchalantly against it, as if waiting for her. In his arms he held her dog Corax.

She stopped in her tracks. "NOO!" she screamed at the top of her voice.

Corax wriggled joyfully at the sight of her, but the man still held him.

Furious, but refusing to cross the street, she screamed again. "Let him go! He's mine! Put him down!"

She was sobbing, seeing how badly Corax wanted to come to her. But she dared not go near. She kept her distance, ready to run if the man came toward her. She pressed the backs of her hands hard against her cheeks. The man had not moved or said a word.

She beat her fists uselessly in the air and stamped her feet. "Corax!" she called. "Let him go!" She was helpless. She could not go closer. But she had to get her dog back.

"Cor- aaax!" Her dog!

The man wouldn't let him go. He started walking toward her. She backed away. "Don't you come near me! Don't!"

He stopped.

"No! No!"

"Anya," he said softly.

"Get away from me! Give me my dog!"

"I'm not here to hurt you."

"I know who you are! I'm never *never* going anywhere with you!"

"Can I just talk to you?" The man held something up. "Look. Your friend Hugh gave me these, to prove who I am."

She stopped. He held her leather bag of marbles.

"And he gave me this. You left it in his van." He showed her a book, *A Child's Garden of Verses.*

She shook her head at him. "You stole those! You *made* him give you those!"

"I know what color the shooter marble is. Blue."

"Oh sure. All you had to do was look inside," she cried hoarsely.

"These used to be my marbles."

"What? I don't believe you."

"I gave you this book, when you were small. I know these verses by heart.

'The world is so full of a number of things, That I think we should all be as happy as kings.'"

He came closer. "Here. Take your dog." He put him down and Corax raced to her.

She seized him and knelt on the pavement, hugging him and crying and pressing her cheek to his head. The man came and squatted near them, but not too near. Anya turned her back and shielded Corax from the man.

"Hey." Jack spoke gently. "It's me. Your dad. You don't have to be afraid of me."

She mustn't weaken. How could she believe the impossible?

"Do you want me to prove I'm your father? I know everything about you. Your birthday is September 8th. You live at 5 Elm Street, and your bedroom is on the third floor, next to Mrs. Wright's. You have a pink piggy bank that's empty, and three overdue library books on your desk."

Anya looked back at him, sobbing aloud. He handed her his handkerchief. She refused it and turned away again, crouching over her dog with her back to the man. Before he showed up, she had known where she was going. She had things all figured out.

Overhead, raindrops hung like orbs of mercury, trembling on the tips of maple leaves and lit by a weak sun. The wind had calmed but an occasional puff of breeze shook some drops loose and showered them to the sidewalk. Crouched on the ground, Anya watched them absently. Raindrops, spreading and disappearing. Kaleidoscope patterns of leaf shadows. Sounds of city traffic from a block away, out on the busy street, where people moved with great purpose because they knew where they were going. She knew where she was going, too. She did.

She could only stare at the pavement, absorbed. Something held her back, would not let her move. How could she turn around to face that man? If she did, there was no telling what would happen. No telling.

"I was so worried about you, Anya."

Her heart slammed its door.

"You're probably mad at me for being away for so long," Jack said to her back.

A pair of maple keys blew out of a tree and whirled to the sidewalk. Now she stared at them. Little wings, finely veined, plump with seeds, looking for a spot of earth where they could grow.

"I feel very badly about us, Anya. You and me. You can't know."

She shrugged. Corax searched her face. She patted his ears back and put her forehead to his.

"Have you been picturing your father as somebody different?"

She wouldn't look at him.

"I bet you were hoping for someone handsome."

She stuck her lip out, shrugged again.

"I guess you're stuck with me, though. I'm here for good now."

How could this be her father? Impossible. How did he get here? How did he find her? Anya felt her face crinkle up. She held her breath and squeezed back another sob. Corax looked over her shoulder and wriggled away.

"No!" she called in panic.

The dog stood between them, looking from Anya to Jack, then padded over to sit in front of the man. His tail swished back and forth on the sidewalk and he looked worriedly up into the man's face.

Jack stroked her dog's head.

"Corax! Puppy!"

"Look," Jack said to Anya, gesturing with his thumb. "Proof of who I am. Over there. There's my car. Surely you've seen it in the garage at home. There aren't that many red Chrysler Imperials around."

It was true. There had been a red car in their garage. Neil had taken it out to a gas station once, and he had let her go with him.

Corax turned and trotted back to her, his tail wagging in a tentative way. Anya rubbed the backs of her hands across her face, pulled him to her, and turned her back again.

Her dog was braver than she was. He wasn't angry. He wasn't afraid to be wrong.

"Mrs. Wright sends you her best. She's getting better. She

didn't slip on a marble, by the way. Just so you know, her fall was not your fault. Her bad knee gave out at the top of the stairs."

What?

Oh. That, that was something. She hadn't been able to let her breath out, she had been holding herself so tightly. Now something released. She went soft, weeping with relief.

"You know what, Anya? You know what I want? I really want to go home." The man held out his hand. "Will you come with me?"

Maybe she'd be able to move. A lump of iron, a hard, hard lump in her heart, was dissolving, draining away.

She couldn't look up, but she made herself stand, very slowly. She kept her back to the man. He stood too.

Gently, he touched her hair.

He rested his hand on her head, a big warm hand.

Slowly he turned her around.

He pulled her into his arms, and the dog went crazy trying to be included.

CHAPTER NINETEEN

*T*he ride home seemed short. They put the top down on the car. Corax found that he loved car travel. He loved the wind in his face. He loved having Anya sitting still in one place so when his wind bath was finished, he could curl up on her lap and go to sleep.

Before they left Syracuse, Jack had to stop to make a couple of phone calls. He hurried back to the car.

"Nobody was home at our house but I talked to Mrs. Wright's doctor," he told Anya. "She's coming home tomorrow with a nurse to help her until she can get around on her own. We'll have to make a bedroom for her downstairs. The sunroom, maybe. A new bedroom for you, too. We'll tuck it in somewhere."

"Really?" She spoke quietly. Did he mean that?

"Then I got the name of your former cook and called her."

"Betty?"

"Yes, and Neil. I hired them back and Betty will be there tonight to make us some dinner when we get home. How does that sound, kiddo?"

"Yes, fine," said Anya. It was wonderful news, but .... She paused, dread swamping her again. Her stomach clenched itself back into a knot. "And Grandmother and Grandfather?"

"They are at Aunt Ida's for a while. I should tell you. I'm thinking of offering to buy the house from them. It's time they moved into something smaller. Mother can get a place closer to her sister, so we can have Elm Street to ourselves."

"But – what about Aunt Helen?" She looked with a long face at Jack. "What about Robert?"

"Yeah, we'll have to work something out there. Do you and Robert get along?"

"No! He's horrible!"

"The thing is, I have a big paper to write. Maybe a book. I'll need some place to work. So if Mrs. Wright runs the house for us and Betty and Neil are there, I won't have too many distractions. I'll make a couple of trips back to Santa Fe during the winter, but mostly I'll be working at home. You can go to your same school, if you like. For this year at least. That's what I've been thinking. What do you say?"

"I just wish Robert weren't there."

"He's back at school now. There's another thing, though. I might as well tell you."

"What?"

"Aunt Helen – Oh great! That reminds me. I forgot to call her last night. Anyway, Aunt Helen has gotten herself into a real mess. I'm not sure what will happen to Robert if she goes to jail."

"What? Jail!"

The little red convertible flew along and Jack told Anya the whole story as Helen had told him. They were opening the door to 5

Elm Street before Anya knew it.

"Anya! Sweetheart!" Betty flew across the hall to hug her. "What happened to your hair! And what is this, I ask you?" She pointed at Corax. Fortunately Betty loved dogs and somehow Corax, wagging happily, sensed that she would be important in his life. He knew, with that dogly intuition, that it's never a bad idea to get friendly with the cook. Neil came into the house especially to give Anya a big hug.

"Am I happy to see you!" he said, ruffling her short hair.

"Mr. Nether – "

"Please, Betty. Call me Jack."

"I don't think I can do that. But here. A telegram came for you."

Jack opened it. His eyes bulged. "What?" He read it three times, then folded it and put it in his shirt pocket.

"Whew!" he gasped, leaning heavily against the hall table for support.

"What is it?" Anya asked.

"It's from your Aunt Helen."

"What happened?" She was suddenly sick with fear again.

"All the stuff I told you about her? She gave that whole story to a reporter. It's going to be in the news any day now."

"Oh no. Will she go to jail?"

"Maybe not."

"Why not?"

"You started something, Anya."

"What do you mean?"

"Apparently it's Aunt Helen's turn to run away. She has fled the country. Run off. Gone. To Canada. With someone – wait." He unfolded the note again. "A policeman named – I don't know – a weird name. Have I heard it before? It says 'Wallhanger' but that can't be right. That must be a typing mistake. Anyway, she's run off to Montreal."

"With a man?"

"With this guy. She's going to live in Montreal."

"*Aunt Helen?*"

"She's switching Robert to a private school up there. And she's paying for it this time. Incredible news, wouldn't you say?"

"Robert's gone? No more Robert?"

Jack straightened up. "You know what, Anya? You've been through a terrible ordeal and I have five new gray hairs from worrying. But it looks like things are going to work out pretty well after all. We should walk up the street and get ice cream cones. I feel like celebrating."

"Me too," said Anya. "Corax too."

They walked along licking their ice creams until they came to the green iron bridge over the canal, and there they stopped to hang over the railing.

"Ah, the old canal. I used to swim in here when I was a kid," Jack told her.

"You did? You were allowed?"

Jack laughed. "No."

"I was never allowed, either. I never dared to."

"You want to see our secret swimming place? If it's still there?"

"Sure."

They inched down the steep bank. Just under the bridge someone had built a very short swim platform out of a couple of old boards and some cement blocks. Jack, Anya, and the dog crowded onto it and looked down into the opaque green water.

Jack slipped off his shoes.

"What are you doing?"

"Last one in is a rotten egg!" With a clean dive, he knifed into the water, clothes and all. Anya waited in horror to see him surface. What? So it *was* a myth, this business about the canal being full of floating cow guts? She kicked off her shoes, opened her arms, and flung herself in.

Corax was frantic. All that water! He pranced up and down on the little dock, pacing and worrying. He barked, trying to warn them. Then he leapt. He just had to. Into the water he went, because he just couldn't stand to be left out.

*T*hen, while Jack and Anya and Corax sat in the warm sun to dry off, a rogue breeze came skittering down this stretch of the canal. It leapt onto the green iron bridge and stirred up a little dustdevil for a playmate. Gathering bits of this and flecks of that, it whirled down past the train station and into a garden at the corner of Elm and Main. After blustering among the late-blooming rosebushes there and scattering petals everywhere, just for a merry prank, it spun past the cemetery with a tricksy little laugh, whipped through the apple orchard and on down the road that twisted into the city. Down the road it went, knocking this askew and leaving that a little bit wrong, a trail of mishaps in its wake. Knowing someone will put things right again, only better. Better, because who with any sense would ever want to waste a perfectly good calamity?

THE END, perhaps

ACKNOWLEDGEMENTS

First of all, my thanks to any gentle reader who contributes a review of this book on the book review site of your choice. Even a couple of sentences would be a great help and very much appreciated.

A novel is an orchestration of happenstance and reveries and figments. The inspiration for *The Adventures of Anya and Corax* bloomed in a moment, on a patio one midsummer evening. Thank you, Dr. Gary C. Woodward, for introducing me to the original Corax.

For use of the image and the spirit of the dog Corax, I give heartfelt thanks to the noble Red Dog his own self, who lives in the ocher-colored house down where the road bends. Thanks also to his minion, Marc Garstein. It is generous of you both to share photos and personas that shaped this Corax, especially a playful willingness to become friends in the blink of an eye.

Most invaluable was my editor, Dorian Kincaid. She fine-tuned the book. She helped me give it definition. As if born and raised to the task, she seems to know better what is in my mind than I myself. For your eagle eye and acute perceptions, and for both of those semi-colons, many thanks.

I have turned to Nancy Dilmore on several projects for help with all things equine, and both she and Lori Dilmore helped with

Raoul's Spanish. *Gracias, pequena. Gracias, cunada.*

Happenstance. When the first draft of this tale was completed, several coincidences came to light. I had found Mertensia, New York on a map of my old stomping grounds, but had no memory of it. I phoned my sister Margaret for help. Not only did she drive through it every day, she said, but her son had more to tell. He said the Mertensia train station, where, in the story, Anya and Corax stand with Hugh's poster, was that old building that had been moved and now sits right behind their house. To me, that was a sign, an approbation, and the charming bit of serendipity I needed. Thank you for that, trainiac Arian Horbovetz. And yes, my sister confirmed there are actually places in Mertensia where wild bluebells, *Mertensia virginicus,* carpet the ground in the spring. In case you wondered.

I couldn't find a suitable image of a little girl in the 1930s, until I looked in the back of my own cupboard and found photos of my mother. She wouldn't be pleased with the digital rearrangement of her hair, but I think she makes a fine Anya.

Reveries. Another old memory surfaced only after I began researching transients. My grandmother once told me that, during the Depression, her mother, Mama Beckwith, cooked an extra chop for dinner whenever she could, ready for that knock on the door that she knew was bound to come. She would hand a plate through the door, and a hungry man was allowed to sit on their back porch and have a hot dinner. Their house, they were told, had been marked by hobos, though they never found the secret symbol. Papa Beckwith, chief of police in their town, directed some of the men to the police station,